BORDER LORDS

AND

ARMSTRONG'S WAR

A WESTERN DOUBLE FEATURE

RIDE THE WILD TRAILS!

LEE PIERCE

Lee Pierce

BARKING RAIN PRESS

Edited by Roger Gilmartin (www.barkingrainpress.org/roger-gilmartin)

Proofread by Robin Wilkinson (www.writingthatsings.com)

Barking Rain Press
PO Box 822674
Vancouver, WA 98682 USA
www.BarkingRainPress.org

ISBN Trade Paperback: 1-935460-72-2
ISBN eBook: 1-935460-73-0
Library of Congress Control Number: 2015952744

First Edition: November 2015

Printed in the United States of America

9 7 8 1 9 3 5 4 6 0 7 2 5

DEDICATION

I dedicate this volume to
my wayward son, Rory McDonald.
Take care, son.

ALSO FROM LEE PIERCE

Bounty Hunter's Moon

Treasure of Peta Nocona

Rough Justice

WWW.LEEPIERCE.INFO

Border Lords

Chapter 1

Mose Kincaid sat in his rocking chair in front of the marshal's office and looked to the south. Although there was little breeze blowing, a huge dust cloud was approaching from that direction. He reached down and scratched behind the ear of the cur lying at his feet. The old dog leaned into the scratching fingers.

"Looky yonder, General Lee," Moss said to the dog. "I believe that's about the biggest bunch of dirt I ever seen flyin' through the air. I wonder what's causing it?"

As the cloud got closer, the old, broken-down horse wrangler planted his callused hands on the arms of the rocker and slowly lifted his protesting body from the chair. Bones creaked and worn-out muscles screamed. With a tight grip on his cedar cane, he hobbled into the marshal's office.

Marshal Dan Cable sat behind his desk drinking lukewarm coffee and going over wanted posters. He looked up as ol' Mose toddled in. "Well, well, Mose," he said, smiling, "must be something pretty big happening outside to get you out of your rocking chair before suppertime. What's going on?"

Cable liked Mose Kincaid. The man had been the first person to introduce himself when the future marshal had arrived in town a little over a year ago. Dan Cable had been a burned-out lawman on the drift, and the small burg in the southwestern part of Arizona Territory seemed like as good a place as any to live out his last years in peace. Before he knew it, he was itching to get behind a badge again. The town council had been more than glad to appoint him marshal. Cable's reputation had preceded him, and the few local rowdies and rounders quickly cleaned up their acts or left town. Lucasville, Arizona was a nice, quiet place, and Marshal Cable liked that just fine.

"Marshal," said Mose, his brow furrowed, "there's a suspicious lookin' dust cloud headed this way from the south, and I thought you'd like to know about it."

Dan Cable bit his tongue to suppress a smile. "Dust cloud, you say?"

"Yes, sir, marshal. It's about the biggest one I've ever seen. I knowed you'd want me to tell you about it."

"Well, well, Mose, I reckon I do need to know about it so I can close my door to keep the dirt out."

Mose lowered his head like his feelings had been hurt. He was headed out the door when the marshal, realizing what he had done, spoke up. "It's about time for me to make my rounds, Mose. Let me get my hat, and we'll check out this great dust cloud. We can't be too careful, living this close to Mexico and all. Shucks, it might be a gang of border raiders coming to rape and pillage our town. We couldn't have that now, could we?"

The old man looked up, and the lights were bright again in his eyes. "No, sir, marshal," he said with conviction. "We surely couldn't have that."

Marshal Cable spun the cylinder of his Colt .45 Peacemaker, and, satisfied, dropped it into his custom-made bullhide holster with "DC" hand carved into the side. It had been a present from his men in Company C of the Texas Rangers when he left Texas three years before. He reached into his gun cabinet and removed a sawed-off, ten-gauge Greener shotgun. He held the nasty little weapon out to the old wrangler. "Mose," he said, "you'd be doing me a real favor if you'd back me up, just in case that dust cloud is bringing trouble with it."

Mose reached out a gnarled hand and accepted the prize. He cradled it to his chest like it was a newborn child. His eyes were misty when he looked up at the marshal. "Much obliged Dan'l," he said, sounding like he had a frog in his throat.

Dan Cable stepped out onto the porch, Mose right on his heels. Outside, the yellow fleabag of a dog hadn't moved since his master went inside. He slept, an occasional snore sputtering through his mangy jaw.

It was Sunday, and the street was empty. Folks were on picnics, enjoying the late spring weather that would soon make way for the dry Arizona summer. Summer brought the heat of Hell to Lucasville, and people relished the balmy April weather while they could. Dan trudged to the edge of the plank sidewalk and looked south. Mose had been right about one thing. The dust cloud was so enormous now it looked like a summer storm blowing in, except the skies were clear and cloudless. The smile left Cable's face, and he rotated his head in a tight spiral, feeling the joints in his neck crackle and pop. Involuntarily, he flexed the fingers on his gun hand. Maybe Mose had reason to be concerned. A dust cloud as big as this one meant a whole lot of hoofed animals were barreling toward

Lucasville. It was either a herd of cattle or, more likely, a bunch of riders. Either way, Marshal Cable didn't like it.

Carlos Macias leaned so far forward in the saddle that the brim of his great sombrero touched the neck of his mustang stallion. He spoke to the big, black charger, urging the beast to gallop faster. He and his men rode hell-for-leather toward Lucasville. A single thought raged like wildfire through Carlos's head: Revenge! Revenge on the *gringo* ranger who had shot his younger brothers to death five years before. He had barely escaped with his own life that day, but the gun battle that had taken his siblings' lives cursed his dreams and haunted his waking hours. Now he would have his chance to take down that son-of-a-dog lawman. Carlos swore a bitter oath to his dead brothers.

"Enrique, Miguelito, blood of my blood, today I will avenge your deaths."

Twenty of the worst cutthroats and gunmen from south of the border rode with Carlos Macias. They didn't give a *peso's* damn about Carlos and his vendetta against the *gringo* bastard. He had promised them an American town full of women, whiskey, and gold if they rode with him on his mission of death. The ex-ranger was the only law for fifty miles. When he was dead, the town would belong to them.

"Mose, you'd best go into my office," said the marshal. "This don't look right." Keeping his eyes on the approaching cloud of dust, he stuck his hand out to the old cowboy. "Here, give me my Greener."

Mose hesitated, then handed over the shotgun. "I'm here to help you, Dan'l. You might need me," he said, stumbling over the words. "I can back you up. Let me stay with you, son."

Still staring at the swirling, brown mass that was rushing their way, Dan spoke in a low voice. "I know, Mose. That's why I want you inside the office. Pop my Sharps 50 out of the gun rack, and back me up from the window in the door." Dan glanced at the old man, and then he looked down at the old, yellow dog, who now stood at his master's side. "Take General Lee with you. I don't want him taking a stray bullet. I'd never hear the end of it from you, you old hell-raiser." The marshal scratched his chin. "Now do what I say, and get that Big Fifty."

Mose snapped a brisk "yes, sir" and retreated into the office. After a moment, he was back at the door, holding the big buffalo gun with the long barrel sticking out a hole in the upper panel.

Marshal Cable heard the barrel scrape along the wood behind him and he grinned. "Mose, you'll do to ride the river with." He didn't look back, but he knew the old-timer was smiling.

When the riders reached the edge of town, Carlos held up his hand, and the outlaw band drew their panting horses to a halt. Brown dirt and stifling dust swirled around them, caught in the dead air. Lathered and grimy from their long run, the horses blew and wheezed, trying to catch their breath. Carlos motioned for the men to stay put while he walked his black mustang toward the sheriff's office. The big man on the black horse looked familiar to Marshal Cable, but he couldn't quite place him. As the man rode closer, the marshal stepped off the porch into the street. He took a deep breath and tried to relax. The mustang stopped six feet away. It snorted and pawed the ground. *"Buenas dias, jefe,"* said Carlos. "How are you, Ranger Cable?"

"How is it you know my name?" said Dan, tensing up. He raised the Greener and laid it across his left arm. "I don't seem to recollect you."

"Ranger Cable, it has been too long since we last met. My name is Carlos Macias. It hurts me that you do not remember our time together. Five years ago you put a bullet into my left shoulder. I almost bled to death. Do you remember me now, *Señor?"*

Memory of the long-ago gunfight sprang into Dan Cable's consciousness. He shifted the shotgun, raising the barrels. He wouldn't be able to make a straight shot, because the horse's head partially shielded Macias. Dan thumbed back the hammers on both barrels on the Greener.

"I remember you now, Macias. You and your two brothers were wanted for crimes against Texas. We tried to bring you in peaceable, but you and your kin had other ideas. I recollect your brothers didn't make it that day."

"I knew it would come to you, Ranger Cable." Carlos smiled, revealing yellow, dirt-stained teeth. "On that day, you and your *compadres* killed my brothers, Enrique and Miguel. Today it is your turn to die."

Even before he finished talking, Carlos flipped open his folded arms, revealing the two Colt .45s in his hands. Sticking both arms straight out, he fired the pistols as fast as he could at the moving target of the marshal.

Dan jumped to his right and threw the shotgun up to his shoulder. When the first bullet hit him, he was pulling both triggers. The lead slug twisted him to the right, and the double aught buckshot flew into the air, missing Macias by two feet. Dan dropped the shotgun and pawed for his .45. He cleared leather and tried to raise the pistol to fire, but his arm wouldn't respond. Bullets screamed into his flesh. Dan Cable dropped to his knees, still trying to raise his six-gun. By sheer will, he managed to lift the heavy pistol. As he looked up to sight his target, a bullet hit him between the eyes. He blinked once and toppled onto the sidewalk.

Carlos knew his adversary was dead, yet he kept pumping lead into the twitching body until his pistols ceased to fire. Acrid smoke swirled above the outlaw's head like strings of wispy clouds.

Carlos sat his saddle and eyed the marshal. He spit in the direction of the dead man and motioned for his men to ride in. He started to turn his horse when thunder cracked from the door of the marshal's office. The black stallion screamed, stumbled sideways, and fell over into the dirt. Carlos dived off, rolled, and came up running for the side of the nearest building. "You son-of-a-bitch!" screamed Mose. "You killed the marshal. I'll shoot your greaser ass to pieces."

Mose reloaded the buffalo gun and peeked out the door hole, trying to spy the killer. General Lee began to howl like he sensed what was going on.

Carlos flattened against the building. A half-dozen of his men drew greasewood torches from the backs of their saddles and fired them up. Carlos directed them toward the marshal's office. Before they could get there, a fat rider on a paint horse rode up, unlimbered a long-barreled, twelve-gauge shotgun, and fired both barrels into the front window of the office. The glass erupted, shards shooting in every direction. Mose ducked at the sound of the shotgun blast and covered his head. After the glass storm settled, Mose's eyes darted all around, searching for General Lee. He spied the yellow mutt lying in a corner, whimpering in pain. Blood had begun to flow from a dozen glass-filled wounds in the dog's body. Dirty tears rolled down Mose's cheeks. "I'm sorry, General Lee," he hollered, "but I can't help you now. Hell, I can't help myself." The old man looked up to see a rider throw a flaming torch through the shattered window. Papers on the desk burst into flame, and the desk and surrounding furniture began to catch fire. Mose crawled over next to the dying dog.

The fat rider with the big shotgun dismounted and fired two rounds point-blank into the office door. The door splintered apart, the pieces falling inward. He reloaded and stepped through the opening into the burning office. Reacting more than thinking, Mose raised the Sharps to his shoulder and fired. The round caught the fat outlaw chest high, sending him flailing back outside.

"Gotcha," Mose whispered. He smiled.

A handful of bad men converged outside the office and fired a hail of bullets through the open window and busted-in door. Lead chunks slammed into Mose, ripping him apart. His body jerked like a string puppet, falling on top of the dying dog.

Carlos ran to the hole where the front door had been. Holding up his hand to shield his face from the growing flames, he peered into the office. He could barely see the crumpled up body lying in a back corner. The rifleman was dead. A hard-edged smile split Carlos's face. Stepping outside, Carlos waved to his men. "*Amigos*, the devil ranger is dead!" he yelled. "The town is yours."

Chapter 2

Silverjack McDonald rode easy in the saddle. Long silver-gray hair cascaded from his hat and fell on his shoulders. He was a big man, rawboned and rangy. Quick with his fists, he was even quicker with a six-gun. On the backside of thirty, he'd punched cows, worked as a constable in Ft. Worth, Texas, fought as a bare-knuckled fighter, and prospected for gold. He'd ridden the outlaw trail for a while in his younger days. Now he was a Deputy United States Marshal working the Arizona territory.

He pulled his horse to a halt in front of the squat, red adobe building. Dirt and trail dust flew in every direction. The big grey mare he was riding shook her head and whinnied. She plunged her nose into the watering trough in front of her and snorted. Tiny bubbles bounced around her nostrils. Jack stepped from the saddle and patted her on the rump.

"Sorry about pushing you so hard, Bess, but Marshal Tolliver's message said beeline it here on the double. When he hollers froggy, well, if we want to eat, we'd better jump."

He tied her reins to the hitching rail and strode toward a rough-hewn wooden door. He hesitated at the entrance and removed his shapeless, brown hat. As he banged the hat against his grimy buckskin clothing, he surveyed the little town of Gila Bend, Arizona Territory.

A dozen varied buildings made out of adobe and wood dotted the landscape. Jack thought it looked like a giant hand had thrown them and they had landed in a disorganized jumble. The newest looking building and the biggest had a large glass window in front. Gold lettering on the window read "Gila Bend Territorial Bank, Wilson T. Cosgrove, President." Jack frowned and spat in the dirt as he read the sign. "Will Cosgrove, you son of a shit beetle," he said through clenched teeth. A half-inch-wide grey scar traversed the right side of his face from temple to jawline. Shaking his head, Jack jammed his hat back down on his head and stomped into the marshal's office.

Marshal Ethan Tolliver and another man were sitting and talking when Silverjack barged inside. "Lord, Jack," said the marshal, "don't you know how to enter a room quietly? I thought you were part Injun."

"Yeah, he is, marshal," said the other man, a wide grin covering his hawk-like features. "But most of the time his Irish blood covers up the Comanche in him."

The room was lit with two coal-oil lanterns, and as Jack's eyes adjusted to the room he recognized the men who were hurrahing him. "Sorry, Ethan," he said, still frowning, "it's just that I see that crook, Will Cosgrove, has got himself a bank. Dang, I hate that yellow-livered, back-shootin', gut-eatin'..."

Marshal Tolliver held up his hand. "All right, Jack, you've made your point. Now shut up and sit down." Silverjack sucked in a lungful of air and opened his mouth to continue his tirade. The marshal pointed his finger at Jack, and the irate deputy marshal stopped, closed his mouth, and obeyed his superior's order. He pulled up a worn-out, old oak chair and plopped onto it next to the other man in the office. For the first time Jack looked at his tormentor. Even sitting, the man looked taller than most. His broad shoulders rivaled Silverjack's, but the thing that set him off from most people was a thick, black mustache that drooped past his chin. The mustache, combined with his sharp features, gave him an evil looking countenance.

"Well, dang me for a shanty Irish gold miner's son," said Jack. "Pharaoh Smith, what are you doin' in these parts? Last time I saw you was in Santa Fe, what, maybe five years ago. You was a big-time bounty hunter." Jack noticed the badge pinned to Pharaoh's faded blue shirt. "Hey, you're wearing a deputy marshal's badge. When did you get so desperate for work?"

Before Pharaoh could speak up, Marshal Tolliver jumped in. "Speaking of badges, Deputy Marshal McDonald, I don't see yours anywhere on you."

"Huh," said Jack. "Oh, I got it here someplace. Just a minute, let me think. Well, durn, I believe I left it in my saddlebags. I'll just go fetch it."

"No, Jack, you won't *just go fetch it*," Marshal Tolliver said, his face a granite mask "I have something to tell both of you." He hesitated. "Dan Cable has been shot to death."

Jack and Pharaoh jerked a glance at each other, then looked back at their boss.

"What happened?" Pharaoh said, his jaw clenched tight. "Wasn't he down at that sleepy, little town close to the Mexican border? I thought nothing worse than a long dry spell ever happened at that place."

Marshal Tolliver leaned back in his chair, sighed, and told his deputies what had happened in Lucasville. "After the raiders killed Dan, they ransacked the town, burning the marshal's office, the post office, and the bank to the ground after they robbed it. Two women were defiled and half-a-dozen men were killed. I don't know how many were wounded."

"When did you find out about this?" Jack asked, rubbing the scar on his face.

"Three days ago. A rider brought the news. That's when I sent for you, Jack. Deputy Marshal Smith was already in town."

"What's the plan?" asked Pharaoh.

"I want the two of you to ride to Lucasville and survey the damage. Take charge of the situation, and help the townspeople put their lives back together. Stay in town until the army gets there."

"Why the army, Ethan?" said Jack. "We can go after those polecats. Give us half-a-dozen deputies, and we'll clean out that border trash."

Marshal Tolliver rubbed a callused hand down his face. "That's just what we're not going to do, Jack. I won't have you starting an international incident over some border scrape just so you can get revenge for Dan's killing." He sucked in a deep breath and let the air slide out of his nose. "Hell, we all liked Dan Cable. He was a damned good man. No one would like to get his murderers any more than I would. But that is not our job."

"Well, goddamn a bear," Jack said. "We're gonna play nursemaid to a town while the cavalry is havin' all the fun chasing down those *pistoleros*. That ain't right."

"Pharaoh, do you feel the same way that Jack does?" Ethan Tolliver's eyes shot fire. Silverjack had pissed him off.

Pharaoh took off his hat and ran his hand through his dark brown, curly hair. He shook his head. "We'll do it, marshal. Jack will be okay once he calms down and comes to his senses. The job will get done."

Jack started to protest when Pharaoh shot him a withering glance. The muscles of Jack's jaw popped out as he ground his teeth together, but his mouth remained closed. He nodded his head.

"When can we leave?" Pharaoh said, adjusting his hat onto his head.

"Get a voucher from the bank for supplies, load up, and head out as quick as you can. I've wired the army, and they should be there within a week." Marshal Tolliver glared at Silverjack. "Deputy Marshal McDonald, if you don't follow my orders, you'll be in a helluva lot more trouble than those border raiders. Understand?"

"Yes, sir, Ethan," said Jack, managing a tight-lipped smile. "I'll act like a church deacon."

The marshal frowned. "One more thing, Deputy McDonald—don't call me Ethan."

"Yes, sir, Ethan," said Jack as he rushed out the door.

After agreeing to leave at dawn the next day, the two men separated. Pharaoh walked toward the bank to pick up a voucher and then get the supplies they needed for the trip. Silverjack walked Bess to the livery stable to have her grained and rubbed down. He and Pharaoh planned to meet for supper later on in the evening. By the time the men finished their chores, the Blue Bell Café was closed. The Busted Hump Saloon served steak and beans all night long, so they headed there for their evening meal.

It was a Wednesday night, and the part-time churchgoers were at one of the two churches in town, so The Busted Hump wasn't too busy. Only the true-blue heathens were at the bar drinking. Silverjack and Pharaoh took a table in the back and ordered steak and beans along with two cold beers. After the waiter brought their beer, they settled back and discussed their mission.

"Hell's bells, Pharaoh," said Silverjack, furrowing his brow, "I know damn well that you feel the same way about Dan Cable as I do. Why didn't you speak your piece in Ethan's office?"

"Jack, if I had opened my mouth, Marshal Tolliver would have taken both of us off this case and found somebody else."

"Naw, he wouldn't do that. We're the best men he's got." Jack fingered the ugly scar on his face. "Do you really think he would?"

"Just as sure as you're hard-headed as an old mossy horn, Jack."

"Hmmm..." Silverjack sighed but said no more.

The waiter showed up with their food and two more beers. They dug into their steaks like starving coyotes and didn't speak again until their plates were clean.

———•——

Come daylight the next day, the two marshals were headed south toward Lucasville. Neither man spoke as they urged their horses to a steady lope. Silverjack's mare, Bess, could eat up ground all day at the pace they set. Texican, Pharaoh's mustang gelding, had equal stamina and heart.

The sun crept over the flat horizon, bathing the rock countryside with a golden sheet slashed with fingers of pink and silver. Spring enveloped the morning air, and the scarce vegetation bloomed in a rainbow of colors, making the desert seem more hospitable than it really was. The cool of the day would soon be replaced with a dry desert heat.

The two riders covered as many miles as possible before the sunlight began to scorch the land. Noon found them searching for a place with enough shade to conceal their mounts from the sun while they rested.

Silverjack tugged on Bess's reins. He pulled off the shapeless mass of beaver felt he called a hat and fanned it in front of his face. "Pharaoh, is that a mirage, or do I see a stand of trees up yonder?"

"Looks like the real thing, Jack, but that's not all I see. Look up in the sky."

"Uh-huh. Looks to be a dozen or so buzzards circling around up there."

"Strange thing is we're downwind and I don't smell anything dead."

"Yeah, but there's something that's gonna die pretty soon. I smell a man down there. Let's ride in real slow. Unhitch your iron; this might be a trap."

Silverjack pulled his Winchester from the buffalo hide scabbard resting under his right leg. Pharaoh flipped the leather thong off his Colt .44 and loosened it in his holster. Jack rode out a few yards ahead while Pharaoh edged his horse to the left and followed his partner into the trees.

"Hello the trees!" Jack yelled out, his eyes flickering back and forth. No answer. He moved Bess closer and called out again. This time a muffled sound caught his attention. He motioned Pharaoh around behind three large cottonwood trees that were clumped together with creosote bushes and prickly pear cactus. The eight-foot-high stand of cactus obscured the lower parts of the trees. Jack cocked the Winchester and walked Bess around the prickly pear. The sight that greeted him caused Jack to jerk his head back. He scanned the area carefully to make sure he hadn't ridden into a trap.

Satisfied everything was okay, Jack called out to Pharaoh to join him in the grove. When the other marshal rode around the trees, he jerked his horse to a halt and stared openmouthed. There, hanging upside down, his feet lashed to a thick cottonwood limb, dangled an enormous Negro man. His hands were strapped behind his back with rawhide strips, and his mouth was gagged with a bloody bandana. All he had on was a pair of grimy black long johns. The man's chest rose and fell in an easy rhythmic manner. He was either unconscious or sleeping.

"God in Heaven, Jack," said Pharaoh. "Who could have done such a thing to a man?"

Jack spat into the dirt and cussed. "Looks like somebody don't like the color of this man's skin."

"A man's a man."

"Not to most people in these parts. If you ain't lily-white you ain't human. Whoever did this is in a heap of trouble if this man lives."

"Do you know him?"

"I reckon I do. He saved my bacon more than once when I was ridin' the owl hoot trail up in Colorado some time back."

"We'd better cut him down before he dies on us."

"Hell, Black Tom ain't gonna die hangin' from a tree, leastways hangin' upside down. He'll live, all right. We've just got to be sure he ain't playin' possum on us. Pull your six-shooter and aim it at him like you mean to blow his head off."

Pharaoh did as he was told. Jack rode to within three feet of the hanging man and laid his Winchester up against the black man's temple. "Tom, this is Silverjack McDonald. I know you're playin' possum. We don't mean you no harm. We intend to cut you down and help you out, so don't be makin' no sudden moves. If you understand me, open your eyes and nod that big ol' nappy head of yours."

The two marshals waited but nothing happened. Pharaoh glanced at Jack with questioning eyes. Jack returned the stare, and then he looked up at the buzzards and shook his head. "All right, Pharaoh, I guess I made a mistake. This ain't the man I thought it was. He sure looks like my old *compadre*, Black Tom Raines, but I reckon lots of folks look alike hangin' upside down. We'll leave this one to the buzzards."

"It's me, Jack," the hanging man mumbled around the gag in his mouth. Two bloodshot eyes glared up at Silverjack.

"Well, I'll be switched," said Jack. "This is my old friend. Pharaoh, help me cut this hard-headed *hombre* down. I can't hardly wait to hear his story."

Chapter 3

Jack and Pharaoh cut Tom Raines down and carried him over to where a small spring bubbled up from some rocks in the middle of the trees. They laid him on the ground and cut his bindings. Jack removed the blood-soaked bandanna and tossed it aside, then put his canteen to Tom's parched lips. The dehydrated man sucked water down his throat, spilling it all over his face and neck.

"Whoa there, *amigo*, you'll strangle yourself if you ain't careful," Jack said, pulling the canteen from Tom's clawing grasp.

Tom struggled to hang onto the canteen, but his feeble strength failed him. His hands dropped to his sides. He groaned as he stretched his neck and tried to rub away the tingle in his arms. He began to quiver as the blood flow caused needles of fire to shoot through his legs. Seeing Tom's discomfort, Jack rubbed one leg while Pharaoh rubbed the other. Tom struggled in silence.

After a few minutes, Tom's body began to relax. He raised his hand, and the two marshals ceased rubbing. Jack handed him the canteen, and this time the black man sipped instead.

"Jack," said Pharaoh, "we're not going any farther today until we find out the situation with your friend. We've got good shade and water here. I'll start building camp. You talk to Tom and find out what happened."

Jack nodded and Pharaoh headed for the horses. Jack removed his neckerchief and dipped it in the cool spring water. Squeezing out the excess water, he mopped Tom's head. Tom lay still as Jack worked the wet cloth.

"Tom, I sure would like to know how a top-notch gun hand like you came to be hangin' downside-up from a tree. There ain't no hurry in tellin' me, though. Take your time. We'll stay with you 'til you can fend for yourself."

"Damn it, Jack, I ain't much on gratitude," said Tom, his voice weak but clear. "But you and your friend saved my bacon *and* my beans. I owe you, old timer."

Fire shot across Jack's eyes. "Tom Raines, you may be my friend, and right now you're not doin' too well, but if you call me that again, there may be some new knots put on your head. You dang well know I don't like to be called that word, and just because my hair's grey don't mean I'm old."

Tom smiled. "Damn, Silverjack, you ain't changed a bit. I surely am glad about that." He tried to lift himself up on his elbows. "Say, pardner, could you help me sit against this rock behind me? I'm tired of lookin' up at you."

Jack stuck his arms under Tom's armpits and lifted him to a sitting position. Tom let out a big sigh and drizzled more water down his throat. "What are you two hard cases doin' in this godforsaken country, Jack? Last time I heard, you were ridin' high in the Texas Rangers."

"I'll tell you about that in due time, Tom. But first, what in blazes happened to you?"

"Well, me and the Compton brothers were ridin' together huntin' bounties. I didn't like those boys too much, but they hired me to help go after Milo Truax and his gang. We caught Milo and four of his boys while they were camped out at night. Got them without firing a shot."

"Y'all were lucky," Jack said, fingering his scar. They're a pretty salty lot. Then what happened?"

"We got to this spring and decided to camp for the night. When we got settled in, Earl Compton decided it would be easier to take the gang in if they were dead. That fool up and shot Milo right between the eyes while he was sittin' there tied up like a Christmas turkey."

"I'll be damned," said Jack.

"Yeah, well hell, I jumped up to stop him from killing anybody else. And when I did, the lights went out. Next thing I remember, I'm hangin' upside down from a tree limb."

"Do you suppose they killed the whole bunch of prisoners?"

"I reckon they must have. When I woke up, everybody and everything was gone. I'm not sure how long ago they left. It seems like a long time but I don't know. Watchin' buzzards fly around lookin' at my toes sort of took up my thinking. I was tryin' to figure a way out of my predicament when I heard you two riding up. I didn't know if it was the Comptons riding back or what, so I played possum. I was sure happy to recognize that whiskey voice of yours."

"Whiskey voice," said Jack. He started to say something else when Pharaoh interrupted him.

"Camp's set up," said Pharaoh. "Arbuckles will be boiling soon. So what's the story on Mr. Raines?"

While Jack set about fixing some grub, he relayed Tom's story to Pharaoh. Tom lay back and closed his eyes. When the story was finished, Pharaoh shook his head.

"Nothing but flat-out meanness would cause Earl Compton to do what he did to those boys. Tom, do you have any idea where the Comptons were headed?"

"We were taking Milo's gang into Lucasville." Tom kept his eyes closed. "That's the closest town with any kind of law in it."

"Not anymore," said Silverjack.

By the time the sun squinted over the horizon the next morning, the three men had already broken camp and headed south. Tom took turns riding with Silverjack and Pharaoh. The sun was casting slight shadows to the east when the riders topped a sandstone knoll, and Lucasville came into view.

'There she is," said Silverjack, reining in Bess. "Sure don't look like much of a town."

"Big enough for a man to die in," said Pharaoh.

"Yeah, *amigo*, I reckon you're right enough there. Let's ride in a little closer. When we get to that grove of trees over yonder, you get down, Tom, and lie low. Me and Pharaoh will ride in and scope the place out before we let anybody know we're marshals. There ain't no way of tellin' if the Comptons are in Lucasville."

"There's a good chance they left already, Jack," said Pharaoh. "With Dan dead, they'll have to ride to Gila Bend to find the closest lawman to get their reward."

"Maybe so. We're wastin' time talkin' about it. Let's go on in."

They rode to the copse of trees, where Tom slid off the back of Pharaoh's horse. Silverjack shucked his Winchester and gave it to him.

"Stay low, Tom. We'll come back and get you if everything is all right. But you come a-foggin' it if any shootin' starts."

Tom nodded and began to settle in amongst the trees. Silverjack and Pharaoh turned their horses toward Main Street and headed them at an easy walk into town. As they rode into Lucasville, both men kept a sharp watch out for anything peculiar. The place was little more than a village. Having a U.S. Post Office and a bank qualified it as a township. Now with both burned to the ground, the future of Lucasville was uncertain.

The town's origins dated back to 1871, when prospector Hezekiah Lucas reported a silver strike in the canyons near the Mexican border. Word of his strike rapidly reached the nearby town of Gila Bend. People looking to get rich quick poured in from all over the territory. Within weeks, the population of Lucasville, as Hezekiah chose to call it, boomed to over two thousand people. A U.S. Post Office was established, as well as a bank, three churches, six saloons, two brothels, and various other businesses.

Lucasville boomed for six months until the silver petered out. By then Hezekiah Lucas had made a small fortune selling shares to his fledgling mine. One day Lucas said he was going to San Francisco to purchase heavy-duty mining equipment to search for the silver lode he knew was there. He left and never came back.

It turned out he had salted his diggings, and there never was any silver to speak of, at least none that came from around Lucasville. Within a short time, ninety percent of the population vacated Lucasville. A few hardy souls decided to stay and make a go of the town. The post office survived as well as the Catholic Church, one saloon, a general store, and a livery stable.

The rest of the businesses, including the bank, did not survive. The bank building remained empty for over five years until Abraham Daggett, a man with a shady past, showed up one day and reopened it. When Dan Cable showed up in Lucasville, the bank had been open for less than a year.

"Pharaoh," said Silverjack, "this place is a ghost town. Why, there ain't even a dog roamin' the streets. This is just plain creepy. Where do you think all of the people are?"

"Inside with the shutters closed most likely, Jack."

"Can't say I blame 'em, what with all that's gone on here in the last bunch of days. I hope the Comptons didn't add to the damage that was already done."

"We'll soon find out. Here's a saloon. Let's see what we can rustle up. Walk soft."

"I'll be quiet as a church mouse on Sunday morning."

Pharaoh walked into the saloon and sidled up to the bar. He ordered a beer. When it arrived, he turned and laid his elbows behind him on the bar. He hooked one boot heel onto the brass rail at the bottom. Diffused sunlight filtered in through dirty windows. Sawdust covered the floor. A dozen men sat at tables scattered about the place. A few of them peeked at the newcomer from under hats pulled low, but the majority did not look up. Pharaoh sipped his beer in silence and waited for Silverjack.

Jack sauntered in, stepping up to the bar about ten feet to Pharaoh's right. He ordered a beer and a pickled boiled egg. The bartender drew a beer and slid it down the bar to Jack. He then pulled a long, two-pronged fork from under the counter and fished around in a massive glass jar filled with brownish eggs. With the deft touch of experience, he speared a big nasty- looking one, pulled it out, and laid it on a small, cracked plate, all in one smooth motion. *"Amigo,"* said Silverjack. "I appreciate you slidin' my beer down the bar, but I believe you ought to walk that egg to me. I would sure hate it gettin' smashed before I got to sink a tooth into it."

The bartender glanced down at the egg on the plate and placed them on the bar. He drew the plate back like he had decided to slide it, anyway. A loud click brought his head up. The muzzle of a Colt .44 stared the brawny barkeep in the face.

"My name's Silverjack McDonald," the pistol's owner said. "I'm a United States deputy marshal sent here to find out how come my old friend Dan Cable got shot to pieces and nobody in this damn town raised a hand to help him."

Pharaoh stared at his fellow marshal. "So much for the church mouse," he mumbled.

Silverjack held his six-shooter steady as the bartender shuffled toward him. By the time the man covered the distance, he was sweating like ten-year-old dynamite. His hand shook, and the pickled egg rolled all around the plate.

Jack stuck his pistol onto the end of the bartender's nose. "Pilgrim, if you drop my lunch on this nasty floor, I will make you lick the whole damn place clean."

The saloon got so quiet you could hear a flea fart. The bartender placed the plate on the bar and backed up to where the jar of eggs was sitting. He chanced a pleading glance at Pharaoh, fear showing in his eyes, hoping for help stopping Silverjack. Pharaoh grinned and flipped open his vest, displaying his deputy marshal's badge. The saloon patrons sat still at their tables.

"Bein' that you're the bartender, *amigo*," said Jack, "I expect you know everything that goes on in Lucasville. I'm askin' you, right now, to tell me all that you know about the day Dan Cable died. I'm only askin' one time. Do you understand?"

The bartender nodded.

"Good." Silverjack kept his eyes on the barkeep as he addressed the patrons. "The rest of you *hombres* sit real quiet like you're doin' now. This other feller up the bar a ways is Deputy Marshal Pharaoh Smith. He's gonna make sure nobody makes any sudden moves."

Pharaoh nodded and pulled iron.

Silverjack laid his .44 on the bar and picked up the vinegary egg. He bit it half in two, chewed, and swallowed. He scrunched up his face. "Don't sell many eggs, do you, barkeep?" he said. Dropping the partially eaten egg on the plate, he chugged his beer. Wiping foam from his mustache with a buckskin sleeve, he pointed at the bartender. "Commence with your story... *amigo.*"

Chapter 4

The bartender stuttered and coughed his way through the events that took place the day Marshal Cable was murdered. The two deputy marshals listened without comment. When the man finished, Silverjack turned to face the rest of the saloon.

"Any of you boys in here got anything to add to that story?"

A tall drink of water sitting at the back of the saloon stood and walked to the front tables. He had the look of a thirty-dollars-a-month-and-found cowboy. When he stopped, he removed his sweat-blackened hat and held it in both hands in front of him. He scrunched up the brim and began to roll it up and down.

"My name is Ollie Dunsmore. I ride for the Slash B outfit up north of here. Most of us here do. We liked Dan Cable and respected him. He was the best thing that ever happened to this town."

The other men nodded and spoke up in agreement. The cowboy looked back at his supporters and seemed to gain confidence in what he was doing. "Those border outlaws hit town on a Sunday afternoon. Folks was enjoyin' the nice weather, and Lucasville was near deserted. The raid was over before most anyone knew what was goin' on. The few people who were in town got wounded or killed." He paused like he wasn't sure what to say next. "Two ladies were hurt real bad. They were, uh, they were..."

"We know what happened to them, Ollie." Pharaoh spoke in muted tones. "You said they were border outlaws. How do you know that?"

"One of the wounded men, Abe Daggett, the banker, recognized the leader of the bunch when they were burnin' the bank down. It was Carlos Macias. Everybody around these parts knows he works both sides of the border, stealing and killing. He's a bad one. People say..."

Pharaoh raised his hand. "We know who he is. Anything else you want to add?"

Ollie nodded his head. "Yes, sir. We gave Marshal Dan a real nice funeral. Ol' Mose, too. Mose Kincaid was an old, wore-out cowboy Marshal Dan kept around as a sort of deputy." He rolled up his hat until it resembled a wad of greasy black rags. "Uh, sorry, marshals. Sometimes I talk too much." His eyes darted around, not focusing on any one thing.

"Where's the banker now?" Silverjack asked. He lowered his six-shooter into his holster and glanced back at the bartender, who was still keeping as much distance between himself and Jack as he could.

"He's at Doc Prater's," blurted the bartender.

"I'll show you where that's at," Ollie said, punching some shape back into his hat.

"Just tell us. We've got another errand for you."

After the cowboy gave out the directions, Pharaoh sent him to the edge of town to bring Tom Raines to the doctor's office.

On the way to Dr. Prater's, Silverjack fingered the scar on his face. "Pharaoh, I'm wonderin' if this was a bank robbery turned nasty or somethin' else a whole lot different."

"What are you thinking?"

"Maybe Dan did get killed tryin' to protect this town, but somethin' else is gnawin' at my gut, and I can't quite figure out what it is. It's damn distracting."

"Yeah, I know what you mean. The name Carlos Macias ought to spark a memory, but nothing has popped up yet. Maybe we'll find out more when we talk to the banker."

They reached the doctor's office, knocked, and went inside. A ten-by-ten room contained an old, scarred wooden desk, a cane-backed chair, a small coal oil lamp, and not much else. A doorway on the left opened into another room. A man of about thirty stood in the doorway. He was tall with an average build. An unruly shock of dark brown hair covered the top of his head. "We need to talk to the doc," said Silverjack.

"I'm Samuel Prater," said the man. "What can I do for you?"

"Doc Prater?"

"Yes, I'm Dr. Prater. If you need something, tell me. I have many injured people to take care of."

"Sorry, Doc. I figured you would be older." Silverjack introduced himself and Pharaoh and asked to talk to Abe Daggett.

"All right," said Dr. Prater, rubbing his fingers on his forehead. "My nurse is with him right now. His wounds will heal, but he needs rest. You can have five minutes with him, no more."

"Yes, sir, Doctor," Pharaoh said, taking his hat off. "Five minutes will be plenty."

He nudged Silverjack and darted his eyes at his hat. Jack glanced up and frowned at Pharaoh, making no attempt at removing his headgear. Pharaoh shook his head and started into the back of the building. Silverjack grinned at the doctor and followed Pharaoh.

Four men lay in narrow cot-like beds in a large room. There were two empty beds. All of the men were bandaged on various parts of their bodies. Abe Daggett lay in a smaller room directly back of the large room. The door to the room was open. The marshals stepped inside. A withered-looking little man lay on the only bed in the room. He stared at the ceiling as the nurse dressed a wound on his chest.

The young nurse was dressed in tan duck pants and a loose-fitting calico shirt. She wore a sleeveless white smock over her clothes. Her blond hair was tied up in a neat bun. She seemed oblivious to the room's new occupants.

Pharaoh cleared his throat. "Pardon me, ma'am. My name is Pharaoh Smith, and this is Jack McDonald. We are United States Marshals, and we need to talk to Mr. Daggett for a few minutes."

"Did Samuel—Dr. Prater—say it was okay?" she said without looking up.

"Yes, ma'am, he did."

"Very well. I'm finished with Mr. Daggett's dressing. You have two minutes, then it's out of here."

"The doc said we could have five minutes with him," Silverjack said, throwing out his best "for the ladies" smile.

A glare that would melt granite greeted his efforts. "Two minutes and you are out of here."

Jack lowered his gaze. "Yes, ma'am," squeaked from his pursed lips.

Never looking back, the nurse walked into the bigger room and headed toward the closest patient. Pharaoh rolled his eyes and, stifling a grin, approached the shrunken man lying in front of him. "Mr. Daggett, I'm a U.S. marshal, and I would like to ask you a few questions about the raid."

Abe Daggett looked at Pharaoh and nodded his head.

"Mr. Daggett, you are the banker, correct?" asked Pharaoh.

"Yes, marshal." Abe Daggett's voice was strong and clear.

Where were you when the raid took place?"

"I was in the bank—working on some important paperwork—when I heard a ruckus outside in the street. The bank was locked, but the safe was open. I had just removed some papers from the vault. I quickly closed and locked the safe and hurried to the front window to see what all the commotion was about. I, er, uh... excuse me, marshal, but will you please hand me that glass of water on the table? Since the fire, I can't seem to drink enough water."

Silverjack handed him the water, and he gulped it down like he'd been in the desert for a long time. "Um, thank you," he said. "Let me see... oh, yes, as I said, I looked out the window just in time to see a man hurling a flaming torch at the bank. I jumped back as the torch hit the window. The glass didn't break, and I ran to my office. When I reached my door, I turned to see a man break the front window—with his rifle I think—and throw the torch inside." The banker took a breath and sighed. "I'm sorry, gentlemen, but I'm a little shook up retelling that horrible incident." He drank some more water.

"We get the picture, Mr. Daggett," said Pharaoh. "How did you get wounded?"

"Yes, of course, I must tell you that." Daggett seemed to be getting a little nervous. "I tried to retrieve some important papers that were on my desk, and before I could get out the back door, I was overcome with smoke and lost consciousness. When I came to, I was in this bed with a bullet wound in my side. I don't know how it got there."

"You were shot, but you don't know when or how," said Silverjack.

"That is what I said," snapped Daggett.

"Your two minutes are long over," said the nurse. She had slipped into the room unnoticed a few moments before. Pharaoh tried to ask another question, but the nurse wouldn't hear of it. She shooed them out to the doctor's office. Dr. Prater was sitting at his desk as they scooted by.

"Sometimes I wonder who's running my office, gentlemen," the doc said, grinning. "Have a nice day."

They stepped out onto the porch. Silverjack scratched the back of his neck and frowned. "Well, if that young lady ain't a pistol," he said, "I don't know what is."

"She's sure protective of her patients, all right," said Pharaoh. "Maybe a little too protective."

"What do you mean, pardner?"

"I can't put my finger on it, but she seemed to show up just when it looked like we might get something of importance out of the banker."

"Yeah, I hadn't thought of that," said Silverjack. "You know, ol' Daggett didn't tell us much we didn't already know."

Pharaoh shook his head and started to say something when Ollie Dunsmore showed up with Tom Raines. The bare-footed bounty hunter slid off the back of Dunsmore's horse. He hopped and skipped gingerly over the rock-strewn street.

"If you ain't a sight, Tom," said Silverjack, grinning. "We need to get you some boots."

Tom grimaced as he stepped on a sharp pebble. "I don't have no money, Jack. You want to lend me some?"

"No, but I've got a spare pair of moccasins in my saddlebags that might fit you okay. You need some clothes, too."

Ollie spoke up. "This here Negro feller looks like he's real close to Marshal Dan's size. All the marshal's belongings are bundled up at the church. I could go get 'em if you want me to."

"Do that," said Pharaoh." We'll be in the saloon."

Silverjack dug the moccasins out of his saddlebags and gave them to Tom. The bounty hunter slipped them on, and the three of them tromped to the saloon.

Silverjack was the first one through the door. "Draw three beers, barkeep," he hollered.

The bartender frogged when Silverjack yelled and dropped a whiskey glass he was wiping. The shot glass hit the hardwood floor and shattered into a dozen pieces. Ignoring the tiny slivers of glass, the bartender made haste to draw the beers. He had two ready and was filling the third when he looked up at the three approaching men. Seeing Black Tom, he froze, not moving until the cold beer overflowed and coursed down his sleeve. He sat the mug down and looked at the trio. "Say, we don't serve nig—"

Silverjack's .44 jumped into his hand. "I appreciate you keepin' your mouth shut, barkeep. This is Tom Raines, just about the meanest bounty hunter in Arizona. He don't care for people who call other folks insultin' names. Makes him madder 'n hell. I reckon I just saved your life. You owe me. Don't you think?"

The bartender swallowed the tobacco he was chewing and nodded.

"You give us those three beers, and I'll call it even. Take 'em to a back table, and make sure the chairs are dusted off."

The bartender's face began to turn green from the effects of the ingested tobacco, but he scurried to a table, placed the beers on top, and wiped down the chairs. Suddenly, his head shot up, and a gurgling sound erupted from his stomach. He beelined it to the door, running into two patrons in the process. His retching could be heard all the way to the back of the saloon.

———

"Looks like that feller can't handle his tobacco," Silverjack said, chugging half of his beer.

All right," said Pharaoh, "let's get down to the reason we came here. The wounded men seem to be well taken care of, and except for the two unfortunate ladies, the rest of the townspeople don't look too much the worse for wear. I say we sit and wait for the Cavalry."

"As soon as I get some clothes, I'm taking off after the Compton Brothers." Black Tom spat out the words. "That cowboy told me they hightailed it toward Mexico once they found out the marshal was dead."

"That was a damn strange thing to do," said Silverjack, tracing his scar. "What do think they did with the outlaws' bodies?"

Pharaoh sipped his beer. "Couldn't say, Jack, but headed south, I doubt the Comptons hauled any excess baggage along."

Black Tom's eyes lit up. "Maybe they buried them somewhere on the trail to Mexico. Hell, I bet I could find the bodies and still collect the reward. Jack, come with me. You've got the best smeller I ever saw. Help me and I'll split the bounty. It'll be like old times."

"Sounds mighty temptin', Tom. I believe I could smell out them boys. They ought to be stinkin' real good about now."

"He can't go with you, Tom," said Pharaoh. He's a sworn U.S. deputy marshal. He has to stay here with me and wait for the U.S. Calvary."

"Aw, Pharaoh, come on," Silverjack said. "You said yourself all there is to do here is to squat on our spurs and wait for them soldier boys to show up. You can do that by yourself. I could make us some extra cash workin' with ol' Tom here. What do you say?"

"There is no way you are going with him." Pharaoh started to get angry. "Dammit, Jack, you swore the same oath to Arizona that I did. As many shady things as you've done in your life, I've never known you to go back on your word."

Silverjack's head dropped, and he blew out a long, loud breath. "Ugh... shucks, Tom, this high-and-mighty do-gooder is right; I can't go back on my word. Sorry, pard."

"Your loss, Jack. I'll go alone."

They had grown silent when the saloon doors flew open, and Ollie Dunsmore came bursting in. Looking around and spotting the men at the back table, he ran to them. "Marshals, come quick!" he shouted. "One of the ladies who was hurt just died."

Silverjack and Pharaoh jumped to their feet and hurried for the door. Black Tom continued to sip his beer. As the three men hustled out the door, Ollie Dunsmore explained what had happened.

"I stopped at the doc's a minute on my way with the marshal's clothes when it happened. Miz Cooney bolted upright in bed and started screamin'. The doc and Miss Boyett, the nurse, ran to her room, but it was too late. Miz Cooney was dead."

Just as the trio reached the doctor's office, the sound of a pistol shot echoed from inside.

Chapter 5

Silverjack bolted through the door of the doctor's office ahead of the pack. Inside he spied the young nurse. She was leaning against the far wall. Her hand covered her mouth, and she was crying.

"We heard a gunshot," Silverjack said.

The nurse didn't respond. Silverjack grabbed the sobbing woman and turned her to face him. She tried to pull away, but he held her tight. Pharaoh and Ollie barged in.

"What happened?" Pharaoh yelled.

"Mrs. Kleegler... Mrs. Kleegler shot herself." She pointed a shaking finger toward a room the marshals hadn't noticed before.

Silverjack stayed to console the stricken nurse while Pharaoh and Ollie hurried into the room. Inside the cramped quarters, a narrow bed held a slender woman entangled in the sheets. A ghastly sight greeted the two men as they reached the foot of the bed—the wall behind it was splattered crimson and gray, and a smoking revolver hung by its barrel from her gaping jaw.

Dead eyes stared to the ceiling. The back of the woman's head was gone. Ollie tore his eyes away from the gore and wretched.

Silverjack gently led the nurse outside. By the time he got her seated on a nearby bench, she had almost stopped crying. She sat staring into space with empty eyes. Silverjack stepped back inside the office, and in a moment returned with a wet cloth. Handing it to the nurse, he sat beside her. She wiped her tears and washed her face.

"What's your name?" said Silverjack.

She didn't look up. "Abby Boyett," she said softly.

"I'm Jack McDonald."

"I can't believe this is happening," said the stricken woman. "Why Lucasville? Nothing ever happens here. This has been a peaceful town ever since Dan got here." She began to sob again.

Silverjack placed his arm around her shoulders. "Dan Cable was a helluva good man and a friend of mine. I reckon you knew him pretty well, too."

Abby raised her head and stared at Silverjack with glistening red eyes. "Dan and I were going to be married a month from the day he was... he was killed."

Silverjack traced the scar on his face. He swallowed hard but said nothing. Momentarily, Pharaoh emerged from the office. He glanced down at Jack and jerked his head toward the street.

Silverjack squeezed Abby's hand and followed his partner into the street. They walked some distance away, out of Abby's earshot.

"Jack," said Pharaoh through clenched teeth, "I've seen the elephant, but I've never set eyes on something like this. My God, those poor women." He sucked in a short breath and purged it just as quick.

Silverjack told him about Dan's and Abby's marriage plans. Pharaoh cursed and spat out the green stomach bile that had surged into his throat. Wiping his mouth with his sleeve, he looked Silverjack in the eyes.

"We goin' after those bastards?" asked Silverjack.

"Yeah, Jack, we're going after those bastards."

———◦———

Black Tom Raines fidgeted as he sat on the bay gelding that Ollie Dunsmore had procured for him. "Hurry up if you're going with me," he hollered at the two marshals who were in the doctor's office talking to Dr. Prater and Abby.

Silverjack stepped outside and walked around Tom's mount. He ran his hand over the horse's muscular rump. "Looks like a whole lot of horse Ollie picked out for you, Tom. That waddy's got a good eye for horseflesh."

"He'll do, but I want my old horse, and I intend to get him back from the Comptons. They're going to pay with blood for what they did to me."

"Does that mean you're going with us to get Macias and his bunch?" Pharaoh had emerged from inside the office and was stuffing an oilskin-wrapped package inside his saddlebags.

"Uh-uh." Tom tensed his shoulders. Thick muscles rippled under his shirt. "I'm going far enough to find the bodies of Milo and his gang. That's it. After I claim my reward, I'll go after the Comptons."

"It don't sound like you've got much confidence in us bringing them in, Tom."

A cavernous laugh rumbled from deep inside Tom Raines. "Jack, you two are as good as there is at trackin' men, but you don't know Mexico like I do. Hell, my mama was born in Juarez. I did half my raising down there. I speak the lingo, and I know the country like a Mexican. Y'all don't have a darky's chance in a KKK meeting of getting out of there with your hides intact. I expect there might even be a reward for the Comptons after you boys disappear."

"Damn, Tom, we saved your life. You're a hard man."

"Yeah, Jack, I am. When you're my color, you've got to be hard to survive." He reined his horse around. "Are y'all going with me, or are you going to talk me to death?"

Silverjack swung up into the saddle. Pharaoh had already mounted. As they turned their horses to leave, Ollie Dunsmore rode up leading two horses.

"Here's your pack animals, Mr. Raines. They'll do the job for you."

Tom nodded and reached for the lead ropes. Ollie pulled back and held onto the ropes.

Tom frowned and dropped his hand to his six-gun.

"Hold on there, Mr. Raines," Ollie said, his voice quivering. "I told you I'd have the horses, and here they are. They're yours to use under one condition. I've been thinking a lot since you fellers came to town. We took Dan Cable for granted. Truth is, we didn't know what we had in the marshal. So…"

"What are you getting at, Ollie?" Pharaoh's patience was growing thin.

"Marshal Smith, I'm going with you."

"Boy," said Silverjack, "you puked your guts up when you saw that dead woman. What makes you think you can go after the men who caused that?"

"I'm goin', marshal, and you can't stop me short of killin' me."

"Well, hell," said Silverjack, unlimbering his .44.

"Put it away, Jack," said Pharaoh, shaking his head. "If he wants to go, he can. But I will tell you one time, Dunsmore: If you go froggy for any reason, I'll run you all the way back to your mama. You got that?"

"Yes, sir, I sure do."

Tom laughed again and gouged his horse in the ribs. The startled animal lurched forward and broke into a run out of town. Ollie grinned and took off after him. Pharaoh looked at Silverjack and shrugged his shoulders. He spoke to Texican, and the mustang gelding took off at a gallop.

Silverjack sat his saddle and watched the three riders kick up a whirlwind of dust. He removed his hat and ran a callused hand through his silver hair. "Well, hell again," he said.

Five miles from town, they found the graves. Six bodies lay in shallow cavities dug in the sand. Dirt, rocks, and broken tree limbs covered the dead Truax gang. Tom saw them first, and he let out a war whoop. Jumping from his horse, he inspected the gruesome site. Satisfied he had found what he was looking for, he jerked off his hat and slapped it against his leg.

"Boys, this is my lucky day!" Tom bellowed. "I'll load these *hombres* up and be in Gila Bend in three days. Then it's onto San Francisco and high times for me."

"Looks like the Comptons didn't waste too much time buryin' these fellers," said Silverjack.

"They must have been in an awful big hurry to get to Mexico," said Pharaoh. He rubbed his chin. "I find it strange that bounty hunters in possession of cash bounties just drop everything and ride into Mexico."

Jack shifted in his saddle. "What are you gettin' at, Pharaoh?"

"I've got a hunch the Compton Brothers are in some way connected to Carlos Macias. I can't figure it out yet, but I bet there's something to it."

"This is beginning to look like more than the sacking of a town," said Silverjack. "You know we didn't ask that banker if they got any money from the bank before they burned it down."

"He said he had locked the safe, and no one has mentioned any missing money," Pharaoh said. "Still, it makes a man wonder." He scanned the southern horizon. "Ollie, how far are we from the Mexican border?"

"As the crow flies, Mexico is about two miles south of here, but there's too much Organ Pipe cactus that way. You can't hardly ride through that stickery stuff. The best place to cross is a wide gulley about ten miles southeast."

Pharaoh sighed. "All right, from now on we ride real careful. Chances are those boys are long gone, but there's no use riding into an ambush. Ollie, you know the country. Lead us to that crossing."

There was an audible gulp from Ollie. His Adam's apple bobbed like a cork on a fishing line, but he nodded and started heading southeast. Pharaoh fell in behind him.

Silverjack stared down at Tom Raines, who was digging like an armadillo trying to get at the source of his future payday. "Wooeee, Tom," said Jack," how can you stand that God-awful smell?"

Not even looking up, Tom answered, "Smells like money to me, Jack."

Letting out a disgusted snort, Silverjack spoke. "Tom, I always knew you liked to live high on the hog, but I never figured you for a polecat that would run out on a *compadre*. Go get your blood money. I hope one of them Frisco whores doses you up real good."

Tom ignored Silverjack's remarks and kept on digging. Silverjack fingered his old knife scar and cursed under his breath. He jerked Bess's head around and took off after his companions.

Chapter 6

The three men rode easy toward Mexico. When they reached the gulley that marked the boundary line, Silverjack rode ahead to scout the surroundings. Pharaoh and Ollie dismounted and walked their horses down the gully, searching for some shade. They found it underneath a narrow sandstone overhang. A half hour passed before Silverjack returned. He came riding down the gully, whistling. Pharaoh stepped from under the overhang and waved him over.

"What did you find out, Jack?"

"Looks like Macias and his bunch made camp about a mile south of here. There weren't any signs of them being in a hurry. I found a separate set of horse tracks, probably the Comptons, but I didn't find any sign of where they might have camped. Those fellers were hightailin' it."

"I've thought a lot on it, Jack, and with what you found, I'm convinced now that the Comptons were supposed to meet Macias in Lucasville. I think they sidetracked to catch the gang they murdered and took too long doing it. That would explain their dumping the bodies in shallow graves and riding on in a hurry."

"Ollie," Silverjack said, "what was in that bank to cause two gangs to attack Lucasville?"

"I couldn't say," said Ollie, tightening his cinch. "There sure wasn't any of my money in there. A cowhand spends all of his pay."

"You ain't got any idea, huh?"

"No, sir, I sure don't." Ollie kept fiddling with his saddle. "Shouldn't we be headin' after those fellas while we have daylight left?"

Silverjack pursed his lips and stared at the lanky cowboy until Ollie swung into the saddle. Silverjack followed suit. "Come on," he said. "I'll lead y'all to where Macias camped."

The three men rode in silence until they reached the cold campsite, and then they searched around until they found some hoofprints leading due south. With Silverjack still in the lead, they moved out in single file, following the tracks. Torn-up sagebrush and trampled ground made the trail easy to follow. They made good time until dusk made the trail too hard to see.

Ollie, who was in the middle, reined in his horse. "Say, fellas, I just now recognized where we are. There's a little spring not too far from here. Got some trees, if I recollect. We ought to camp there."

Silverjack jerked Bess around and urged her up abreast of Ollie. He leaned over and stuck his nose in the cowboy's face. "Say," he said, "I was wonderin'. How come you know so blame much about Mexico, boy? You ride down here a lot, do you?"

"Aw, marshal, heck, we have to ride over here all the time and round up strays. Don't none of us like it, but it's what we get paid for."

"Sounds like these Slash B boys do a whole hell of a lot for their pay, don't it, Pharaoh?"

"Ollie, take us to the spring," said Pharaoh.

Ollie glanced at Pharaoh and back at Silverjack.

"Goddamnit, Pharaoh!" said Silverjack, "When I'm talkin' to somebody, don't you ever interrupt me. I don't trust that boy no farther than I can throw him."

"Jack," Pharaoh said, raising his voice, "Marshal Tolliver put me in charge. If you don't like the way I'm handling things, ride. I can do this job without you. Do you understand me?"

"Yeah, I understand you, boss." Silverjack spat into the dirt. "You're still Mr. High and Mighty Pharaoh Smith. I thought you'd changed, but you ain't. This ain't over." Jack spurred Bess in the ribs and took off.

The spot Ollie had picked was a near perfect place to set up camp. Evidence of that lay in the remains of over a dozen old campfires scattered about the area. A tiny spring gurgled from under a flat rock into a gravel basin less than two feet across and a foot deep. The clean, clear water nourished ocotillos, desert sage, and a small stand of stunted mesquite trees.

When Ollie got to the campsite, he jumped off his horse and tied her reins to one of the mesquites. "I'm gonna gather up enough dead wood for a fire," he hollered. "I'll be back in a jiffy." He trotted around the knoll.

Pharaoh and Silverjack dismounted and led their horses to the spring. They filled their canteens and then let the horses drink their fill. Silverjack took off his hat and ran fingers through his hair. "Pharaoh, somethin' ain't right about that waddie. For a man who didn't throw in with Dan Cable when the marshal needed him, he sure seems anxious to get some revenge. I think he may be in cahoots with them outlaws."

"You could be right, Jack. This whole mess is getting more confusing. If Ollie is in on the deal, I wonder who else might be involved."

"Makes a man think. That's for sure."

"Here comes Ollie back with an armload of wood. We'll keep a close eye on him without tipping him off."

"I'm gonna do this my way," said Silverjack.

"Wait, Jack, let's take this easy." Pharaoh reached for Silverjack's arm, but Jack shook him off.

The cowboy dropped his load of wood at the marshals' feet. "We're in luck, fellas. I found a bunch of nice dry firewood just the other side of the knoll. We'll have us a cook fire in no time."

"There won't be a fire," said Silverjack. "It's too dangerous. We'll make do with a cold camp."

"Aw, now, marshal, I got to have me a fire. I get cold real easy out in these chilly desert nights. My old, broke-up bones give me the rumatiz somethin' awful. Shucks, there ain't nobody within miles of here. I'll just make a little fire."

Silverjack stepped over to Ollie, who was bending down and stacking some wood. He reached under the cowboy's head, grabbed his bandana and jerked him to his feet. Jack wrapped his hand around the bandanna and twisted it tight enough to choke off Ollie's breathing. The cowboy's eyes bulged out like a squashed toad frog, and right away his face started turning purple. Pharaoh started to intervene, but Silverjack threw up a hand, and he backed off. Ollie looked on the verge of passing out.

"Ollie, I'm gonna loosen this necktie and ask you a few questions. If I don't like the answers, I'm gonna squeeze it so tight your head will fall off. If you understand me, do a little jig."

The purple-faced cowboy's boots flopped around in the dirt. Silverjack loosened the bandanna, and Ollie gasped in a bucketful of air. He almost fell over, but Silverjack held him up.

"First question, Ollie. Are you in cahoots with Macias and the others?"

Ollie hesitated, and Silverjack wrenched the bandanna tighter. "Okay, okay," the stricken puncher squeaked. "Please don't choke me to death. I can't stand any more." Tears welled up in his eyes and balled up in the dirt caked on his face. "I'll tell you everything I know."

Silverjack smiled and relaxed his grip on the neckerchief. "All right, Ollie, start at the beginning, and don't leave anything out."

———

Carlos Macias and one of his men, Pedro Quintano, sat at a back table in the only cantina in Villa Lobo, Mexico. The place was dark and dingy. Four tables with mismatching chairs sat about the place. A fat Mexican dressed in greasy clothes sat behind the plank wood bar, dozing in a rickety chair. Two old wine barrels held up the six-foot-long bar top. Macias and his man were the only customers.

They sipped warm *pulque* and watched three *gringos* stomp in, throwing back the curtain that passed for the bar's front door. "*Dios mio,*" Carlos muttered. "Why is it all *Norteamericanos* act like they own the world?"

Pedro shrugged his shoulders and kept drinking. As the men approached the table, Carlos nodded to his companion, who stood up and retreated into the shadows behind his boss.

"Sit down, *señores,*" Carlos said. His tone belied his contempt for the men.

"Hey, bartender," yelled the first man to sit down. "Bring us three glasses of that horse piss you Mexes call whiskey."

The Mexican outlaw eyed the three men and appraised them for what they were: American bounty-hunting trash. He had killed many men himself, but never for the price of their hides, as though they were sheep-killing coyotes or wolves.

The oldest of the three was Burl Compton. Big, mean, and ugly, he respected no man or woman. Burl had a full beard and was beginning to gray at the temples, even though Carlos suspected he was not yet thirty years old.

Anse Compton was tall as his older brother and built like a scarecrow. His left eye wandered all over the place, never seeming to focus on anything. He wore a thin gambler's moustache and a thin goatee. A narrow scar traversed his nose horizontally.

Petey was the youngest. Short and pudgy, even his clean-shaven, fair features and long, straggly hair had already begun to show the strain of riding the hard trails.

Burl put a finger to his left nostril and blew his nose. Mucus spewed onto the hard-packed, dirt floor. He wiped his nose and looked at Carlos Macias. Defiance filled his eyes. "Damn, Carlos, if you bean eaters ain't got the dirtiest country I ever saw." He grinned. What few teeth he had were twisted and brown.

Carlos curled his lip at the insulting gesture but said nothing about it. "You are late, amigos." He sighed as he thought how much he would enjoy killing these three men once their purpose was served, then managed a weak smile. "Were you not told by *el jefe* to be at Lucasville to help with the gold?"

Burl always did the talking for the brothers. "Yeah, we was, but somethin' important came up, and we couldn't get there right away. We rode through there. Looks like you boys tore the town up pretty good. Did you get the gold?"

"*Si,* we recovered the stolen gold."

"Damn, how much is there? When can we see it?" Burl squirmed in his chair like red ants were racing up his leg.

"It is safely hidden. Only Pedro and I know where it is. When I receive word from *el jefe*, I will turn your share over to you."

"Well, I guess that's okay, as long as it don't take too long. Me and my brothers don't want to spend any more time than we have to in this stinkin' country of yours." Burl downed his tequila in one gulp. He winced and screwed up his face as the tepid liquor burned its way into his stomach. "We'll wait—for a while. Now we need some food."

He turned to the fat bartender, who was eavesdropping through droopy eyelids and repeatedly wiping the same spot on the bar with a filthy rag. "*Gordo,* hustle us up some beans and tortillas. We ain't eat nothin' all day."

Chapter 7

Rubbing his throat, Ollie said, "All I know is that Mr. Burdock told all us Slash B riders that if we went into town that Sunday, we wouldn't have a job when we got back. When Mr. Burdock says something, don't nobody question it."

"Is Burdock the big he-wolf around Lucasville?"

"Yessir, marshal, he is. Don't nobody cross him."

Silverjack jerked up on the bandanna with both hands. The cloth went taut.

Ollie lurched and fell backwards over a log he was standing next to. "Oh, Lord," he moaned, "I'm gonna die today." He started crying again.

"Calm down, Ollie," said Pharaoh. "You're not going to die. Jack always pushes too far. This time he's crossed the line. I'll make sure this is his last job as a territorial marshal. Come on, let me help you up." Pharaoh reached for the stricken man's hand and pulled him onto the log.

Silverjack's head shot up; his eyes locked on Pharaoh. Jack's hand dropped to his six-gun. "You sayin' I ain't a good lawman, Pharaoh? I've killed men for less."

Pharaoh's right hand brushed his pistol grips. He returned the stare. "That's part of your problem, Jack. Stand down or pull iron."

Silverjack stood still for a few moments, then his body relaxed, and he turned his eyes away from Pharaoh. "This is the last time you talk down to me, Pharaoh," he said. "Next time we'll settle it." He stomped off, disappearing around the sandstone knoll.

Pharaoh watched him until he rounded the big formation, and then he returned his attention to Ollie. He made a big deal about brushing the dirt off the cowboy. "This isn't good, Ollie," he said, frowning.

"What do you mean, marshal?" Ollie's eyes darted in every direction like he expected to be ambushed at any second.

"I'm going to ask for Silverjack's badge in the morning, but I can't do anything tonight while we are asleep."

"You've got to protect me, marshal! That feller's crazy. I think he wants to kill me."

"The best thing you can do, Ollie, is to be completely truthful with me. I mean don't leave anything out. And I might be able to protect you from him. I might even speak to the judge and keep him from hanging you."

"Hanging me!" For the third time, tears formed in the frightened man's eyes, this time coursing down his cheeks like muddy little waterfalls. "I swear, marshal, I won't lie to you. Just, please, you have to protect me from that maniac."

Silverjack stood by the knoll, out of sight, but not out of earshot. "Maniac," he said, laughing to himself. "I reckon I'm a pretty good play actor. This 'good guy, bad guy' routine works every time. Pharaoh will have that younker spillin' his guts in no time." He took off his hat and leaned back against the knoll. A cool breeze drifted in from the west.

———————

Wilson Cosgrove stepped out of Dr. Prater's office, followed by Abby Boyett. She looked at him and stuck out her hand. "It was very nice of you, Mr. Cosgrove, to come and visit Mr. Daggett. I'm sure that will go a long way toward his recovery."

"The least I could do, Miss Boyett. I've known Abraham for a long time. I'm so glad he survived."

"Are you returning to Gila Bend soon?"

"Not right away. I must conduct some business that I have been avoiding because of the long trip here. Now, I have no excuse but to get it done." He reached over and caressed the nurse's hand. "Don't worry, Miss Boyett," he whispered. "I'll do my best to take Dan's place."

Abby yanked her hand away. "What?" she said, shocked. "What do you mean by that, Mr. Cosgrove?"

"Oh, I'm sorry, Miss Boyett. I didn't mean to startle you." His voice sounded strained. "I only meant I would be here if you needed a shoulder to lean on. Nothing more. And please, call me Will. I would really like that." He smiled, flashing four gold teeth in the front of his mouth. "Now, my dear, I must go and take care of my business. Remember, contact me if there is anything I can do." He tipped his hat and was gone.

Abby shuddered as the banker strutted across the street and into the saloon. "Not now, not ever," she muttered, and turned back into the doctor's office.

———•———

Will Cosgrove stepped into the saloon and hurried up to the bar. He waved the bartender over. When the man reached him, Wilson glanced around. Finding the saloon empty, he smirked and turned to the bartender. Both men leaned over the bar and spoke in hushed tones.

———•———

Sleep escaped Ollie as he tossed and tumbled in his bedroll all night long. By the time the sun rolled over the horizon, he had saddled his horse and was itching to ride somewhere—anywhere—as long as it was away from the crazy marshal. His teeth chattered from the morning chill, but he dared not start a fire. Watching the lawmen beginning to stir in their soogans, he breathed a sigh of relief as Pharaoh rose first. "Mornin', marshal," he said, waving. "Sure is cold, ain't it?"

Pharaoh grumbled and frowned at the cowboy. "How come you haven't started a fire yet, Ollie? If Jack gets up and there isn't any coffee boiling, he'll be mad as a nut-cut bull."

Ollie blanched and began to scramble around, hunting the wood he had gathered the night before. With shaking hands, he got a small blaze going and water on to heat. The Arbuckles was boiling when Silverjack emerged from his bedroll.

"Something sure smells good," Silverjack said. "Ain't nothing like a strong cup of Arbuckle's to get a body goin'." He put on his hat, shook out his boots, pulled them on, and jumped up. Holstering his revolver, he stretched his arms across his body and back as he stomped over to the fire. Giving Ollie the evil eye, he poured himself a cup of the molten brew.

"Jack," said Pharaoh, "You overstepped the line for the last time last night. I'm gonna need your badge."

"The hell you say."

"Jack, don't make this hard. You've threatened your last prisoner. Give me the badge."

Silverjack's hand dropped to his .44. His fingers wrapped around the butt of the six-shooter. His eyes darted between the two men facing him. Turning the tin cup up, he drained its contents. Dropping the cup on the ground, he took his hand off his .44. "Ain't either one of you worth a pinch of dirt. Y'all deserve each other." He spat coffee grounds, turned, and strode to his horse. Stepping into the saddle, he nudged Bess over next to Pharaoh. "I ain't got no badge, marshal. I lost it a long time ago." He laughed, ripped Bess around, and took off at a gallop, throwing up a cloud of dirt and rocks.

"He didn't give you his badge, marshal."

"What?" said Pharaoh, watching Silverjack disappear around the knoll.

"He didn't turn in his badge."

"Didn't you hear him say he lost it? Besides, we need to break camp and head back to Lucasville."

"Okay, marshal, whatever you say." Ollie scratched his rear end and smiled.

———————

In Lucasville, Will Cosgrove sat at a corner table in the Ocotillo café and dug into his bacon and eggs like he hadn't eaten in days. He was a large man with broad shoulders and big hands. He had worked hard to get to the position he now had and, in his mind, had earned his developing paunch and graying hair. His mood was jovial, and he greeted everyone who came through the door.

As he took a biscuit and sopped the last of the egg from his plate, he looked up to see Abby and Dr. Prater enter. He waved them over to his table and stood up as they arrived. "Good morning, folks," he said, flashing his gold teeth. "Please sit down, and let me buy you breakfast."

Abby frowned as Will pulled a chair out from the table. "Hello, Mr. Cosgrove," she said, her voice barely above a whisper. She sat down and turned her attention to Dr. Prater. "Samuel, perhaps I should go back and stay with our patients. I'm concerned that Mrs. Wheeler won't know what to do in case of an emergency."

"Nonsense, Abby," said the doctor. "Mrs. Wheeler doctored people here long before I came to town. Chances are she knows as much or more than I do about taking care of our patients. Relax and enjoy your coffee."

The waitress brought two fresh cups of coffee and refilled the banker's cup. Abby usually used cream and sugar, but on this day she drank her coffee black. Dr. Prater stirred two heaping spoons of sugar into his cup and took a sip.

"So, Mr. Cosgrove, did you finish that business you were telling Abby about?"

"Yes, yes, I believe I did. I should be hurrying back to Gila Bend, but the quiet solitude of your little town and the breathtaking scenery around here is compelling me to stay a few days longer." Will smiled at Abby when he mentioned the scenery. She did not smile back. "As a matter of fact, I was thinking about renting a buckboard and taking a ride out to the countryside. Abby, would you do me the honor of guiding me around to the most scenic sites? I'm sure you know all the best places to ride."

Abby's eyes darkened. "I'm sorry, Mr. Cosgrove, but I have work to do at the office. I can't go with you."

"Abby," said Dr. Prater, "I think that's a dandy idea. You need to get out into the fresh air. You've been cooped up in my office ever since Dan was..." His voice trailed off. "Ever since the tragedy. I believe a ride would do you a world of good. Besides, I think Mrs. Wheeler and I can hold down the fort for a little while without you."

Abby glared at the doctor and bit her lip.

"Well, that's settled then," said Will. "I will make haste to the livery stable and see what might be available for our trip."

"Mr. Cosgrove," said Dr. Prater, "there is no need for you to rent a rickety buckboard. I have a nice buggy and a splendid horse boarded at the livery. I want you to take it. Your ride will be much more enjoyable."

"Thank you, Dr. Prater, for your generosity. I will accept your offer." The banker turned to Abby, gold teeth sparkling. "I will pick you up at the doctor's office in half an hour." He stood up, said goodbye, and sauntered out the door.

Dr. Prater bid him goodbye and went back to his coffee. He smiled at Abby. "Mr. Cosgrove seems like a nice man. You should have an enjoyable afternoon."

Abby stood up and glared down at the doctor. Her lips were squeezed together so tight that they turned white. She sucked in a deep breath and looked like she was about to have a fit.

Shaking a clenched fist at Dr. Prater, she stormed out of the café.

Silverjack followed the bank robbers' trail south. No attempt had been made to hide the hoofprints, and he found them easy to follow. He dug a thick piece of jerky out of his saddlebag and gnawed on it as he rode. "Bess, I hope Pharaoh learns somethin' from that waddie." He patted the mare's neck. "I know one thing—I ain't too thrilled to be ridin' into the lion's den by myself. That's for dang sure."

The sun was a blinding ball of fire overhead when Silverjack topped a slight rise and spied a small adobe hut below. A rickety-looking corral housing half a dozen goats and a tired looking burro stood beside the hut. Needing fresh water and hoping for a hot meal, Jack rode Bess at a slow walk down the hill.

As he rode up to the door, he saw no sign of life around the place. "Hello, the house," he said. "*Hola la casa. Yo cuero agua, por favor.*"

The door cracked open, and a long-barreled musket appeared. "I speak English, *señor*. You are a *Norteamericano*. We have no water for you. If you do not leave *muy pronto*, I will shoot you."

"Damn," Jack said under his breath. "Okay, *amigo*, I will go, but how about some water for my horse first?"

"Go now or I shoot you. I mean it, *señor*."

"Okay, *hombre*, I'm leavin'." Jack nudged Bess and they started away. "Sure do admire this South-of-the border hospitality, don't you, Bess?"

The mare didn't answer.

Chapter 8

ilverjack rode on until the middle of the afternoon, when he found a little shade behind an enormous boulder. It was the only boulder for miles. He tied Bess to a small clump of sagebrush. Taking out his canteen, he drank a small sip and poured the rest into his hat. Bess quickly slurped up the small amount of water. Jack sat down and leaned in against the rock. Pulling his wet hat over his eyes, he was asleep in no time.

Bess whinnied. Silverjack opened his eyes. He heard something besides the mare. Straining his ears to listen, he could barely hear voices. After listening for a minute, he decided it was two men talking in Spanish and broken English. He closed his eyes just enough so he could see through his lashes. "We should shoot this one, Juan?" said one of the men who sounded American.

"No, Blacky," said the other, "I want his clothes. We bash in his head with a rock. *Mucho sangre, pero es* okay."

"Hell, yeah, it'll make much blood. Let me do it. Draw your gun, Juan—just in case he's playing possum." Blacky picked up a large rock and crept toward Silverjack. Standing over the prostrate man, he raised the rock above his head. Silverjack kicked him in the groin and rolled away, pulling his .44 as he did. Blacky doubled over and fell on his face, retching into the sand. Juan fired but missed. Jack fired and hit the Mexican in the knee. Juan dropped to the ground, firing as he fell. Jack emptied his six-gun at the fallen man. Reaching for his boot gun, Jack came to one knee and fired once more. It was a wasted bullet. Two of the rounds had buried in Juan, one in his chest, one in his throat. The chest shot had killed him.

Silverjack reloaded his pistols as he looked around for any more assailants. Finding none, he turned his attention to Blacky. The man lay in the dirt, groaning, covered with his own vomit. Jack walked over to him and removed his pistol. Then he walked over to Bess to make sure she was okay. He patted her neck and then turned back to Blacky.

"What are you two doin' out here in the middle of nowhere?" he asked.

Blacky had managed to sit up and was wiping his face with his bandana. He looked up at Jack but did not answer

Silverjack aimed his .44 and fired. Dust jumped up between Blacky's legs, and he scrambled backwards. "I just kicked you in the balls a while ago," he said. "If you don't answer my question, next time I'll shoot you down there. What are you doin' out here?"

"We was just ridin' around and we saw you sleepin', so Juan decided we ought to rob you," said Blacky, a sullen look covering his face.

"Aw, to hell with it," said Silverjack. "I've had enough of this. I'm gonna shoot you in the head and be done with it." He thumbed back the hammer on his .44 and aimed it at Blacky's head.

"Don't shoot!" hollered Blacky, sliding backward on his rear end. "We ride for Carlos Macias. We scout the area to make sure no laws or *Federales* are prowling around."

"Are we close to where Macias stays?"

"We're about five miles from where he is. Can I have my canteen? I need to wash this puke off my face."

"I ain't gonna waste no water on your face. Get up. You're gonna bury your *compadre*, and then we're gonna go see Carlos Macias."

After the dead outlaw was placed in a shallow grave, Silverjack tied Blacky's hands to his saddle and tied Juan's horse behind him. He mounted Bess and instructed Blacky to lead the way to Carlos Macias.

They rode for a few hours until the outlaw halted his horse. Silverjack rode up beside him. "What is it?" he said.

"There's a small village over the next hill," said Blacky. "Carlos should be there."

"That's just fine. Let's go see him."

"No. You have to let me go. If he finds out I led you here, he will kill me."

"You should have thought about that, *amigo*, before you tried to rob me." Silverjack lifted his left leg and kicked the outlaw's horse in the rump. The animal took off at a trot up the hill.

At the top of the hill, Blacky stopped again. Several stunted mesquite trees grew all over the hill. "See," he said, "I told you the truth. Carlos is down there in the cantina. Now, you've got to let me go. I tell you, Carlos will kill me. He's a ruthless cutthroat."

Silverjack drew his .44 and rode up next to Blacky. "I'm gonna cut you loose," he said. "You get down and walk over to that tree yonder. Make a move, and I'll be bringing Macias your dead carcass."

Blacky got down and trudged to the tree. Silverjack followed him. He made the outlaw face the tree, and he ran several strands of rope around it. Jack knotted up the rope just enough so that Blacky could get loose in a couple of hours if he worked hard at it. He remounted Bess and grabbed the reins of Blacky's horse. "See you," said Silverjack as he dug his heels into Bess's ribs.

"Wait, you can't leave me like this!" hollered the outlaw.

"I believe I just did," said Silverjack, smiling.

Riding down the gentle slope of the hill, Silverjack stuffed the last of his jerky in his mouth as he scoped out the village. Maybe two dozen adobe huts baked in the afternoon sun. A larger building on the near edge of the village had *tienda*, or "store," written on it in bright red letters. Riding into the village, Jack noticed a whitewashed building across from the tiny town square with *cantina* written on it. A wooden well stood in the middle of the square. Two women wearing colorful but faded dresses were drawing buckets of water and pouring them into large earthen jars. Jack tipped his hat as he rode up, and the women grabbed their jars and scurried up the street. Jack dismounted, drew a bucket of water, and drank his fill. He removed his bandanna and dipped it into the water. He washed his face and neck and put the bandanna back on. A small wooden watering trough stood at the corner of the well. He poured the remaining water into the trough and led the three horses to it. As the horses drank, he retrieved another bucketful of water and dumped it into the trough.

Silverjack stretched and looked around. "Hard to believe people can live like this," he said. These Mexicans are some *muy* tough folks."

After the horses were watered, he led them to the cantina and tied them to a post in front. Two other horses were tied there. Jack stretched, his muscles complaining. "Hell," he said, "I hope I ain't makin' a big mistake." He fingered the long scar on his face and stepped inside.

Chapter 9

The sourness of the cantina assaulted Silverjack's nose. He curled his lip as he looked around the dimly lit room. The place was empty except for two men sitting in the shadows at a back table. Wide-brimmed *sombreros* obscured their faces. A foul smell emanated from the direction of the bar, where a short, round sweat-soaked Mexican stood. Sullen eyes stared at Silverjack from under a tangled mop of mud-colored hair. Silverjack hitched up his gun belt and strode toward the man. He placed both hands on the dirty wooden plank disguised as a bar top.

"Give me a shot of tequila, *amigo*."

Silverjack kept his eyes on the bartender. The stinking man glanced at the two men at the table. His head bobbed and he reached under the bar. Silverjack tensed but kept his hands in place. A gush of air escaped his lungs as the bartender's hand rose above the bar, clutching a bottle of tequila.

The bartender scowled as he poured two fingers of the fiery brew into a dirty glass. Silverjack threw the tequila down his throat and shook his head. "Whooee, that's hot stuff, *amigo*," he said, grinning. "But it sure tastes good. Pour me another one. I'll be back directly." Pitching a silver coin on the bar, Silverjack sauntered over to the two men sitting at the back table. Fingering his scar, he pulled a chair out from the table, spun it around backwards, and dropped into it. "How you boys doin' this afternoon?" he said. Sure is hot, ain't it? Can I buy y'all a glass of *pulque* to celebrate?"

"*Que paso con este gringo*?" said the man sitting to Silverjack's right.

"What are you celebrating, *señor*?" said the other man.

"Well, pardner, I'm celebrating the death of that dirty lawdog, Dan Cable."

"*Señor*, why should we celebrate a man's death?"

"Why?" Silverjack's eyes narrowed and he smiled. "Because you're the ones who killed him."

———·—

The afternoon sun glared down on Pharaoh and Ollie as they rode into Lucasville. The deputy marshal held up his hand, and they reined in their horses in front of the burned-up shell of the town marshal's office. Pharaoh stared for a long time at the charred remains, and then he looked over at his riding companion.

"Ollie." His voice was grave. "You're not officially under arrest, but I aim to keep you with me until this mess gets sorted out. Do you understand me?"

"Yes, sir, marshal. I'll stick to you like a blood tick on a hound dog's hind end."

Pharaoh scowled. "See that you do. We'll take our horses to the livery. After that, I want to talk to that wounded banker, Daggett. He knows more than he's telling."

"Say, marshal? Talkin' about Banker Daggett made me think of something you might want to know." Ollie scratched behind his right ear. He pulled his hand away from his head and mashed a tiny spider between his fingers. Wiping the spider's remains on his shirt, he continued. "I remember about two weeks back, me and some of the boys were in the saloon throwin' a few beers down our gullets. All of a sudden, a big commotion caused us to look out in the street. Well, sir, there was a freight wagon sittin' in front of the bank with one of its wheels busted all to pieces. Dangedest thing you ever saw."

"What broke the wheel?"

"That's the funny part, marshal. That ol' banker was out in the street just a-cussin' the driver to beat the band. And that driver was shakin' like he was scared to death. Right away some fellers came up and started unloading the wagon."

"Was the wagon's cargo gold?"

"Everything was sealed up tight in crates, and I reckon nobody knows except the banker, and he ain't sayin'. But I'm with you, marshal. Whatever it was, the men who unloaded it had to bend their backs to carry the stuff into the bank. You want to know what I think, marshal?"

"No."

———·—

Dr. Prater was saying goodbye to Mrs. Wheeler, the local midwife, when Abby entered his office. Her straw-colored hair whisked in every direction, and her face flushed crimson. Mrs. Wheeler nodded to Abby and hurried out the door. Abby never looked at the woman. She stomped up to the doctor, stopping when her nose almost touched his.

"Hi, Abby. How was your ride with Mr. Cosgrove?"

"Samuel, you had better not decide who I go buggy riding with again. That Cosgrove is nothing but an old lecher."

"But I thought—"

"I don't care what you thought then, and I don't care what you think now." Abby stood on her tiptoes and pushed her face forward until her nose mashed against the doctor's nose. "He kept trying to put his hands all over me." She shuddered. "He told me he would buy me anything I wanted if I would go to Gila Bend with him."

Dr. Prater stepped back and put his hands up between himself and his attacker. "I'm sorry, Abby. I had no idea that Cosgrove was that kind of man. I will speak to him immediately."

Abby closed her eyes and forced her rapid breathing to slow down. She ran her hands through her unkempt hair and stretched her neck. "You don't need to talk to anyone, Doctor. I made it damn clear to that old fool that if he even spoke to me again I would geld him like a worthless bull."

"Excuse me, is someone getting gelded?"

The distraught nurse jerked her head around to see Pharaoh and Ollie standing in the doorway. Pharaoh was smiling, while Ollie stood behind him peeking over his shoulder.

"Humpf," she said, and stormed past the two men and out the door, almost knocking Ollie over as his feet got tangled up trying to get out of her way.

Pharaoh watched her until she disappeared around a corner, and then he turned toward the doctor. "I reckon my timing's not too good, Doc, but I need to ask your banker a few more questions."

"No, your timing isn't good, marshal. I just gave Mr. Daggett a sedative, and he will be out until tomorrow morning."

Pharaoh pursed his lips and rubbed his neck "I guess I'll have to wait, then. Doc, do you mind telling me what got Miss Boyett all riled up?"

Dr. Prater chuckled. "I don't know much, except she sure doesn't like Will Cosgrove. From what she told me, he's not quite what he appears to be." He paused. "All of my patients are resting now, marshal. May I offer you a cup of hot coffee?"

"Sounds good, Doc. We need to talk, anyway. You know Silverjack doesn't like Will Cosgrove, either. He's always said the man was a crook, but nobody's ever caught him doing anything illegal. He bears watching. Let's get that coffee, and we'll talk about Cosgrove, Daggett, and a few other things I've got on my mind. Ollie, don't leave this room. I'll call you if I want you." Ollie looked around until he spied a cane back chair in the corner. He mumbled to himself as he crossed over and plopped down in the chair. Pharaoh ignored him and followed the doctor into his office.

A small, scarred desk, two old chairs, and a tall, narrow file cabinet took up most of the space in the doctor's tiny office. Pharaoh sat at the chair across from the desk. In a moment, Dr. Prater walked in carrying two steaming cups of coffee. After handing one to Pharaoh, he grabbed the chair behind the desk and spun it around to face his visitor.

"You have questions for me, marshal?"

Pharaoh got right to it. "How long has the banker been in Lucasville?"

"Daggett or Cosgrove?"

"Daggett."

The doctor ran bony fingers down his small moustache. "Let's see. I guess he came to Lucasville a bit over two years ago. Said he was going to put Lucasville on the map. Nobody paid much attention to him accept Buck Burdock."

"Burdock owns the Slash B ranch."

"Yes, he does. That and most of the land for miles around."

"I'm guessing that he had something to do with the bank coming to Lucasville. How does Burdock fit in with the rest of the people around here?"

"That's a good question, marshal." Dr. Prater drained his coffee cup. He offered Pharaoh a refill, but the marshal declined. The doctor got up and stepped around the corner. A blue enamel coffee pot gurgled on the wood stove in the corner. He refilled his cup and stood for a minute staring at the wall. He shook his head and went back to his office. Easing into his chair, he took a sip of his coffee. "Most folks here don't care for the man. They believe he is after their land and wants the town as his own."

"Are they right?"

"I think they are. There is something unsavory about Burdock, but I can't quite put my finger on it."

Pharaoh nodded his head and called Ollie into the room. The cowboy didn't respond, and he called again. Still no answer. "If that boy's gone, he's in a world of trouble," said Pharaoh. He stood and walked into the front room. Ollie sat in his chair with his head down. His hat was pulled over his face.

"Wake up, Ollie," Pharaoh said, disgusted.

Ollie didn't move. The marshal lifted Ollie's hat. Ollie's head lolled back; round, lifeless eyes stared up at the ceiling. A thin red line creased Ollie's throat from ear to ear, and a steady flow of crimson pumped down his neck, soaking his shirt with blood.

"Damn!" said Pharaoh. He stepped to the door and searched in all directions. Not even a dust devil disturbed the empty streets. Lucasville looked as dead as Ollie Dunsmore.

Chapter 10

As Silverjack spoke, Pedro Quintano tensed up, and his hand moved across his belly to his six-gun. Carlos Macias reached over and put his left hand on his friend's arm. He put his right hand on the table.

"*Señor*," said Carlos, "you should be more careful of who you accuse of murder. Pedro here, he does not care for *gringos*." His eyes narrowed like a rattlesnake about to strike. "For sure, ones who carry badges, Marshal McDonald."

Silverjack had taken a big chance in accusing these men of Dan Cable's murder. From their reaction, he knew he had hit pay dirt. What he hadn't expected was to be recognized. He had to play out the hand he had been dealt, but one wrong move and he would be an ex-badge toter.

"And you are Carlos Macias. I heard you were *El Hombre Grande*, the big man in these parts. I didn't know you needed a nursemaid to protect you. Maybe I've got the wrong man after all."

Carlos barked something in Spanish and waved two fingers at the bartender. Pedro stood up and faded into the shadows. The bartender waddled over with two glasses of *pulque,* and then he disappeared as well. Carlos removed his hat and laid it on the empty chair beside him. He stuck a hand in a pocket of his maroon vest and pulled out a shabby deck of cards.

"*Señor*, now we are alone. As you see, I do not fear you or your badge. As a *Norteamericano*, in my country your badge is worthless. I spit on your law. But, as a man, I respect you. Many of my fellow countrymen fear you. You are well known in Mexico, Silverjack McDonald."

"Well, how 'bout that." Silverjack grinned and removed his hat. He ran fingers through his silver-gray hair and rubbed the back of his neck. "I never knew I was famous down here. Hell, I might just move to Mexico and get me a job with the *Federales*. I bet they would appreciate a man as well-known as me ridin' with them. You could even put in a good word for me, *señor*.

Carlos couldn't help but smile at the crazy *gringo*. "Call me 'Carlos,' *señor*, and, *con permisso*, I will call you 'Jack.'"

"That's all right with me, Carlos." Silverjack stared into Carlos's intense black eyes and tried to use his peripheral vision to watch the shadows. The room seemed to be empty, but his body tensed up like it was spring loaded. In spite of the heat, a dirty, brown icicle oozed down his back.

"*Bueno*, Jack, let us play poker. I know how much you *Norteamericanos* like to play this game. We will play one hand, and it will be, as you say, 'winner take all.'"

"What are the stakes? I ain't got much money."

Carlos laughed and began shuffling the cards. "I do not want your money, Jack. I want your life. If you win, you may ride back to Arizona unharmed. You have my word on it. If you lose, I will feed you to my hogs."

In spite of himself, Silverjack swallowed hard.

"Well, hell, Carlos, them ain't exactly my choice for stakes, but bein' that we're playin' with your cards, I reckon we'll play house rules. Deal them pasteboards."

Carlos nodded and pushed the deck toward Silverjack for him to cut. Jack waved the opportunity away, and Carlos snatched the deck from the table. He began to deal. His long, deft fingers flicked a card, face up, to Silverjack. An Ace of Spades. Carlos dealt himself a king. He looked over at Silverjack, face expressionless. He spun a deuce in his opponent's direction and laid his second card down beside his king. Another king.

Silverjack blinked, but he kept a straight face. He downed a long swig of pulque and made a sour face.

"You do not like our national drink, Jack." Carlos looked at the deputy and spat on the floor.

"It ain't one of my favorites, but it'll do to clear the dust out of my gullet." Silverjack fingered his scar. "Since we're playin' for my life, how 'bout you answerin' a couple of questions for me?"

"Sure, Jack, I am in no hurry to kill you. Ask your questions."

"Why did you kill Dan Cable?"

"I expected this question, Jack. Many years ago, Ranger Cable shot my brothers to death. Enrique and Miguelito were all the family I had." Carlos breathed deep and shook his head. His eyes glistened. "In a few seconds, Ranger Cable ruined my life. I swore to avenge my brothers someday, and now it is done."

Carlos slid a card to Silverjack. Six of diamonds. He dealt himself an eight of hearts. "I can't abide by it, but I understand why you killed Dan. Why'd you rob the bank?"

"Ah, this I should not tell you." Carlos lifted his glass of *pulque* and chugged down the fiery cactus juice. "But, because I respect you, and you are not going anywhere, I will tell you why.

"The bank was full of gold. We took it for a man I do not know. That is the truth. A *gringo* came to me, maybe two weeks ago. He would not tell me his name, but he said that if I help him rob Lucasville, I would have *mas oro,* more gold, than I could ever spend." Carlos ran a finger under his nose and pursed his lips. "I have plenty gold, *señor,* so I tell him no. Then he tell me Ranger Cable is the law in this town. I change my mind. I tell him, if he give my men gold, I will go, but the ranger is mine. That is all there is."

"Where is the gold now?"

"Jack, you ask questions like you think you will not be dead soon."

"It's not over 'til the last wolf howls, and I ain't even close to my last holler."

Carlos cackled with laughter. He raised his left hand and flipped it forward. Pedro emerged from the shadows to stand beside his boss. A fleeting smirk crossed his lips as he stared down at Silverjack.

"Pedro," said Carlos, still smiling. "What do you think of this *gringo?"*

"I think we should kill him now, *jefe.* He is too dangerous to let live."

"*Señor,* I think Pedro likes you." Carlos laughed again. "But he is right. It is a shame, but we must kill you. You know where we stay, and if I let you leave, perhaps the *Federales* will soon know, too."

While Carlos hee-hawed, Silverjack eased his .44 out of its holster. He sucked in the foul air—maybe his last breath on earth—and braced his feet on the floor. He leaned a bit to his right, ready to dive sideways and shoot at the same time.

As he coiled to make his move, a loud commotion outside the cantina caused him to stop. Pedro again stepped back into the shadows. Two massive hands appeared at the door and ripped down the curtain there. Burl Compton barged through the entrance with the curtain in hand. His two brothers stepped in behind him and spread out. Burl wadded up the curtain and tossed it aside.

"Macias, there has been a change of plans." Burl Compton pawed at his face like something was on it. "The boss sent a man to tell us to get the gold and take it to him. Tell me where you've got it buried, and we'll dig it up and deliver it."

Carlos dropped the cards and slid his hands under the table. "*Señor* Compton, I know nothing of this. I will not turn the gold over to anyone until I hear from *el jefe* himself."

Burl wiped his face again. "Hell, Macias, you don't even know who he is. Give us the gold now, or we will bury you right here in this stinkin' cantina."

"No, *hombre*, I will not give you the gold."

"After what you did in Lucasville, there's got to be a right smart reward for you, Macias. If you don't tell us where the gold is, we'll kill you and claim the reward." Burl's lips curled into a crooked smile. "After we kill you, I think your pepper belly sidekick will tell us where the gold is hidden."

Pedro emerged from the shadows. "Piss on you and your mangy brothers, *maldito*. You are dead men." All hell was about to break loose, and Silverjack was caught in the middle. He had to make a decision whether to throw down on Carlos and Pedro, or side with them against the Comptons and take his chances later. Burl Compton snarled an oath, and Silverjack made his move. He straightened his coiled legs and spun around in his chair at the same time.

The Compton Brothers pulled iron and started shooting. The Mexican outlaws commenced firing at the same time. Silverjack raised his pistol, took aim, and fired two bullets into Anse Compton's chest. Anse fell back against the cantina wall and slid to the floor. Everyone was firing, with lead flying in every direction. Oblivious to the screaming bullets, Pedro stood with a flaming six-gun barking from each hand. Carlos had flipped the table over and was slinging lead from behind it. The two remaining Comptons kept moving around, shooting from the hip. Pedro took a bullet above his right eye. He died before he hit the floor. A slug shattered Petey Compton's right kneecap, sending him screaming to the floor. He dropped his six-gun and grabbed his wounded knee. While he writhed in pain, a bullet tore through his brain, tearing out a fist-sized chunk of his skull. Burl dropped to his knees, blood oozing from half-a-dozen holes in his body. Despite the wounds, he kept firing until a bullet tore into his heart and ended his life. In less than a minute, four men were dead.

Carlos rose from behind the table and dropped into the closest chair. He began to reload his pistols. When he finished, he eased the six-guns into his holsters. Looking down at his dead friend, he closed his eyes and shook his head.

Silverjack looked around and realized he still sat in his chair. "Damn," he said. His hat lay on the floor behind him, and a searing pain pounded his left ear. He reached up. Blood trickled through his hand as he felt around. His ear was still there, at least most of it. A half inch of the top was gone. "Son-of-a-bitch," he said as he removed his bandanna and held it against his ear to staunch the blood.

Using his free hand, he checked his body for other wounds. A bullet had gone clean through his buckskin shirt without touching him. He found a slight graze on his neck that burned like the dickens but didn't draw blood. He removed the bandanna from his ear and stuck it in his pants pocket. Reloading his pistol, he looked over at Carlos. He stood up and moved away from the chair. The outlaw stared at him, but his eyes were not focused.

"Pardner," said Silverjack, "seems we didn't get to finish our card game."

"It makes no difference now, *señor*; everyone is dead. Pedro is dead. All because of filthy gold. Such a waste." Silverjack was about to speak when Carlos jerked his six-gun and pointed it at Jack's stomach.

"Hey, now, Carlos, what is this?" Silverjack backed up a step and raised his hands. "We just shot a bunch of bad guys to worm food, together. How about an even chance? You owe me that."

Carlos frowned. "I owe you nothing, *señor*, but I will give you something, anyway." He tried to laugh but the sound died in his throat A trickle of blood ran down his chin. "These *gringo* fools died for gold that was not theirs. I will never understand *Norteamericanos*. The gold is behind the bar. Poncho, the bartender, will find you some burros to load it on."

"Behind the bar all the time. Well, I'll be damned if that ain't a hoot. Wait a minute—you're giving the gold to me?"

"Shut up and listen, Jack. The gold belongs to your *Americano* government. It was stolen many years ago from a military train."

"Hell, I recollect that. Jessie James and his gang was supposed to have robbed that train up in Missouri. Nobody ever found the gold, and the James boys swore they didn't pull that job."

"They did not rob the train. The ones who did fought over the gold and killed each other until only one man was left alive. This one kept the place where the gold was hidden a secret for many years. He never went back." Carlos coughed into his hand. More blood poured through his lips. Silverjack could tell by the way Carlos was acting that he had been gutshot, but he said nothing.

"The *hombre* was killed in Tucson two years ago. As he died, he told one man where the gold was buried. That man is *el jefe* of the bank robbery in Lucasville. He is the one who told me that Ranger Cable was there."

Silverjack fingered his scar. "Carlos, why ain't you keepin' the gold?"

"Dead men have no use for gold, Jack."

"What do you mean?" Jack cocked his head.

"I have been shot in the belly. I am dying." Carlos coughed again. "Take the gold back to your country. I believe you are an honest man, Jack. You can get this job done. *Buenas suerte,* good luck. I think you will need it. The man behind the robbery—his name is Burdock."

"I thought you didn't know his name."

"I lied," said Carlos, trying to smile but failing.

"Let me look at your wound, Carlos." Silverjack started toward the wounded man. "Maybe I can help you with it."

"Stop," said Carlos, waving his pistol at Silverjack. "I will not die slowly." He stuck the pistol in his mouth and pulled the trigger.

Chapter 11

Pharaoh had been quiet ever since McCorkle, the undertaker, had removed Ollie Dunsmore's body. He sat on a bench outside the doctor's office and reassessed the situation. Dan Cable had been murdered by Carlos Macias, whose gang ransacked Lucasville and stole an undetermined amount of gold. Where had the gold come from? He had to wait until tomorrow to ask Abe Daggett, who had been sedated by Dr. Prater. Two women were dead, and Ollie had been murdered right under his nose. Silverjack, if he was still alive, was somewhere in Mexico searching for Carlos Macias. This had turned into a tough case with way too few clues.

He removed his hat and ran a hand through his short-cropped hair. Was Daggett a suspect? Buck Burdock threw a wide loop in the area. Was he involved? What about Will Cosgrove? Jack didn't trust him, and he had a nose for bad men. The whole situation gave Pharaoh a headache. Standing up, he started inside to ask the doc for a headache powder when he noticed Abby Boyett running up the street. Her clothes were disheveled, and as she got closer, he could tell her face was flushed. She looked like she had been crying. When she stepped up on the porch, Pharaoh stood in the doorway and confronted her. "Miss Boyett, are you okay?" he asked.

Fire raged in her eyes as she tried to push her way past Pharaoh. Tears streamed down her red cheeks, and she drew back her fists. She stood like that for a moment, then she collapsed against Pharaoh's chest. Pharaoh caught the fainting woman and lifted her in his arms. He turned sideways and carried her into the doctor's office, then into the room where the two dead ladies had been. Laying Abby on the nearest cot, Pharaoh hurried to get Dr. Prater from his office.

"Doc, Miss Boyett has fainted. Her clothes are messed up, and she's been crying."

Both men hastened to the stricken woman's side. Dr. Prater knelt and took hold of Abby's wrist. "Her pulse is racing, but I believe she will be okay. Bring me a glass of water, marshal."

By the time Pharaoh returned with the water, Dr. Prater had loosened Abby's clothing, and her pulse had returned to normal.

"Marshal, please raise Abby's head while I give her a little water."

Pharaoh complied, and Dr. Prater separated Abby's lips. He trickled water down her throat and she swallowed. Within a few moments, the young woman's eyelids fluttered, and she opened her eyes. She lay unmoving, staring at the ceiling. All at once, her eyes flicked left and right, and she jerked to a sitting position. The doc took hold of her shoulders and held her firm.

"Abby," he said. "You are okay. This is Sam. You're safe in my office. Relax."

"Sam, oh, Sam," Abby's voice quivered, and she trembled. "Thank God I made it here."

"Miss Boyett," said Pharaoh, "can you tell us what happened? You walked into my arms and collapsed."

Abby glanced over at him. "I fell into your arms?"

"Yes, ma'am."

She turned from Pharaoh's gaze, color creeping into her pale features. "Oh, I'm sorry, marshal. I must have been so upset I didn't know where I was."

"Abby." Dr. Prater's voice was soft but firm. "Tell us what happened."

"Cosgrove attacked me."

"What!" said Pharaoh, straightening up. "Where did you last see the man?"

"In the stable. I punched him in the nose and ran out of there."

Pharaoh charged out the door and headed toward the livery stable. He reached the wide, wooden door and stopped. The door stood open, and noise echoed from inside. The racket sounded like a scuffle was going on. Pharaoh palmed his six-gun and stepped around the door.

He glimpsed a shadowy figure running out the opposite side of the stable. "Stop!" he yelled as the figure disappeared out the back. Instead of following the person, Pharaoh ran back out the front door. A man emerged from the alley and jumped for a horse that was standing with its reins trailing the ground. He scooped up the reins and mounted in one blurred motion. He jerked the horse's head sideways and kicked it hard in the ribs. The terrified animal's knees buckled, and it almost fell. As the horse regained its balance, Pharaoh shot the rider out of the saddle.

The riderless horse galloped down the street. Pharaoh cocked his .45 and stepped toward the downed man. His bullet had caught the man in the back of the neck. The body lay motionless in the dirt, his face buried in fresh horse manure. "Cosgrove, looks like you fell right in it," Pharaoh said, curling his lip at the pungent odor. Avoiding the man's flop-covered face, he stuck a boot toe under the body and rolled it over. He leaned down and stared into the face of a stranger.

"Dang, you're not Will Cosgrove. Who in blazes are you?"

Pharaoh noticed a long skinning knife sticking out of the man's boot. He stared at the hilt a moment and realized there was blood on it. He grunted and quickstepped back into the barn. Will Cosgrove lay in a back stall. He was on his back and his legs were spread out, his head positioned at an impossible angle. When Pharaoh stepped up to the body, he realized Cosgrove's head had almost been severed. Only a small strip of bloody flesh joined the head to the body.

Pharaoh rounded up a few men, who carried the two bodies to the undertaker's office. Before the corpses were taken away, Pharaoh threw a bucket of water into the face of the killer. He was identified as Tiburcio de la Hoz, a local horse wrangler who was known to be good with a knife. No one knew who he might have been working for.

Pharaoh felt relief as he stepped back into the doctor's office. Abby was sitting in a chair talking to Dr. Prater. Her demeanor was something less than cordial.

Dr. Prater lowered his gaze and held his hand up. "I know, I know, Abby. I was wrong, and I'm sorry. I'm sure if Cosgrove is still in the area, the marshal will find him. That bounder will not get away."

Abby and the doctor looked up as Pharaoh approached them. He explained what had happened and told them about Will Cosgrove and his apparent murder. Both were shocked at the turn of events.

"Doc," Pharaoh said, taking off his hat and scratching his head, "any idea who de la Hoz might have been working for?"

"Not offhand, marshal, but I'll tell you who might know. Casey, the bartender, knows everything that goes on in Lucasville. When his patrons get a little liquor under their belts, they tell him everything they know. The man's a good listener."

"Casey, huh? We had a little run-in with him when we first got to town. I'll go over and prod him a little bit—see what I can find out."

"Marshal," said Abby, "I want to thank you for helping me earlier. I don't know what would have happened if you hadn't been here to catch me. It isn't like me to react the way I did. I guess the thought of Dan being gone, plus everything else that has happened, upset me more than I realized."

"I just happened to be there when you fainted. Anyone else would have done the same thing. Now, if you would excuse me, I have a bartender to scare."

Pharaoh walked into the street and headed toward the saloon. Abby's eyes followed him until he disappeared from sight. Her lips were parted and, just for an instant, her tongue flicked out and moistened them. Pharaoh stepped through the swinging doors of the saloon and observed the place. Except for the bartender, and four men playing cards at a front table, the place was empty. Pharaoh sidled over to the card players and, with his hand resting on the butt of his .45, spoke to them in soft tones. The men looked around at each other and, almost on cue, rose as one and exited the saloon. Their gambling stakes were left where they lay.

The bartender watched the scene play out and kept wiping the same glass like he was trying to rub the clear off of it. He was sweating a river when Pharaoh approached the bar.

"Give me a cold beer, Casey," Pharaoh said in a menacing tone.

"Sure thing, marshal. Anything for the law." Casey's hands trembled as he drew a mug of beer. "Here you go. No charge."

Pharaoh chugged the whole brew and slammed the mug down on the bar. Casey jumped like he was poked with a stick. Keeping his eyes locked on the bartender, Pharaoh removed his hat and set it on the bar. He rubbed the left side of his face and sighed.

"Casey, I'm going to make this real simple. I'm going to ask you some questions, and you're going to answer them truthfully. If I sense you're lying, even one time, I'll quit asking and tell Silverjack you called his mother a real bad name. The last man who said something bad about his mama is still missing. Are we clear?"

Casey looked like he was about to bawl, but he nodded his head. "What, uh, do you want to know, marshal?"

"Who was Tiburcio de la Hoz working for?"

"He worked for a lot of people, marshal, now and then. Mostly, he just hung around town and bragged about how good he was with that pig sticker of his."

Pharaoh inhaled through his nose and blew the air out his mouth. "Last time, Casey. If you think I'm bluffing, go ahead and mess with me. Who was de la Hoz working for when he cut Will Cosgrove's throat?"

Casey's tremble turned into a full-blown shake. "Marshal, they'll kill me if I spill my guts. I can't tell you."

Pharaoh stuck his hat on his head, making a big deal out of straightening it and getting it just right. "Casey, I'm disappointed in you, but you made your choice. Jack should be back in town anytime. I'll be sure to let him know how uncooperative you've been." He took one step toward the door when the bartender blurted out a name.

"Burdock. The chili eater worked for Burdock. When the old man needed some dirty work taken care of, de la Hoz was his man. He could use that knife better'n most men can use a six-shooter. Cosgrove, Daggett, and Burdock were in cahoots to share that Yankee gold. Cosgrove got greedy. He thought him and me were partners because we went way back, and he tried to hire me to kill Burdock and finish off Daggett."

"Why didn't you?"

"Hell, marshal, I ain't no fool. I sent word to Burdock about what was goin' on. I reckon he did the rest."

"I don't know why, Casey, but I'm inclined to believe you." Pharaoh fumbled through his shirt pocket until he came up with a few coins. He pitched a nickel and two half-cent pieces onto the bar. The coins rolled around until they fell over in a neat pile. "Two things, Casey. First, I'm paying for my beer. Second, just to be sure, I'm going to tell Silverjack to come have a talk with you, just in case you might have left something out." Pharaoh touched his hat brim and sauntered out of the saloon.

Casey stood for a moment with his mouth agape. Then he reached behind him and tried to undo the knot in his apron. Frustrated that he couldn't get the thing untied, he ripped it off and threw it on the floor. Hurrying to the cash register, he popped it open and dug out all of the bills. Stuffing the money in his pocket, he reached under the bar, grabbed his hat, and headed for the back door.

Chapter 12

Silverjack had no idea how much the stolen gold was worth, and the less he thought about it the better. Except for stopping long enough to untie Blacky and send him on his way, he had made good time since leaving the cantina, and he figured he could make it to Lucasville in less than two days if the gold-laden burros cooperated. So far, they were clopping along at a steady pace. His biggest worry was running across bandits or *Federales*. Either would try to take the gold away from him. He wasn't going to let that happen.

The sun was a shimmering ball of red fire dropping in the west when Silverjack rounded the knoll where he and the others had camped the night before. He decided to make a cold camp, so after picketing his horse and the burros, he hunkered down and feasted on cold beans and tortillas he had picked up at the cantina. Afterwards, he laid out his bedroll and made it look like someone was in it. Then he grabbed his extra blanket and rifle and moved into the shadowy darkness of the trees to sleep.

As he sat leaning against a small tree, listening to the sounds of the night, Silverjack thought about Carlos Macias and what had taken place back at the cantina. The outlaw had carried a grudge against Dan Cable ever since his brothers were killed. The gnawing rage in his gut had kept him alive while he searched for the ranger. After he'd killed Dan, Carlos had lost his reason to go on. What makes a man yearn for revenge so much it becomes his only reason to live? Silverjack pondered these thoughts as he closed his eyes for a moment to rest them.

The smell of coffee boiling caressed Silverjack's nostrils. He lay for a moment enjoying his dream, when he realized he was awake and the coffee was real. He kept still with his eyes shut. Someone had started a fire in his camp. He had no idea who it was, but the odds of it being a friend were less than slim.

Silverjack mentally cursed himself for sleeping so hard. He dared not move for fear of alerting the person in his camp that he was awake. He was trying to decide what to do when the decision was made for him. A leg cramp caused him to move his leg.

"Antonio," said a greasy voice that Silverjack recognized. It was the bartender from the cantina. "The *gringo* is awake. He is playing like a little possum."

The scattered laughter made Silverjack shiver. More than one man occupied his camp. He had no choice but to open his eyes and face his destiny. His eyelids lifted, and he stared up into the bartender's ugly face.

"I see you ain't found no bathtub yet, Poncho," Silverjack said, waving his hand in front of his face. He tried hard to look unconcerned. Sitting up, he rubbed his eyes and tried to make out a man standing over a small fire a few feet away. "I appreciate you boys fixin' me some coffee this mornin'. I'm a real bear until I've had me a couple cups of hot black Arbuckles."

Silverjack didn't recognize the man at the fire. The Mexican was tall with narrow shoulders. He wore a loose-fitting blue shirt over striped gray pants tucked into high leather boots. His sombrero was thrown back on his head, and a two-gun *buscadero* rig encircled his waist. "*Buenas dias, señor,*" said the man. "I am Antonio Contreras. I believe you have taken something that belongs to my *amigos* and me. We have come for its return."

As he stood up, Silverjack glanced round for his guns. None were in sight. He looked over at Poncho, who was grinning at him like a crazy man. The bartender's crooked teeth were as nasty as his body. His breath was foul with the odor of onions and chilis eaten long ago. Silverjack's stomach rumbled at the man's stench. Silverjack reached down, picked up his hat, and began stumbling toward the fire. His body was stiff from sleeping sitting up, and his wounded ear hurt like hell. Furthermore, he had no clue how he could get out of this mess.

Antonio Contreras held a tin cup full of coffee. Steam billowed from the cup as the heat from the mud-colored liquid clashed with the early morning chill. Silverjack's mouth watered at the thought of a fresh cup of the black brew. "Since that's my Arbuckle's you're enjoyin' there, pardner, you reckon you can spare me a cup?"

"No, *señor*, I cannot. It would be a shame to waste coffee on a dead man."

"That's pretty harsh, Antonio." Silverjack tried to smile, but it came off as a crooked sneer. "You're gonna kill me for gold that don't rightfully belong to either one of us."

"*Si, señor.*"

Silverjack fingered the scar that traversed his face. Out of the corner of his eye, he caught the rising sun's rays flickering off a metal object sticking out of a pile of rocks fifty yards away. "That don't hardly seem right, *amigo*." Silverjack tried to buy some time and hoped he'd guessed right about the shiny object protruding from the rocks. "You're drinkin' my coffee, and I expect you're gonna eat my food, too." Jack scrunched up his face like he was mad. "And another thing, I'm tired of folks tellin' me I'm a dead man and me still walkin' around breathin'. Man, you ain't got no heart at all."

Silverjack's statement was prophetic, as the sound of a rifle shot echoed off the rocky knoll, and Antonio's heart exploded. The Mexican's face bore a questioning look as he dropped to his knees and pitched forward into the fire. Silverjack dove for the dead man's pistols. He jerked them from the *buscadero* rig and rolled away. Screaming lead chunked up around him, and he came up firing. By the time he drew a bead on one of the outlaws, the hidden rifle man had shot two more of the bandits. Jack aimed and twice squeezed the trigger of one of the nickel-plated Colt .45's. The bullets tore into Poncho's belly, gutting him open like a slaughtered hog.

Both pistols cocked and ready, Silverjack spun on one knee, searching for another target. Horses were bolting in every direction, kicking up a mountain of dirt that made seeing impossible. Jack stayed low, trying to clear dirt from his eyes. As he did, he realized all was quiet. The gunfire had ceased as quickly as it had started. Jack stood up and turned in a slow circle. Four bodies lay around the camp. He shook his head and spit out a wad of dirty brown saliva. He shaded his eyes as he gazed toward the pile of rocks. A rider approached from that direction, but Jack couldn't make him out. Whoever it was could sure shoot the hell out of a rifle.

The shooter reached the camp, reined in his big bay gelding, and stepped to the ground. Silverjack stuck out his right hand. "Howdy, Black Tom," he said. "It sure is nice to see you standin' right side up."

"You're damn lucky I came along when I did, Jack, or you'd be on your way to being buzzard dung. I was riding south, searching for the Comptons, when I heard a commotion and stopped to check it out."

"I sure was in a fix," said Silverjack. "Now I'm real glad I cut you down the other day."

"Consider us even, Jack."

"Even it is, Let me find my guns, and then help me round up those burros, and we'll be on our way north."

Tom rubbed his stubbled chin. "Didn't I hear something about gold?"

"I'll explain everything while we ride. Come on, before more bandits show up."

———

Pharaoh narrowed his eyes at Dr. Prater. "Doc, I need to talk to Daggett."

"I believe Mr. Daggett is sleeping now, marshal. I suppose when he awakens, you may speak with him for a short time. He needs to rest quietly."

"I'll speak to him now." Pharaoh pushed past the doctor and strode toward Abe Daggett's cot. "If what I think is true, he's got a long rest ahead of him." The marshal reached the bed and pulled his six-shooter. He stuck the barrel of the .45 against Daggett's nose and pressed down hard.

The banker awoke with a start and began to squirm. His eyes crossed, trying to focus on the pistol mashing his nose. When he realized what was up, he froze. Daggett's eyes shot to the hand holding the pistol and on up the arm. They widened as he recognized Pharaoh holding the pistol.

"Daggett people are getting killed around here in bunches today." Pharaoh cocked the .45. "I'm tired, and I'm mad, and I'm not in the mood for another lie. I'm going to ask you some questions. You blink your eyes twice for yes and once for no. Blink."

Abe Daggett blinked twice.

"Marshal," said Dr. Prater, "what are you doing?"

"Stay out of this, doctor. Your banker helped get the gold stolen from his own bank. Will Cosgrove and Buck Burdock were his partners. Is that the truth, Daggett?"

Daggett closed his eyes and opened them. A tear meandered down his cheek, puddling at the corner of his mouth. He blinked again.

"What is going on, marshal?" Dr. Prater looked confused. "What you are saying is absurd. I know little of Cosgrove, but Abe Daggett is one of Lucasville's leading citizens. And you know I don't like Burdock, but I'm certain he is not a criminal. Both have done wonderful things for this town. You are mistaken about them. What proof do you have that they committed this crime?"

Pharaoh stepped away from Daggett and holstered his six-gun. "I have enough information to ride out to Burdock's ranch and arrest him on suspicion of robbery and murder."

Dr. Prater dropped his head and walked into his office.

Abby had entered the room and was watching in horror as the two men talked. "Marshal, I'm like Samuel. I can't believe what you're saying is true. That would be awful."

"Gold corrupts a lot of people, both good and bad, Abby," said Pharaoh. "No one knows how they will be affected by that temptation until they are exposed to it."

"I still can't believe it, marshal."

"When Jack gets back in town, we'll ride out to Burdock's and get this situation under control. Maybe then you'll believe it, Abby."

Unnoticed, the doctor re-entered the room. "Marshal Smith, you are a smart man and good detective. It's a shame you discovered the truth—or at least part of it."

Chapter 13

A short-barreled .41 revolver rested in Dr. Prater's grasp. He cocked the pistol and aimed it at Pharaoh's chest. Abby's eyes saucered in disbelief. "Samuel, what are you doing?"

"I am about to solve a problem, Abby. Marshal Smith has stumbled upon Lucasville's best kept secret."

"I don't understand."

"In a moment you will. Marshal Smith, remove your revolver with your left hand, and pass it to me, pistol grips first."

Pharaoh grit his teeth and cursed himself for being a fool. But he did as the doctor ordered and, barrel in hand, thrust the six-gun forward.

"Abby, my dear," said Dr. Prater, "you are a sweet girl and an excellent nurse. However, your naivete is equal to that of your dead ex-fiancée, Marshal Dan Cable."

Abby shrieked and lunged at the doctor, fists flailing. He sidestepped her attack, and as she stumbled by, he slammed his pistol barrel to the back of her head. Abby fell forward onto an empty cot and lay still.

Pharaoh stepped toward the doctor, but he was too far away to make it to Abby's aid in time. Before he could take a second step, Dr. Prater had his pistol pointing at Pharaoh's chest again.

"Marshal, take another step, and I will kill you right here."

"If that girl is bad hurt, Prater, there won't be a rock big enough for you to hide under. I'll forget my badge and hunt you down like the devil's spawn you are."

"Devil's spawn!" Dr. Prater laughed. "My God, man! You talk like a Bible toter at a backwoods camp meeting. Oh, my, Marshal Smith, you are as simple as Abby and that dead fool Cable."

Pharaoh breathed hard, trying to remain calm. "What are you going to do with Abby and me?"

"There will be one more tragic accident in Lucasville. You and my former nurse will be burned to death along with all the other patients in this building while I am out at Burdock's ranch making a house call."

"That's insane!"

"No, marshal, actually it is a foolproof plan. Cosgrove is dead. Daggett will perish in the fire along with everyone else, leaving the gold to be split between Burdock and myself."

"What's going to happen when Silverjack gets back in town and finds out about the accident? He won't buy it for a minute. When he catches you, you'll wish you'd given up to me. Jack was raised Comanche. Your death will take a long time."

"I have taken measures to assure that fool will not be returning to Lucasville. I am sure that by now he is ample dinner for a pack of hungry coyotes."

Pharaoh's eyes caught movement behind the door. He grinned. "You don't think much of Jack, do you, Doctor?"

"Of all of you, I believe he is the dumbest of the lot." Dr. Prater chuckled.

"Well, Doc, why don't you turn around and tell him to his face?"

"You best turn slow, sawbones," said Silverjack.

Dr. Prater whirled at the sound of Silverjack's voice. He recognized the marshal's silhouette in the doorway and tried to aim his pistol to fire, but his arm wouldn't cooperate. He looked down to see two smoking holes marring the neat appearance of his clean, white shirt. "Oh, dear God," he whispered as he dropped to his knees. He rocked backwards and then slumped forward with his arms crossed in front of him.

"Damn fine shootin' for a lawdog, Jack," said Tom Raines, standing beside Silverjack, pistol in hand.

Silverjack ignored the comment and walked over to Pharaoh. "What in Beelzebub's crooked pitchfork is goin' on here, Pharaoh?" he said, surveying the room.

As soon as Dr. Prater's body had hit the floor, Pharaoh scrambled to the bed where Abby still lay unmoving. He checked her pulse. It was weak but regular. "You're sure a tough one, Abby," he said, then turned to Silverjack. "I'll explain later, Jack. Right now, I have to take care of Abby. She took a nasty rap on the head."

Silverjack grabbed a sheet from a vacant cot and helped Tom pick up Dr. Prater's body. They carried the dead man outside and laid him on the sidewalk. Tom wrapped the body with the sheet, tucking it in at the corners to keep the flies out. When he finished the grisly task, he stood up, rubbed the back of his neck, and stretched his tight muscles. "Do you think there might be a reward out for this chunk of maggot meat, Jack?"

Silverjack looked at his companion and shook his head. "You ain't ever gonna change, Black Tom. It's always about the money for you."

Tom put a finger on his left nostril and blew a big, green chunk of mucus onto the corpse. He wiped his nose on his sleeve. "Yas, suh, boss," he said, hard black eyes staring at Silverjack. "If you don't got no money, you don't have no freedom."

Silverjack nodded and sent Tom to round up Mrs. Wheeler, the town midwife, so she could check on Abby.

Abby opened her eyes and quickly shut them again. The brilliant light blinded her, and her head ached like it did when she was kicked by Papa's mule. She took a deep breath and opened her eyes again—this time slower. After a moment, she was able to keep them open and focus. The first thing she saw was Marshal Pharaoh Smith standing over her. She thought he looked funny with his face all squinched up. She tried to laugh and regretted it right away. Flaming arrows of pain tore through her brain. She tried to scream, but no sound came out. Her only thought was that if this was death, please let it happen quickly. The fire raging in her skull was more than she could stand. She passed out again.

"So that's pretty much all I know, Jack." Pharaoh sipped from the white porcelain coffee cup in his hand. "Added to what you've told me, I think if we round up Burdock, we'll have this situation well in hand."

"When do we hit the ranch?"

"Just as soon as I know Abby is going to be okay. Then we'll head out." Silverjack fingered the scar on his face. "This sure didn't turn out to be the picnic I thought it would be. What are we gonna do with all that shiny stuff? I ain't a greedy man, but a new rig would look right nice on 'ol Bess. I've been usin' the same saddle for nigh onto ten years."

Pharaoh's features hardened, and he stared Silverjack in the eye. "Jack, I don't like talk like that. As much gold as we've got, anybody might be tempted by it."

"Yeah, *compadre*, anybody but Deputy Territorial Marshal Pharaoh Smith. He don't care about the gold, because he's already got more money than a normal man could spend in a lifetime."

"That's enough, Jack. I'm warning you. No more foolish talk about the gold."

Silverjack smiled, but his eyes showed no mirth. "Hell, Pharaoh, I was just joshin' you. What would a broken-down old gunfighter like me do with a bunch of tainted gold but spend it?"

"What about Tom Raines, Jack? Can we trust him not to turn on us and try to take the gold?"

"I've been cogitatin' on that. I think if he was gonna try for the gold, he would've shot me when he ambushed those *Mexicano* outlaws back yonder. He's a strange one, but in his own way, I think he's loyal."

"Speaking of Black Tom, he should be back now with that midwife, Mrs. Wheeler."

While the two men were talking, Abby had awakened again. She lay there taking in the conversation and letting her senses ease into service. Her head still ached, but the pain was bearable. She tried to speak, but her mouth felt full of cotton. She closed her eyes and rolled her tongue around until enough saliva loosened up her vocal chords. Pushing the pain to a remote part of her mind, she opened her mouth. "How about a drink of water, boys?"

"Abby's awake," Pharaoh said, rushing to her side.

Silverjack grabbed a glass and filled it from a pitcher sitting beside the coffee pot. Reaching Abby's bedside, he handed the glass to Pharaoh, who poured a trickle through Abby's dry lips.

"How do you feel, Abby?" Pharaoh asked as he gave her some more water.

"Like I got kicked in the head. What happened?"

Pharaoh explained what had transpired. Before he was finished, Tom showed up with Mrs. Wheeler in tow. Assured by the midwife that Abby would be okay, Pharaoh joined Tom and Silverjack on the sidewalk.

"Did you get the gold hidden in a safe place, Jack?"

"Yep, only Tom and me know where it's hidden."

"You best help keep us alive, marshal," said Tom. "It would be a shame if that gold went lost again, right after we found it."

Pharaoh scowled at both men. Tom stared back at him. Silverjack turned his head. "We ain't gonna get the bad guys standin' here talkin' about no gold," he said. "Let's get this fandango over with."

Pharaoh nodded, and all three men started for their horses. Pharaoh swung into the saddle. He looked back into the doctor's office, trying to catch a glimpse of Abby. He was unsuccessful. "All right, boys," he said, "y'all better be loaded for bear. Check your weapons. We don't know what to expect when we get to Burdock's ranch. Just let me do the talking."

"What are you gonna say, Pharaoh?"

"I'll know when we get there, Jack. Let's ride."

They turned their horses into the street and galloped out of town in the direction of Buck Burdock's Slash B ranch.

The Slash B lay ten miles north of Lucasville. The trail there was rocky, and the terrain was dotted with large stands of giant yuccas and lesser groups of prickly pear and ocotillo cactus. The three riders picked their way among hills and arroyos that covered the arid landscape. Mid-afternoon was upon them when they reined in their horses on a small hillock overlooking the ranch headquarters.

"From what I've been told," said Silverjack, "this spread covers a whole lot of southern Arizona."

Pharaoh removed his bandanna and tried to wipe some of the trail grime off his face. "I expect we've been on Slash B property for some time now."

Tom stood in his stirrups and looked around He settled back into his saddle with a puzzled look on his face. "Something's bothering me. It's awful dry around here, and we haven't seen any cows. A big ranch with no livestock—that don't make no sense."

"I can answer that," said Pharaoh. "While Ollie Dunsmore and I were riding back to Lucasville, I grilled him about Burdock's operation. He said they never did have much stock here. What they had was sold off over a month ago. Burdock let most of his men go right after the bank robbery. The ones he kept were more gunmen than cowboys."

"Any idea how many men are down there, Pharaoh?" "Ollie told me Burdock had six gunhands on the payroll. I killed one in town, so there's probably five, maybe more."

"Good," said Black Tom. "That means we can shoot anybody on sight."

"No, it means we have to be careful that we don't get shot on sight." Pharaoh cut his eyes toward the black bounty hunter. "Burdock is the only one we want. We're going to try and take him out of there without any bloodshed."

"Here y'all go again," said Silverjack, "jawin' when we should be workin'. How are we gonna play this, Pharaoh?" Pharaoh stretched his neck, looking around. "See those rocks about fifty yards to the right of the house? Tom, you set up behind those with your Winchester ready."

"Why am I always the one to hide in the rocks?" Tom said, frowning.

"Because we're marshals," said Silverjack. "It's our job. Besides you could hit a jackrabbit's tail feathers at a dead run with that Winchester '73 of yours."

"Tom," said Pharaoh, "you should be able to see the front and back of the house. I don't intend to go inside, but we may have to, so I want you covering both ends."

"We," said Silverjack, "means I'm goin' with you. All right, let's go."

Tom held his horse back as the other two picked their way down the hill. The ranch house was a rambling, one-story adobe structure. Besides the rocks where Tom was headed, little else but scrub cactus and creosote lay within a hundred yards of the house. A small barn and pole corral stood behind the house.

Silverjack and Pharaoh counted six horses in the corral. Whether more were in the barn, they couldn't tell. As they approached the house, two men stepped outside and spread out six feet apart. Both were heeled and carried the look of death. The two marshals walked their horses to within a few feet of the men.

"What do you want?" said the shorter of the two men. His tobacco-stained handlebar moustache drooped below his lantern jaw. He wore two pistols butt-forward, with another stuffed in his belt.

"We're here to see Buck Burdock," said Pharaoh. "We're deputy territorial marshals."

"Howdy, Silverjack", said the other man standing in front of the house. He was built like a grizzly bear and almost as big. A wiry, black beard dotted with patches of gray seemed to sprout from his face like a noxious weed. A filthy bandanna crossed his face, covering his left eye. His clothes were no cleaner than the bandanna. A shiny scarlet sash wrapped around his considerable girth. An enormous Bowie knife rested behind the sash, along with two .36 Navy pistols. A short-barreled, twelve gauge shotgun almost disappeared in his paw-like hands.

Silverjack leaned forward and squinted his eyes. "I'll be damned—Hunk Threadgill. I thought I killed you in Nacogdoches."

———◆◆———

Chapter 14

unk Threadgill lifted the filthy bandanna covering his left eye to reveal a puckered empty eye socket. "Yuh damn near did kill me, Jack. Besides losin' the eye, I got a bunch of places all over me where you stuck your pig sticker. You just missed my gizzard."

"Well, Hunk, I'm glad you lived through our tussle." Silverjack ran a finger down his scar. "My face still gives me some trouble now and then."

Hunk grinned. "That's good to know, Jack."

Pharaoh fidgeted in the saddle. "We need to see Buck Burdock right now."

"He ain't here," said Handlebar.

Hunk turned to the little man. "Buford, don't be lyin' to Silverjack here. He'll put your candle out before you can spit your cud. Burdock's in the back of the house, Jack. There's two hardcases with him. They're playin' moon. The old man sent us out here to kill y'all." He turned the shotgun toward the marshals.

Silverjack's hand dropped to his six-gun, but he made no move to draw. "Burdock's a lyin' son-of-a-bitch, Hunk. You gonna stand with him?"

"When I hire on for a job, Jack, I generally stay with the brand."

"That's admirable of you, Hunk, but this feller ain't worth the horse flop on your boots. Besides killin' a bunch of innocent people, his men raped two women. You don't belong with that trash."

"Aw, hell, Jack, I didn't know. That trumps all deals with me." Hunk shifted the shotgun, pointing it at Buford. "Buford, I reckon we need to take a little walk. Go on and head for those rocks out yonder where Black Tom's pointing that Winchester at us."

Buford jerked his head toward the rocks. Then back to Hunk's shotgun. Without saying a word, he started shuffling off the porch away from the house.

"I saw y'all when you topped the rise, Jack," said Hunk. My one eye's better'n most folk's two. After y'all finish the dance, me and Buford will help you pick up the pieces." He stepped from the porch and followed the smaller man.

Pharaoh looked at Silverjack, who rolled his eyes and grinned. Pharaoh nodded and stepped out of the saddle. Silverjack followed suit.

"Jack, give me a minute to sneak around back. Then you kick in the front door and holler your ass off. We'll trap these boys between us." Pharaoh ducked low and started creeping around the side of the house.

Silverjack gave Pharaoh enough time to get in place and stepped onto the porch. He pulled his .44. Then he reached down and slipped his hideout gun from his left boot. Sucking in a deep breath, he raised his boot and drove it into the door. The cheap pine door busted in two big pieces, splinters and small chunks of wood careening in every direction. "Give it up, Burdock!" yelled Jack. "Territorial marshals got you surrounded. You ain't got a chance."

Flattening himself on the porch, Silverjack just missed being riddled by the fusillade of lead spitting from the house. He covered his face against the chunks of wood and adobe that showered him.

At the back of the house, Pharaoh hollered. "Drop your guns, Burdock! Surrender and you'll get a fair trial!"

Scrambling to his feet, Silverjack snuck a peek around the door jam. The gunfire rained toward the back of the house. He cocked both pistols and stepped inside. A bullet screamed in front of him, tearing his hat off. Both pistols came up firing, and a loud groan echoed from behind a half-closed door. Silverjack poured more lead into the door. The bullet-riddled panel swung open, and a body pitched forward. Silverjack kneeled and reloaded his pistols.

Pharaoh snapped off a series of shots into the back of the house. His six-gun clicked on an empty chamber, and he dropped to one knee behind a rock-walled well to reload. Before he could get a shell in the chamber, a man came running out of the house, firing at his position. Pharaoh ducked his head and rolled around the well. He managed to cram one bullet into his six-gun before the charging man burst upon him. A fiery chunk of lead tore into the meaty part of his right arm. He border shifted his six-gun to his left hand. When the wild-firing gunman loomed over Pharaoh, the marshal fired his one bullet into the man's chest. Pharaoh tied his bandanna around his arm and reloaded. Readying himself to fire again, he realized the gunfire had ceased. "Burdock, this is your last chance. Give up, or face the consequences."

"Okay, marshal, you've got me. I'm done. All my men are dead. I'll come out with my hands up."

"No, stay where you are. Throw out your weapons, and lie down on the floor."

A .44 Smith and Wesson and a .45 Colt flew from the house and bounced in the dirt.

"That's all I have, marshal."

"Jack, are you all right?"

"Yeah, looks like I might get out of this alive."

"Good. Get Burdock, and bring him out the back way. And be careful."

Silverjack eased into the room where Buck Burdock lay. The rancher cringed on the floor, his arms outstretched in front of him. "Get up real slow, Burdock. My pardner wants to take you in alive, but I'd just as soon shoot you and get it over with."

Burdock placed his hands under him and pushed himself to his knees, then to his feet. He stood with his back to Silverjack. He started for the back door and staggered to one side. "Marshal, I'm sick," he murmured. "I think I'm going to pass out."

The rancher weaved like he was about to fall. Silverjack started to step back and give the stricken man some room. His boot heel caught on the curled edge of a rug, and he stumbled and looked down. As he regained his balance, he looked up in time to see a blur whistling toward his head. He ducked, but something caught him on top of his head, and he dropped to the floor.

Burdock squeezed the piece of firewood that he had clobbered Silverjack with, watching the marshal crawl around dazed on the floor. When Silverjack tried to stand up, the rancher picked up both of his pistols.

"Now you get up, marshal. You're sure not too careful for a lawdog. That suits me fine.

You just gave me a chance to get out of here with my hide. I said get up!"

Silverjack tried to shake the cobwebs away with little success. He managed to reach his feet, but he was in no condition to fight Burdock. The rancher jabbed him in the ribs with his own .44, and Silverjack staggered out the back door. Burdock stuck to him like a shadow.

"I got your pardner, marshal." Burdock's voice exuded confidence. "You try to stop me, and I'll blow him to little bitty pieces. Drop your iron and get on your feet."

"Aw, Jack," Pharaoh said, laying his pistol on the ground and standing up. "Burdock, you won't get away with this. We'll hunt you down wherever you go."

"Hard for dead men to hunt anybody down, marshal. This one's clumsy." Burdock again jabbed Jack in the ribs with the .44, eliciting a groan. "And you're so stupid, you actually dropped your gun when I told you to. I reckon they don't make lawdogs like they used to."

Buck Burdock reared back his head and let loose an evil laugh. A Winchester cracked, and the rancher flopped over on his side. A thumb-sized hole dribbled blood just in front of his ear.

Chapter 15

Pharaoh said, "Well, Lieutenant Cardigan, that's about it." He eyed the shave tail lieutenant, who had ridden down from Fort Apache with a detachment of men to temporarily take over the running of Lucasville. "With Buck Burdock and the rest of his conspirators dead, except for Abe Daggett—whose confession tied up all the loose ends—we're done here. This affidavit I just signed turns the temporary running of Lucasville over to the Army." Pharaoh stood up and offered his hand to the lieutenant.

Lt. Cardigan shook his hand. "Thank you, Marshal Smith. You can be sure the United States Cavalry will do their best to help the people of Lucasville rebuild their town. Now, about the reward, are you sure you want it handled the way you said?"

"Absolutely," said Pharaoh. "Also, I would appreciate it if someone kept a close eye on Abby Boyett. She's been through a lot these last few weeks."

"Yes, sir," said Lieutenant Cardigan. "I will handle it personally."

"Excellent, lieutenant. I thought you might."

The lieutenant's cheeks turned pink, but he said nothing.

"Now," said Pharaoh, "with our job here done, we'd better be riding back to Gila Bend. Good-bye, lieutenant." Lieutenant Cardigan saluted, and Pharaoh smiled and stepped outside. Silverjack and Black Tom were saddled and waiting. Pharaoh patted Texican on the neck and mounted.

"What about the reward?" asked Black Tom.

"Your share will be wired to Gila Bend in ten days to two weeks," said Pharaoh.

"Outstanding," said Tom. "It's been a pleasure working with you boys. If you ever make it to San Francisco, look me up. The drinks are on me. *Adios*." He spurred his horse and took off at a gallop.

"Reward," said Silverjack. "I never knew how sweet that word could be. Let's see, $5,000 split up three ways means my share comes to—over $1,600. That's right, ain't it?"

"Uh, yeah, that's about a third of five thousand, all right," said Pharaoh, looking down at his saddle horn.

"You know," said Silverjack, "I reckon we should have given some to Miss Boyett to help put the town back together. That would have been the thing to do."

"I did give her some, Jack."

"Really." Silverjack fingered his scar. "That's good, Pharaoh. I'm not a greedy man. How much did you give her?

"All of it."

"All of it!" Silverjack's mouth dropped open. "You mean all of *your* share, right?"

"I mean all of it, Jack—your share, too."

"Pharaoh Smith, what right do you have giving away my money? I put my life on the line for that dough."

"No, Jack, you put your life on the line for fifty bucks a month, and besides, it was the right thing to do."

"The hell it was. Pharaoh Smith, you sorry, no-good—"

Pharaoh kneed Texican, and the big horse took off. "See you in Gila Bend, Jack!" Pharaoh hollered as he rode away.

Silverjack gouged Bess with his heels, and they took off at a hard gallop after Pharaoh. "When I catch you, you dadgum do-gooder, I'm gonna tear off your—"

The rest of Silverjack's words disappeared into the wind.

-THE END-

Armstrong's War

Chapter 1

The crack of a pistol shot shattered the morning silence. Jim Butler jerked his mount to a halt, his hand dropping to his six-gun. He was high atop a rocky ridge that overlooked a long, sandy arroyo. The shot had come from below. Dismounting, he hunkered down and trotted toward the edge of the ridge. A few feet from the rim, he dropped to his belly and crawled the rest of the way. Peering over the precipice, he frowned at what he saw.

Four cowboys with pistols drawn sat horseback on the edge of the arroyo. Three of the riders were men from Jim's past. Below the men, kneeling in the dirt, were four Mexicans and a half-butchered longhorn steer. Another Mexican lay on his back; blood oozed from a gunshot wound on his side. Of the four riders, the youngest one with the blond hair was bellowing like he was in charge.

"I told you my daddy was making a big mistake letting them Mexes start farming on our property."

One of the cowhands, a scruffy-looking puncher, nodded in agreement. The other two glanced at each other, saying nothing.

"You're sure 'nuff right about that one, Chris," said the nodding cowboy, punctuating his statement by launching an enormous glob of stringy tobacco juice that hurtled through the air in the general direction of the Mexicans.

"*Señor* Armstrong," said one of the Mexicans, "We do not kill this cow. It was dead when we found it. The neck was broken, maybe from a fall into this arroyo. We did not want the meat to go bad, so we butchered as much as we could carry to our families. We would have told El Patron when we saw him next. This is *verdad, señor.* The truth, I swear it."

"Don't lie to me," said Chris Armstrong. "You stinking bean eaters ain't worth the spit in my mouth. Get your sorry carcasses into that cart yonder and head out toward our ranch house. When my daddy finds out about this he'll make sure you heathens get to dance on the end of a short rope. I heard you boys love to dance. Ain't that right?"

The scruffy cowboy laughed like he thought his boss had said about the funniest thing he'd ever heard. The other two sat stone-faced.

"Say, Chris," said the larger of the two silent cowboys, a barrel-chested man with a gray bush of a beard. "See the way that old steer's neck is all twisted back. That sucker's broke clean. Maybe these fellers are levelling with you?"

"Shank Halsey, how long have you worked for the Double-A-Slash?"

"Chris, you know I was with your daddy when he rode into this country. Shucks, son, I've been here forever."

"If you want to stay here, old man, you had better shut your mouth."

The last of the riders, a lanky mass of freckles named Rusty Puckett, started to say something, but Shank nudged him, and he backed off.

From his perch above the scene, Jim watched with growing concern. He had known Shank Halsey and Rusty Puckett all of his life. He wanted to speak up, but decided to watch some more before committing himself.

"*Señor*," said the Mexican who had spoken before, "what about Manuel? We must get him to a doctor. He is bleeding too much. He might die here."

"Bleed to death or hang, it don't make any difference. He's going to die anyway," said Chris. "Didn't I tell you to get in that wagon, Mex? Now, go!" He turned to the scruffy rider. "Val, you make sure these boys get to the house in a hurry. I'm going ahead to tell Bale what we found and to get the ropes ready."

Not waiting for an answer, Chris Armstrong dug his spurs into his horse and took off at a gallop toward the headquarters of the Double-A-Slash ranch. Seconds later, Shank Halsey headed out in the same direction.

Jim waited until all the men were out of sight, climbed aboard his steel dun mare, and worked his way down the embankment to the arroyo. When he got there the wounded Mexican was still breathing, but the man had lost a lot of blood. Jim rummaged through his saddle-bags until he found a pint bottle of whiskey and a clean shirt. He wrapped the shirt around the wound to staunch the flow of blood. He then gathered up a few pieces of wood and started a small fire. After putting a pot of water on to boil, Jim looked over at the unconscious man. The Mexican farmer's breathing was coming in shallow, ragged gulps. Jim had removed more than his share of lead chunks in the last fifteen years, but never from a man this close to death.

"Amigo," said Jim, "I don't hold much chance of you living through the night, but I'll do my best to fix your wound. Then it'll be up to the man in the sky to decide whether you live or die."

Jim unsheathed the knife he wore on his belt and placed it by the fire. He cleaned the wound with hot water. Then he poured some of the whiskey over the knife blade. Straddling the still unconscious man, using great care, Jim probed into the bullet hole.

I think I feel it, *amigo,"* said Jim. He was sweating but not from the heat. He reached the tiny piece of lead and, with a little effort, popped it out.

"You're lucky, pardner," he said. "It doesn't look like the bullet hit any vitals." Afterwards, he packed the wound and wrapped it with strips torn from his clean shirt.

Jim reckoned he was two hours north of Two Bucks City, Texas. He had planned on reaching the town by early afternoon, but the shooting of this Mexican farmer had altered his plans. He couldn't leave the wounded man, and moving him was out of the question. He unsaddled his horse and picketed the big mare over a large patch of green grass. He arranged his gear on the ground and checked on the Mexican. The man's breathing had become more regular since the bullet had been removed. He seemed to be resting.

"Amigo," said Jim, "you survived my butchering well enough; you just might make it after all. I made camp and I'll stay with you through the night. I can't promise anything beyond that. It's been a coon's age since I had me a fresh beefsteak, so I believe I'll carve me a big ol' hunk of this steer and cook it for my dinner. I'll save some to make a broth for you, if you make it."

———

Chris Armstrong charged up to the Double-A-Slash ranch house like the devil himself was chasing him. He jumped off of his horse before the animal stopped, bounded onto the porch, and stomped inside.

"Dad!" he hollered. "Dad, are you here?"

An answer came from the kitchen. Chris entered the room to find his father sitting at the table drinking a cup of coffee. Maria, the Mexican cook, was washing dishes.

"Señor Chris, would you like some coffee?" said Maria. She wiped her hands on her apron and started toward the coffee pot sitting on a potbellied stove in the corner.

Chris ignored the offer and ripped into his father. "Dad, I told you, letting those greaser farmers squat on our land would cost us. Well, now they have gone and killed a steer and tried to butcher it. I'm going to teach all of those Mexican peons a lesson."

"Whoa, there, Chris," said Bale Armstrong. The chair under him protested, squeaking loudly, as Bale tried to straighten his bent frame up to face his irate son. "Calm down. Sit here, get you a cup of coffee, and tell me what's going on. That's a pretty strong accusation you just made. Did you see these Mexicans kill the steer?"

"No, I didn't see them, but they did it. They had already killed it and were butchering it when we got there."

Maria's slender body stiffened at the accusations. "Excuse me, *Señor* Bale, but I must go to the henhouse for a few minutes." She didn't wait for Bale Armstrong's answer.

Throwing a tattered shawl around her narrow shoulders, the old woman hurried outside. The screen door banged shut behind her. Bale looked up as she left, and then back at his son. His eyes were hard.

Placing both hands on the table, using great effort, Bale pushed himself to a standing position. His worn-out legs creaked like rusty hinges as he stood. "Was anybody with you when you found the steer?"

"Shank and Rusty were with me. Val Rose was there, too."

"Where are they?"

"Bringing in the rustlers. I'm going to hang them. That ought to keep the rest away from Double-A-Slash livestock."

"Hang 'em! That's a little bit harsh, isn't it?"

"Bale, those greasers have got to learn once and for all who is boss around here."

Bale looked Chris in the eye. "You had better not forget who is boss around *here*, either, Chris. I don't like it when you call me by my first name. It shows disrespect. Ever since you started hanging around with that Quarry bunch, son, you have been making some mighty poor decisions. You know Mort Quarry wants this ranch, and he will stoop to anything to get it."

Chris opened his mouth but nothing came out. He sat for a moment, and then stood up. "I don't have time for this. I'm going to the barn for some rope. I've got a bunch of Mexicans to hang."

Before Chris could go out, Shank Halsey strode into the room. He stood in the doorway blocking Chris's exit. Chris tried to go around him, but Halsey stood his ground.

"Boss, we got to talk, and I'd just as soon Chris be here to listen to what I've got to say." He shot a withering glance toward the younger Armstrong. Chris backed up against the cabinet and stood silent.

"I'm sure you already got the story from Chris, boss, but I want to make sure he didn't leave nothin' out."

Bale Armstrong looked at Chris and back at Shank. He cocked his head to the side and motioned for the old wrangler to continue.

"Boss, them farmers was butcherin' that steer when we came up on 'em. The dumb thing was in the arroyo with its neck all twisted back. They said they found it there with a broke neck, and they was just tryin' to save some of the meat. One of 'em said he was goin' to tell you, next time he saw you."

"Is this true, Chris?" said Bale, narrowing his brow.

"They said that, but everybody knows a Mex would rather tell a lie than eat tortillas and chilli peppers."

"That ain't all, Boss," said Shank, in a low voice. "Chris shot one of 'em. The feller didn't have no gun, either."

"Good Lord, Chris," said Bale, his face blanching white. "You shot an unarmed man?"

"Come on, Dad, it was a stinking Mexican."

Bale looked at Shank. "Is the man dead?"

"Don't know, boss; Chris made us leave him there and bring the rest of 'em here to hang."

"Where are the rest of the men who were doing the butchering, Shank?"

"Rusty and Valentine are bringin' 'em in. They ought to be here any minute, now."

"Shank, you get Maria to take a wagon, and you two hightail it back to the arroyo. If that man is still alive, bring him back here."

Bale Armstrong turned to his youngest son. "Chris, you tell the boys to let those Mexicans go and tell Rusty to escort them back to their homes. I'll go out there tomorrow and apologize to them. And boy, you had better hope that man you shot isn't dead."

Chris looked at his father, disbelief covering his face. "*You* tell them, Bale. I'm done working here. Mort Quarry offered me a job, and I'm going to take it. He knows how to treat his men, and he always needs another gun." He turned toward the door. "Get out of my way Shank, or you'll be the next man I shoot." Shank stepped aside, and Chris stormed out of the kitchen.

Shank looked down at his boss and old friend. "He'll come back, Bale. He just ain't quite growed up yet. Maybe him bein' away for a while might help, it sure can't hurt. I'll get one of the hands to hitch up a wagon, and, on our way out, I'll tell Rusty what to do with them farmer fellers."

Shank headed for the front door. Bale Armstrong dropped into his chair and bowed his head.

Chapter 2

Jim was moving to check on the wounded man when the clatter of an approaching wagon caught his attention. Standing up, he loosened the thong on his .44 and stood relaxed as the wagon pulled up to the edge of the arroyo. Shank Halsey rode beside the wagon, and Jim was surprised to see a woman driving the rig. As the woman pulled the team of horses to a stop, the big puncher reined his horse in to her left.

"Howdy," said Jim. "Sit and rest a spell, coffee's hot."

"Gracias, señor," said the lady.

"Usted son Mexicana?" said Jim.

"Yes, I am, but I speak English."

"Good," said Jim. "Maybe you can help me, *señorita.* There is a Mexican man here. He has been shot. I took the bullet out and did my best to help him, but I don't know if he will live or not."

Maria hopped down from the wagon seat and scurried over to the wounded man. "It is Manuel, *por Dios,* he is alive."

Shank glared down at Jim. "I know you from somewhere," he said. "What's your name?"

"Most folks call me Jim Butler. What's *your* handle?"

"It don't matter who I am. What's your interest in this hurt feller?"

"No special interest, I was just ridin' by, looked down into this arroyo and noticed the steer. When I rode down, I saw the wounded man. The rest you know."

"You had a fire. Did you cook up some of that animal?"

"Well, him being dead and all, just wasting away... Yes, sir. I did have me a big chunk of beef. It sure was good, too."

"You're on Double-A-Slash land, feller. That steer belongs to Bale Armstrong."

"He must be the big 'he coon' around here, then."

"Has been for thirty years and will be for another thirty," Shank said. "You the Jim Butler who was involved in that little ruckus up in Oklahoma about a year ago?"

"Yep, that's me."

"You got yourself a reputation, Butler. We don't need no more two-bit gunfighters around these parts. You saddle up and shuck it for somewheres else."

Jim smiled at the old cowpoke. "You people sure ain't too friendly around here, *amigo.*"

Before the conversation could heat up anymore, Maria called out, "You two quit wasting time and help me get Manuel into the wagon."

Jim looked at Shank, winked, and turned to help Maria with Manuel. Shank sat his horse, his hand resting on the butt of his six-gun, and watched.

With the wounded man loaded and settled in as best could be expected, Maria clicked her tongue and the horses started off toward the ranch headquarters. Shank stayed behind with his eyes on Jim, until the wagon was thirty feet away. He started to turn his horse to follow, when Jim spoke.

"Shank, hold up a minute. I want to talk to you."

Shank Halsey stopped cold. Turning his horse back around, he rode to within spitting distance of Jim. There was a puzzled look on his face.

"How come you know my name, Butler? Where'd we cross trails?"

"Shoot, Marion Charles Halsey, why shouldn't I know your name, you old mossy horn?"

Shank jerked back, almost falling off his horse. "Ain't nobody around these parts knows my Christian name. Who *are* you?"

"Get down off that hay burner, and have a cup of Arbuckle's with me. The coffee's been on the fire for a couple of hours so it ought to be just the way you like it."

Jim dug a tin cup out of his saddlebags, filled it with the strong, hot brew, and handed it to the big cowboy. He took off his hat and ran a rough hand through his bushy hair. "I'm Bale Armstrong, Jr., Shank," Jim said. "I've come back from the dead."

Shank's face turned to chalk. The tin cup dropped from his limp fingers and clattered across the hard-scrabble ground. He stood motionless, staring into the cobalt-blue eyes of Jim Butler. "By the Lord Almighty, you are Bale Armstrong, Jr. Badger, it's you!'

"Nobody's called me Badger in fifteen years. It sounds strange, but it sounds pretty good. How are you, old *compadre?*"

Jim Butler stuck out his right hand, and Shank grabbed it, jerking it like a pump handle. Both men briefly embraced, and then backed off. Shank kept on shaking his head.

"Doggone it, Badger, the old man told us you was dead; it was nine or ten years ago. He said you got killed in some sort of gunfight down Arizona way. Why, he even went down there to see your grave. What in tarnation happened?"

Jim smoothed out his hair and put his hat back on. "Let's get over yonder next to the fire, and I'll tell you a little bit about it."

They hunkered down, and Jim began his story.

"When Poppa kicked me off the ranch, I drifted south into Mexico, and ended up throwin' in with some rough *hombres*. We ran cattle back and forth across the border and raised Cain on both sides. One night in Tombstone, one of the gang came out second best in a disagreement with Doc Holliday."

"Holliday kill him?" asked Shank.

"Yep, that's when I got the idea."

"Idea for what?"

"Back then, I was still mad at my father. I had some papers on me that said who I was, and when nobody was looking, I slipped them inside the dead man's coat. The undertaker buried Bale Armstrong, Jr., the next day. I took the name Jim Butler after James Butler Hickok—Wild Bill—and that's what I've gone by ever since."

Jim got up and stretched his legs. He took his hat off and raked fingers through his hair. Telling his story to Shank had brought back unsettling memories.

"By durn, Badger," said Shank, rising to his feet, "everybody knows about Quick Jim Butler. Some say you're the fastest man with a handgun that there is. I heard you killed over a hundred men. Is that right, Badger?"

"No, it ain't right, Shank. I've killed some men, but only when there was no other choice. I hope I'm through with killing. That's one of the reasons I came back home. I want to settle down on the ranch, if my father will let me."

"Say, Badger. We got to get on back to the ranch and tell Bale you're alive. Man, I can't hardly wait to see the look on Rusty's ol' freckled face when he hears the news."

"No, Shank, I don't want anyone else to know I'm back—at least not yet. I was up on that ridge yonder, and I saw what happened with those Mexicans. Something's not right."

"Badger, it's that dad gum Mort Quarry and his bunch. They're tryin' to get your daddy's ranch, and they don't pay no never mind how they do it. Quarry owns most of Two Bucks City already, but that ain't enough for a greedy crook like him. He wants it all."

"Shank, what happened to Chris? He shot that man for no reason. Since when has it been a crime to butcher an animal that was already dead?"

"Aw, Badger, over the last year, Chris has turned into somebody I don't know any more. He's been hangin' out with that Quarry gang, and not hardly doin' anything to help on the ranch. A little while ago, he told Bale he was quittin' the Double-A-Slash because Bale wouldn't let him hang them farmers."

Jim rubbed his hand down his mustache. "Shank, I'm going to ride into Two Bucks City tomorrow as Jim Butler. I don't want anyone else to know who I am. As far as I'm concerned, right now, Badger Armstrong died in Tombstone. I'll let it be known who I am when I'm ready."

"Whatever you say, boss."

Jim raised his eyes upon hearing the word "boss."

Shank Halsey was grinning like a possum full of pawpaws, and stayed on for awhile talking to Jim about what was going on in Deaf Smith County. The more he heard, the more Jim became concerned he had arrived home too late to save the family ranch.

Bale Armstrong, Jr., might have died in Tombstone, but Quick Jim Butler was alive and well, and he intended to turn over every rock in the Two Bucks country until he found the right snake to stomp on.

Chapter 3

The sun was a glaring yellow orb staring out of a cloudless Texas sky when Jim Butler rode into Two Bucks City. Recent spring rains had turned the panhandle country green. Swathes of orange, red, blue, and yellow flowers shot up everywhere, gracing the landscape with a rainbow of colors. In spite of the trepidation Jim was feeling about coming back after so many years away, he felt good.

The first thing he did was look for the telegraph office. He was surprised to find it in the same old building. Dismounting, he tied the mare to a rail and stepped inside the office. The place reeked of rotting wood. Buckets had been placed at various spots on the floor to catch rain from a leaky roof. A telegrapher sat behind a scarred wooden desk in the far corner. He did not look up when Jim entered the building.

"I need to send a telegram," Jim said in a soft voice.

"Paper and pen's on the table. If you can't write, it will cost you a nickel for me to scribble it out for you." The young man never looked up.

"I can write, *amigo*. Can you read?"

"'Course, I can read," the man said, looking up at Jim. A piercing black stare greeted him, and his lips froze in place.

"Pardon me, sir." The telegrapher's voice squeaked like a trapped mouse. "I meant no disrespect."

Jim wrote out his telegram and handed it to the man. "How much?" He said, reaching into his pocket for change.

The man read the telegram and looked up. "Do you work for Mr. Quarry, sir?"

"What if I do?"

"There would be no charge to send this telegram."

"In that case, I do work for the man. Where could I find him right now?"

"Mr. Quarry could be anywhere, sir. He owns almost all of the town. Dude Miller is usually in the Golden Ace saloon this time of day."

"Who is Dude Miller?"

"Why, he's Mr. Quarry's foreman. I thought you said you worked for them? If you don't, you will have to pay for this telegram."

Jim stared at the telegrapher until the man lowered his eyes. "You calling me a liar?"

"No, sir, I just thought—"

Jim took a step closer to the man. "Send the telegram."

"Yes sir."

The man was pounding the telegraph key when Jim stepped back out on the sidewalk. As he walked up the street, Jim saw the Golden Ace two blocks down the way and across; he turned and headed in that direction. Before he reached the saloon, Jim noticed the bank half a block away and veered off toward the native stone building. He looked up at the sign above the entrance:

Deaf Smith County Bank

M. Quarry, Pres.

Jim stepped inside and felt instant relief from the pounding Texas sun. A young woman behind the teller's cage had her back to him. She seemed oblivious to his presence. Jim put his hand to his mouth and coughed twice. The young lady gave a start and whirled around.

"Pardon me, sir," she said. "I didn't hear you come in. May I help you?" Two shimmering emerald eyes, a petite upturned nose, and a perfect pair of cherry lips in a flawless oval face combined to strip Jim of his powers of communication.

"Sir? Sir, are you okay?"

"Uh, yes, ma'am. I think so."

"You look like you've seen a ghost."

"No, ma'am, just the prettiest girl I have ever seen in my life." Jim Butler was never one to mince words.

The young lady blushed, and Jim thought how she looked like a pink prairie rose, all fresh right after the dew had fallen.

"I'm sorry, ma'am. I need to transfer some money to this bank from the Territorial Bank of New Mexico in Albuquerque."

"How much would you like to transfer, sir?"

Jim told her, and after receiving the proper information, she wrote up the transfer document and handed it to Jim to sign.

"May I help you with something else, Mr. Butler?"

"No, ma'am, I believe that will do it."

"It's not ma'am, Mr. Butler. It's miss—Miss Melinda Quarry."

"Yes, miss. Must be my Texas upbringing that causes me to address all ladies as ma'am."

"Please don't apologize, Mr. Butler. Gentlemen are scarce out here on the prairie. I appreciate your manners. Are you going to be long in Two Bucks City?"

"That depends on a lot of things, Miss Quarry. If there is enough to hold me here, I might just stay for awhile."

"Let's hope you decide to stay. My father has big plans for our little town. Opportunities abound for the right men. We will someday be as big and beautiful as Fort Worth or even Dallas."

"I don't know about the getting bigger part, Miss Quarry, but from where I stand, Two Bucks City has already got both those towns beat in the beauty department. Good afternoon." He walked out into the sunshine, leaving Melinda Quarry again blushing like a rose.

Jim ambled down to the Golden Ace saloon and stood at the swinging doors, letting his eyes grow accustomed to the dim interior light. Satisfied with what he saw, he strode inside. The place looked like a thousand others Jim had seen. A hardwood bar stood out from one wall with a long, gilded mirror hanging behind the bar. A few tables were scattered about and a faro table stood idle in a far corner. Four cowboys sat at a corner table playing penny ante draw poker. One man stood drinking a beer at the far end of the bar. He wore a brace of pistols cinched up high around his waist. Instead of pointing down, as was common, the two holsters pointed inwards toward the man's belt buckle. Jim pegged this one as a gunfighter: one who considered himself an important man in these parts.

"Is your beer cold?" Jim said to the string bean bartender.

"Coldest in town," said the barkeep, who was almost seven feet tall and skinny as a green twig. The man had a perpetual smile on his homely features. He drew a tall mug of draft and handed it to Jim, who chugged every bit of the cool amber liquid and slammed the empty mug down with a loud *thunk*. The gunman at the end of the bar jerked his head in Jim's direction.

"'Scuse me there, fella," said Jim. "It's just that I haven't had a cold beer in about a week and that one tasted mighty good. Can I buy you a mug, *amigo*?"

The man stared at Jim for a moment, and then went back to his drinking. Jim took off his hat and ran his fingers through his hair. He glanced at the bartender, who motioned for Jim to lean over the bar. Jim turned an ear in the barkeep's direction.

"Mister, you're new here, so maybe you don't know," said String Bean.

"Don't know what?"

"That feller yonder is Dude Miller. He's the ramrod for Mort Quarry, the most powerful man in these parts. Dude's a curly wolf with his short guns on his fists. He's best left alone. The man's been drinkin' in here all mornin', and he's festerin' up for a fight. I was you, I'd leave him be."

"What's your name?" asked Jim.

"Most folks call me Stretch. That'll do, I reckon."

"Stretch, I appreciate the warning. But with all due respect, you're not me." Hat in hand, Jim sidled up to the bad man. "Say, there, pardner," he said. "I reckon you didn't hear me offer you a beer."

Dude Miller spun toward Jim, his right hand streaking for his pistol. As the gun came up, Jim knocked it away with his hat and smashed a straight right hand that splattered the man's nose. Miller staggered back and Jim bore in on him, throwing left hooks and right crosses to the rib cage. Miller tried to fight back, but his feeble efforts were useless as Jim pounded him into unconsciousness.

Jim Butler stepped back and let Miller slide to the floor. The card players had stood up at the beginning of the fight, and three of them were now muttering amongst themselves; the fourth one was nowhere to be seen. Jim picked up his hat and took a deep breath. He put the hat back on his head and was turning to leave when a human blur careened in through the swinging doors. The blur, Chris Armstrong, stopped long enough to get his bearings.

Seeing Dude Miller lying crumpled on the floor, and a stranger standing close to him, Chris dropped his hand and let it hover over his six-gun. "You the one who shot Dude?" said Chris. He was trembling.

Stretch, the bartender, flipped a sawed-off Greener shotgun out and laid it on the bar. "There ain't gonna be no shootin' in this saloon, boys. That's the rule and, by heaven, I intend to enforce it." He turned his attention to Chris Armstrong. "Chris, you ain't under your daddy's protection anymore, now that you're ridin' for the Quarry brand. You take Dude out of here and go get him fixed up at Doc Whithers. He ain't been shot, just beat up. He started it, and if Mort Quarry asks me, I'll tell him the truth. You know he likes his boys to behave proper here in town. Now, a couple of you hands help Chris get Dude out of here."

All three of the card players rushed over, picked up the battered man, and hauled him outside. The fourth man, who had run for Chris, was Charlie Pratt. He followed along after the other three, muttering to himself.

Chris Armstrong still had his eyes set on Jim Butler.

"Chris," said Stretch, "I said get out. Besides, son, on your best day, you couldn't beat this man. He's Jim Butler. I was tendin' bar in Nogales when this feller and Jesus Campo Santos shot it out with the four Carlyle brothers. Now there's just one of them Carlyles left—and he ain't got but one good arm. Butler's way too salty for the likes of you, kid. Beat it."

Chris looked at Jim Butler and spat on the floor at Jim's feet. "Another day, Butler," he said. Chris backed out the saloon doors and took off at a trot toward the doctor's house.

Stretch watched Chris leave and then he put away his shotgun. He stuck another beer in front of Jim. When Jim started to protest, Stretch raised both hands in front of his face and shook his head. "You were right, friend," he said, wiping his brow. "I ain't you. And I durn sure don't want to be."

Chapter 4

harlie Pratt ran over to a red brick building with a sign that read, "Quarry Land and Cattle Company." He burst in the front entrance and beelined it to a large, ornate oak door in the back. He knocked and went in without waiting for an answer. "Lordy, Mr. Quarry, we got us a big problem," he said, yanking his hat off.

The huge square man sitting behind an oak desk that matched the door in opulence looked up at this intruder and frowned. The oversized leather chair moaned as the man lifted his enormous body out of it. Moving with remarkable grace for a man of his size, Mort Quarry paced over to the cowboy. His right hand streaked out and grasped the man by the throat, lifting him up on his tiptoes. Charlie Pratt's eyes bulged out and his face turned blue.

Mort Quarry stuck his face up next to Pratt's. "Pratt, if you barge into my office again without being invited, I will choke you to death. If you understand me, nod your head."

Pratt complied.

Quarry dropped him, strode back behind his desk, and sat down. "Now, Mr. Pratt, what is all the ruckus about?"

Charlie Pratt gripped his throat and gagged. Tears rolled down his face as he struggled to breathe. When he gained enough control to speak, his voice screeched like a dying bullfrog. "Mr. Quarry, we have a big problem."

"You said that already, Charlie. Only problem you have right now is that there had better be a real good reason for you disturbing me today. Now, spit it out."

"Yes, sir, Mr. Quarry. There was a fight over at the Golden Ace. Some drifter beat the daylights out of Dude Miller. Three of the boys done toted him to the doc's to get fixed up. But that ain't all, sir. That Armstrong kid tried to call the stranger out, but the feller wouldn't have none of it."

"What did the new man look like?"

"He was a big one—big as Dude, and quick. I ain't never seen a man throw punches like that. Two minutes, tops, and he had Dude out on the floor."

"Anybody get his name?"

"Yes, sir. The barkeep seemed to know him. Called him Jim Butler."

Mort Quarry's change of attitude was imperceptible to the human eye. "Where is this Butler now?"

"I reckon he's still in the saloon, leastways, he was when we left."

Searching through his breast pocket, Quarry came up with a Silver Eagle and pitched it to Charlie. "You have been very helpful, Charlie. I appreciate your coming straight to me. I want you to keep this just between us. Do you understand?"

"Yes, sir," said the lackey, backing out the door and shuffling to the street.

Quarry leaned back in his desk chair, and pondered this new state of affairs.

Jim Butler was a gunman, as dangerous as they come. It was apparent Dude Miller was no match for the man. He had to find out fast if Butler had been hired by Bale Armstrong, or, if by some coincidence, was just passing through. Mort Quarry didn't believe in coincidences. He had a hunch something was up. He had to get a note to his man on the inside of Armstrong's camp, and he had to do it pronto.

Jim Butler rode out of Two Bucks City heading for his father's ranch. He had poked the hornet's nest today and started the nasty little boogers to buzz around a bit. The first step in his plan to stop Mort Quarry from stealing the Double-A-Slash had been put into action.

Jim intended to keep his identity a secret for the time being. Shank knew, but he wouldn't tell anyone. Jim rode onto the ranch and angled his horse toward the eastern part where Panther Creek cut across it. Shank had told him that was where the Mexican farmers were settled in. He had said Bale Armstrong gave the farmers permission to live and raise crops on part of the Double-A-Slash. In return, the Mexicans were to clean out the brush and diseased trees on the northeastern part of the ranch.

Jim knew why Mort Quarry wanted his family's ranch. The person who ran the Double-A-Slash controlled the best water in four counties. Water was like gold in the dry Texas panhandle country. He also knew Bale Armstrong would fight with all he had, but his father was seventy years old, maybe older. Shank had told Jim the ranch crew would stand with Bale, but, outside of Shank and Rusty, none of them were gun handy.

The thing that worried Jim the most was his brother. Chris had always been Bale's favorite, and as far as Jim knew, Chris worshipped the old man. He had seen Chris shoot a man in cold blood, and, in the saloon, Chris had been ready to draw on him for no good reason. Something was wrong with his little brother, and he had to find out what before Chris crossed over the line for good.

There's no doubt Mort Quarry is a greedy man, Jim thought as he rode. *How far he will go to get what he wants is still a mystery. And what about Melinda? Where does she fit into this?*

Jim reined up his horse under a large, leafy cottonwood tree. He propped his right leg up on the pommel of his saddle and took off his hat. Running a hand through his hair, he thought about Melinda Quarry. He tried to keep his mind on the problems at hand, but the young lady's face kept popping up in his head. She was beautiful. No, more than that; his encounter with her at the bank convinced him that she was gorgeous, intelligent, and educated. He fought to get her out of his mind, but nothing seemed to work.

Jim had never been in love before and he wondered about how it felt. All he knew was when he thought about Melissa Quarry, he experienced a feeling that was new to him. He pulled his leg back down and took off at a trot for Panther Creek. His mind was rolling around like the cue ball on a pool table, and he felt like someone was about to strike that ball hard.

He counted ten adobe huts, all linked together by a wide pathway. The place looked more like a small village in Mexico than an unorganized farming community. He reckoned six of the buildings served as housing while the rest were for storage and animal shelters. He was at the edge of the village when a woman called out to him.

"Señor, señor, buenos tardes." It was the woman who'd hauled the wounded man's body away. She was waving at Jim to ride to a hut she stood before. "Hello, *señor*, come over here, please, please."

Jim walked his horse over to the hut. "Yes, ma'am. How is the man who was shot?"

"Come inside, *señor*, and see for yourself."

Jim stepped out of the saddle and followed the woman into the adobe shelter. The wounded man lay on a bed in the back. He was covered from the waist down with a gray woolen blanket. A wide strip of white cloth covered his wound. Jim saw no sign of blood.

"I see the bleeding has stopped," he said.

The woman smiled up at him, took him by the arm, and led him to the man's bedside. The farmer opened his eyes as they approached.

"*Señor*, this is Manuel Cardoza," said the lady. "Manuel, this is the man who saved your life."

Manuel reached up; calloused fingers took hold of Jim's hand and squeezed. His grip was weak but steady.

"My name is Jim Butler. How are you doin', *amigo?*"

"*Buen, Señor* Butler, *gracias.* I wish to thank you so much. You have saved my life. I am your servant."

Jim grimaced. "I'm glad you made it okay, *amigo*, but I don't know about this servant business. I travel alone."

"Manuel, you must get plenty of rest. You can talk to *Señor* Butler sometime later. Go to sleep." Before Manuel could protest, the woman grabbed Jim by the arm and whisked him outside.

Once they were in the open air, she introduced herself to Jim. "*Señor* Butler, I am Conchita Consuelo Maria Lopez de San Martin. I am the housekeeper for Mr. Armstrong at his big *rancho*. Please call me Maria."

"Howdy, Maria. Since you have such an important job with Mr. Armstrong, and you also seem to be well respected here at this village, I bet you know pretty much everything that goes on in these parts."

"*Señor* Butler, do not waste your flowery compliments on this rose. I have more thorns than you could ever imagine."

Jim laughed at Maria's candor. "I apologize, ma'am. You caught me in the watermelon patch."

"Who are you, and why are you here, Mr. Jim Butler?"

The questions caught Jim flat-footed, and he jerked his head back. "Excuse me, ma'am?"

"Was my English so poor that you did not understand what I just said, Mr. Butler?"

"No ma'am, you kind of caught me off guard is all."

"Do you have something to hide, *señor?*"

Jim felt like he was under investigation for a crime. "Ma'am, Maria. I was just passin' through this country when I chanced upon them fellers harrassing Manuel and the others. I tried to be a Good Samaritan and help out a wounded man. Why are you questioning me like I committed a crime?"

"Very well, Mr. Butler—if that is your name, and I feel that it is not. I have certain powers, or visions. Intuition, you might call it, but that would be incorrect. Sometimes I can see into a man's heart and even his soul. I do not know you, Mr. Butler, but I know of you. I had a vision of a large man coming back into this country. He seemed a stranger to all, but he had lived here many years ago. Although he did not know it at the time, he was meant to be the savior of this land."

"Whoa, there, Maria. You're givin' me goosebumps. I think I better skedaddle out of here right now before you spook me real good. You sound like a *bruja,* a witch."

"*Señor* Jim, at one time you were called Badger because you would never give up. I pray that you are the man I think you are. Mr. Armstrong needs your help. His health is not good. His bones no longer support his body. The time is not so far away when he will cease to walk. Please, *por favor,* help us save the ranch."

"Maria, I don't know what to say, except you've got me all wrong. I'm just driftin'. That's all."

Jim quick-footed it outside and swung into his saddle. He tipped his hat to Maria, and dug heels into the steel dun. The big mare took off at a fast trot away from the Mexican village.

Chapter 5

Early the next morning Mort Quarry rented a buckboard and drove out to the Double-A-Slash. His reason for going was to get word to his spy at the ranch, but since he had to make the trip anyway, he decided to make Bale Armstrong one final offer. If the old fool didn't accept the deal, he would put himself in harm's way. It wouldn't start today, but tomorrow Mort Quarry would turn his men loose. He had over a dozen hard cases working for him, each one picked for his prowess with a six gun. All Armstrong had was a bunch of cowboys. Quarry did not expect much competition.

Chris Armstrong and Dude Miller rode alongside the buckboard. Quarry didn't expect trouble, but he was prepared for anything that might happen.

"Dang your sorry hide, Valentine. You're the laziest son-of-a-gun I ever worked with. If we don't get this fence fixed today, Mr. Armstrong will have our behinds."

"Rusty Puckett, how many times I got to tell you, don't call me Valentine. Val is my name, and I ain't lazy; I just like to work real careful like so I don't have to come back and do a job twice."

Rusty started to reply when out of the corner of his eye he caught a glimpse of movement down by a ranch gate that was a quarter mile from where they were working.

"Look yonder, Valentine. Can you make out them *hombres* over by the gate?"

"Why sure I can. I got eagle eyes. Let's see, that looks like." He paused for a moment. "One of them riders is Dude Miller, the other one is Chris."

"Them two," said Rusty, "means Mort Quarry must be drivin' the rig."

"Yep, Rusty, there ain't no mistakin' that big old galoot. Wonder what they're here for."

"It sure ain't no social call. Val, I'll stay and work on this fence. You fork your bronc and beat it to the ranch house. Mr. Armstrong needs to know them polecats are comin'."

Val Rose didn't hesitate. He hit leather and was gone.

———————

Jim Butler sat horseback high on a tree-covered knoll and watched the Double-A-Slash rider take off in the direction of the ranch house. Jim rode in a zigzag pattern down through the trees, never losing sight of Val Rose or the buckboard and its two outriders. He watched as the buckboard slowed down and stopped. The driver got down and walked over behind an ancient pecan tree. In a moment, the massive man climbed back aboard the rig, and resumed his journey.

Jim started to continue on when the actions of the Double-A-Slash cowhand stopped him cold. Instead of riding straight to the ranch, the man veered his horse to the tree where Mort Quarry had been just minutes ago. The puncher dismounted and also went behind the huge pecan. In a moment he reappeared with a note in his hand, which he shoved into his shirt pocket. Then he was back on his horse and riding again.

———————

Quarry drove the buckboard up to the front door of the ranch house. He pulled a handkerchief from an inside pocket, wiped the sweat from his face, and brushed the dust off his clothes as best he could.

"Dude, go knock on the door and see if anybody's home." Quarry laughed at his little joke. Bale Armstrong was always home. Too many hard falls from breaking wild horses had crippled him up.

Dude leaped to the ground and sauntered to the house. He banged on the heavy wooden door. "Anybody here?" he yelled. "Hey, open up." He slammed his fist against the door over and over again. "Come on and open this door before I bust it to kindling."

Maria jerked the door open. Hate and anger smoldered in her eyes. "You people do not belong here. You must go, now."

"Now, now, Maria, control yourself," said Quarry. "If you want to keep your job when I take over this ranch, you are going to have to show my men and me a little respect."

"I spit on your respect," said Maria. "*Hombre,* you have much money and power, but other people have power, too. You are crossing a line that should not be crossed. If you live, it will be with many regrets. You have angered the wrong people. The spirits do not lie."

"Don't worry about her babblings, Mr. Quarry," said Chris Armstrong. "She's about half crazy. The Mexicans think she can tell the future. I think it's a lot of bunk."

Mort was about to tell the woman off when Bale Armstrong appeared beside her. He was carrying a double-barreled twelve gauge shotgun.

"Quarry, you and your trained monkey get off my property." Armstrong leaned on a heavy wooden cane. His face distorted with the pain that wracked his body; his eyes shone with another kind of pain. "Chris, son, get down and come in and let's talk."

"I ain't got nothing to say to you that hasn't already been said." Venom dripped from Chris Armstrong's words. "I work for Mr. Quarry now, and when he takes over the Double-A-Slash, I'll be running the outfit. Then you'll see how a ranch ought to be run."

Dude Miller stood like a rock, staring at the twelve gauge shotgun, ready to shoot Bale Armstrong if he tried to pull the triggers. His face twitched when Chris said he would be running the Double-A-Slash; otherwise, he was a statue.

"Hold on now, Bale," said Mort Quarry, smiling. "There's no need to go waving a weapon around and threatening anyone. We are here to plead with you to sell us your ranch. Be reasonable, man. You are in no shape to run a property like this, and you aren't getting any younger. One of your sons is dead, and the other one has left you. Who are you saving this ranch for, the Mexican squatters over by Panther Creek?" An ugly laugh escaped through Mort Quarry's chunky lips.

"I swear on my dead son's grave," said Bale, his face white from the pain. "I will blow you to kingdom come if you don't ride out of here right now." He wavered and almost fell, lowering the shotgun as he struggled for balance.

Chris Armstrong leaped from his horse and ripped the twelve gauge from his father's weakening grip. As he glowered down at the shell of a man, pity and disgust enveloped his mind, but fear showed in his eyes. Bale Armstrong had always seemed indestructible; now he seemed so small and insignificant. Chris hated him for his roughshod ways, but he loved this man as only a son could. He stood transfixed, shotgun in hand, his mind racing. Had he made the wrong decision leaving his father? He was beginning to see Mort Quarry for what he was, a ruthless, greedy monster. Was it time to go back to his father?

While he stood there bewildered, Dude Miller made his move. "Shucks, this old man ain't worth the air he's breathin'," said Dude. "I'm gonna solve everybody's problem. I'll just kill him right here."

Dude started toward Bale Armstrong when a screaming chunk of lead tore his hat from his head. Dude dropped to one knee and ripped his pistol from its holster. "What in blazes is going on?" His voice was shrill, filled with fear.

Chris Armstrong pulled iron and crouched beside his father. Maria ran to Bale and tried to shield his body with her own. Mort Quarry made no movement toward shelter. He sat immobile in the buckboard.

"Put your guns away, boys," he said. "Whoever is shooting at us intended that shot as a warning." He turned to scan the area where the gunshot had come from. "Come out and show yourself, friend. I believe there is a misunderstanding here."

Another bullet burned in inches from Mort Quarry's hand, burrowing into the side of the buckboard, slinging splinters in every direction. The horse started to buck, but Quarry got the animal under control.

"Dude, Chris," he said, "mount up." He turned and looked out toward the tree-lined ridge that edged across the west side above the house. "I hope we meet again, my friend. Perhaps next time, I will have the upper hand."

Quarry turned the buckboard around and headed away. The horse taking off at a brisk trot. Dude Miller mounted his horse, gun in hand, and rode after his boss. Chris Armstrong stood looking down at his father.

"Chris, your father—he needs you," said Maria. "He cannot live without you on the ranch. Please stay, Chris, *por favor.*"

Chris stared at his father with blank eyes, confusion tearing through his mind. He took a deep breath, then turned and mounted his horse. He rode away without looking back.

Chapter 6

Jim forked the steel dun and headed off in the direction of the mystery tree. Things were happening too fast. He had begun developing a plan as soon as he'd found out what was going on in the Two Bucks country. He now realized there was not enough time to implement his scheme. Drastic measures would be needed without delay. He rode along rethinking everything until he cleared a rise that was above the stand of pecan trees. Scouring the countryside and discerning no movement, Jim trotted his horse down into the *Bosque*.

Mort Quarry was furious. He swung the buggy whip and popped blisters on the back of the buckboard horse as they made their way back to Two Bucks City. His plan to take over the Double-A-Slash ranch had been foolproof. Things had been falling into place like stacked dominoes. Now a wild card had been thrust into the mix.

Quarry had an idea that the man who'd buffaloed Dude Miller was the same one who fired from the ridge today. But who was this stranger? If it really was the gunfighter Quick Jim Butler, where did the man come from, and what were his motives for protecting Bale Armstrong and his ranch?

Dude Miller rode in front of the buckboard; Chris Armstrong brought up the rear. Dude slowed his horse down, allowing the wagon to catch up with him. He sidled his mount over close to Mort Quarry.

"What do we do now, boss?" he said.

"I'm thinking about that right now, Dude. I figured that old fool was too proud to hire protection. Looks like I underestimated him." Mort Quarry considered Bale Armstrong in a new light. "Let's assume Jim Butler is on the Double-A-Slash payroll."

"Let me have him, boss." Dude had lost a lot of respect from the Quarry men after the beating Jim had given him. "I owe that gunslick a whippin'. He caught me off guard when I'd drunk too much of that snakehead whiskey Stretch Cassidy peddles in his saloon. I'll bust him up good, then I'll kill him."

"Hold your horses, Dude. There'll be plenty of time for Butler. What bothers me right now is there might be more gun hands coming in to join him. It doesn't seem likely that Armstrong would hire just one man."

"I hear tell he's a cheap old bird, boss. Maybe he figures one *hombre* is enough."

Quarry ran a thick finger up and down the side of his nose. "Yes, maybe so, but the man has enough money to hire a considerable army if he chooses to."

Quarry didn't like being in the dark about his opposition. He needed information from his man on the inside at the Double-A-Slash, and he needed it now. Out of sheer anger, he jerked the buckboard reins back hard, causing the horse to rear up and fight the pressure of the bit tearing at its mouth. Crazed with pain from the whipping Mort Quarry had administered, the poor animal squealed in agony, bucking and fighting to break free from the restraining harness. Quarry bounced all over the buckboard seat like a rag doll. His knuckles whitened as he held on tight to the reins to keep from getting hurled to the ground.

"Shoot the stupid beast, Dude!" Quarry yelled. "Shoot it!"

Dude Miller peeled his six-gun from its leather pocket and blasted six chunks of lead into the crazed horse. One slug pierced the animal's brain. It dropped to the ground, quivered for a moment, and lay still.

Chris Armstrong reeled in his saddle, a look of horror masking his face. He had just witnessed the execution of an animal whose only fault was being scared and in pain.

"Filthy, evil beast," said Mort Quarry, spitting blood from where he had bitten his tongue during the commotion. He removed a handkerchief from his breast pocket and wiped the scarlet residue from his lips. Tossing the soiled cloth aside, he removed a small notebook and a pencil from an inside coat pocket and scribbled out a message.

"Dude," he said, "take this paper to the tree. I'll ride double with the boy and we'll meet you in town. Chris, bring your horse over here and get off. I will ride in the saddle, and you can get on behind me."

Tight-lipped and shaking, Chris rode over next to his boss and lurched to the ground. Mort Quarry swung his considerable bulk aboard Chris's mount. When Chris climbed up behind him, the horse shuddered at the extra weight.

Quarry kicked the horse's ribs, and the animal bolted forward toward Two Bucks City.

When they reached the edge of town Quarry dismounted. "Chris," he said, "go to the livery stable and tell Old Man Parker where he can find his buckboard. And Chris, tell him that the next time I rent a rig from him, it had better have a decent horse."

Quarry walked to his office building next to the bank and checked for messages. Upon finding none, he stepped into his private office and sat down behind his desk. He was pondering the Armstrong ranch problem when his thoughts were interrupted by a faint knock on the door.

"Come in, Melinda," he said, smiling. Melinda Quarry danced through the door. "Daddy, how did you know it was me?"

"Melinda, my dear. I can always tell by your knock that it is you. You have the soft, unobtrusive ways of your mother, God rest her blessed soul. What can I do for you today, angel?"

"I brought you the documents that you asked for on the Double-A-Slash property, and there are some loan papers that need your approval also."

"Excellent, Melinda, you are becoming quite an astute businesswoman. Anything else new?"

"Why, yes, there is. We had a new depositor today, a new young man in town. His name is Jim Butler, and he is quite attractive in a cowboy sort of way. Although I doubt he is a cowboy. He transferred five thousand dollars from New Mexico to our bank."

"Young, handsome, and with money. My goodness, daughter, I had better meet this fellow and see what his intentions might be. He could be after my most precious asset."

"Oh, Daddy, you are such a silly. I just met Jim."

"Jim, is it? Well, well, now I know I *must* meet Mr. Butler. Is he staying in town?"

"I have no idea where Mr. Butler is staying, and I don't care." Melinda said, looking flustered by her father's response. "I have too much work on my desk to be gossiping with you, Father. If you need me, call." With that, the young lady made a rapid exit.

Mort Quarry rubbed his chin as his daughter stomped out of the room. "Yes," he said. "I will check out Mr. Jim Butler."

Late in the afternoon, Jim rode into Two Bucks City. He was dusty and near worn out. After settling his horse into the livery stable, he walked to the Quarry hotel and got a second-story room. He ordered a bathtub and lots of hot water to be sent up to the room. Waiting for the tub, he lay down and took a short nap.

———

Darkness lay like a shroud over Two Bucks City; dense cobalt-blue clouds rolled in, promising much needed rain. Jim Butler, all clean and spiffy after his bath, stepped out of the Calico Kitchen restaurant and breathed in the cool, damp air. Inhaling brought about a chill that started in his lungs and ricocheted throughout his whole body. He shivered. The shiver was not entirely caused by the liquid night air. Jim's father was in a tight situation, and it was going to take all of Jim's cunning and resourcefulness to pull him out. Chris was setting himself up for trouble, also.

Jim's steps were heavy as he plodded along the creaking plank sidewalk toward the Golden Ace. When he reached the saloon, he recognized two of the horses that were tied to a hitching rail out front. Peering over the swinging doors, he saw the owners of the horses standing at the bar. He swore under his breath, hitched up his gun belt, and stepped inside.

Chapter 7

The saloon was brimming with patrons. Jim recognized some of the men from his previous encounter with Dude Miller. Over in a far corner, he noticed his old friend Shank Halsey playing cards with three other men. One of the other card players was Rusty Puckett. The third man was the cowhand who had retrieved the note Mort Quarry had left in the pecan tree. The fourth player was unknown to Jim.

Down at the far end of the bar were two rough looking *hombres*. They were the ones whose horses Jim had recognized. The two men were drinking beer and talking loud. Jim sidled up to the end of the bar that was closest to the swinging doors.

"Howdy there, feller," said Stretch. "How 'bout a beer on me? It's still the coldest in town."

"I thank you, sir," said Jim, "but there's no need to give away your profit. I can pay." Jim plunked a handful of coins onto the bar.

"Next round, my friend. This one's on me. I never thought I would see the day when Dude Miller got his comeuppance. A word to the wise, though. There's Armstrong men in here tonight, and Quarry men, too. They don't get along none too well. Chris Armstrong's over in the corner gettin' pie-eyed drunk. It could get real ugly in here tonight. I'm keeping my Greener right close at hand, just in case. Better not drink too much so's you lose your edge. It just might be fatal."

"Thanks for the warning," Jim answered.

Stretch Cassidy nodded and moved away. Jim began to drink the beer, lost in his thoughts.

Out of nowhere, the face of Melinda Quarry sprang into Jim's consciousness. He gave himself a mental slap to drive her from his thoughts and chugged the remaining contents of the mug. He was about to order another one when

Stretch appeared, fresh mug in hand. Jim insisted upon paying for this second mug and, after mild protest, the bartender accepted the payment.

The lanky bartender leaned down until his long hound dog face was inches from Jim's. "You see those two gunnies at the other end of the bar? They're a couple of real bad ones. The big one is Hack Bonner. Man, he must weigh near two hundred and fifty pounds. They say it's all muscle and he knows how to use it. Cat quick with a short gun, too. Fast as he is, he ain't near as swift as that skinny one standin' beside him. That one's name is McCafferty, but he goes by the handle of the Irish Kid. Some say he's the fastest man with a short gun anywhere. They rode in this afternoon. Rumor has it they are here to run Bale Armstrong out of the country. If that's true, there's gonna be a whole bunch of innocent people in a lot of trouble. Bale Armstrong is the last chance this town has to keep Mort Quarry from owning everything. He wants my saloon, but I ain't sellin' unless Armstrong gets whipped. If he loses his ranch, well..." Stretch Cassidy's voice trailed off into silence. Fear showed in his eyes. He lowered his head and walked away.

A loud commotion from the opposite end of the bar grabbed everybody's attention, including Jim's. The big gunslinger and the little one were arguing.

"I know you're fast, Kid, but there are those that's faster." The sound rumbled like thunder rolling from the mouth of the big man, Hack Bonner.

"Ain't nobody faster than the Irish Kid," said the skinny one in a thick Irish brogue. He was shuffling his feet and wiggling his long, bony fingers.

"There's one for sure who is," Hack Bonner said.

"I said there ain't a livin' soul who can pull iron with me."

"I heard you crawfished to Jim Butler over Arizona way a year or two back."

Cormac McCafferty, alias the Irish Kid, turned purple. "That's a bald-faced lie. I never even seen Jim Butler. And if I ever did come up against that faker, I'd back him down so quick it would make his dear sainted mother's head swim. That's a fact, boy."

Chris Armstrong was headed up to the bar for another bottle of red eye when he overheard the gunmen's conversation. He had seen Jim Butler come into the saloon, but hadn't had the nerve to approach him.

"Say there, fellers," he said, his speech slurring. "I heard you boys talkin' about the great Jim Butler, and how fast he was with a six-gun."

"You got a problem with that, son?" Hack Bonner towered over Chris's six feet like some malevolent giant.

"No, sir, I sure don't. It's just that I thought you'd like to know that ol' Jim Butler, himself, is right here in this saloon this very night." Chris beamed like he'd just swallowed the prize canary.

"Where's he at?" said the Irish Kid. He was all business.

Chris pointed a wobbly finger at Jim. The bar top cleared in an instant with everybody moving into the crowd around the poker tables. Shank Halsey grabbed Rusty Puckett by the shirtsleeve and yanked him out of his chair. Playing cards flew in every direction. Puckett started to protest when Shank whispered something into his ear. Rusty Puckett gasped and stared at Jim Butler. His eyes slowly filled with recognition, and a smile cracked the corners of his mouth. The two old cowboys edged up closer to the front of the crowd.

Jim stood rooted in place. The saloon got coffin quiet as the Irish Kid swaggered toward Jim. Stretch Cassidy let his hands rest on the Greener shotgun under the bar.

"You Jim Butler?" asked the Kid.

Jim didn't answer.

"Look at him, Irish," said Bonner. "He's too danged scared to talk."

"You a coward, Butler?" It was the Kid again. "You don't look like no big time killer to me. I think your reputation must have been made on farmers and store keepers. That sound about right? Yeah, I think that's right. What do you think, Hack?"

"He don't look like no bad man I ever seen, Kid. He looks, to me, like he wants to leave this fine gathering."

Jim Butler still did not move or speak.

"All right, boys, the party's over. No one gets killed in my place if I can help it." Stretch pointed his Greener right at the Irish Kid's belt line. "Butler, you best back out of here and ride while you still can. I'll hold off these boys. Go, now."

Jim hesitated a moment then began to slide backwards out through the swinging doors. Once outside, he disappeared into the night.

"I'll be hog-tied if I ain't ever seen a man run so fast in my life," said Hack Bonner. "It was sure a sight to see." He was laughing and slapping the Irish Kid on the back. "Come on, Irish, I'm gonna buy you the biggest piece of cow they got in this town."

Both men headed out of the Golden Ace, spurs jangling and jaws flapping, headed for the Calico Kitchen.

"Did you see it, boys? Did you see it?" Chris Armstrong was roaring drunk and spouting off. "Mr. High and Mighty Jim Butler has a yellow streak when he has to face a real man. I should have gunned him down the other day when I had a chance. Next time I see him, I might just make him eat dirt. That sure would be a funny sight, wouldn't it, boys?"

Shank Halsey and Rusty Puckett stomped out of the saloon. They had just seen their old friend 'Badger' Armstrong crawfish, and their night of fun was over.

Chris whispered something to the men closest to him and they erupted with laughter. He raised his hands for them to be quiet and then he weaved his way up to the bar. "Say, there, Cassidy," said Chris, trying to look serious, but not succeeding. "How come it is that you always pull out that old shotgun every time somebody sneezes in your saloon? We all know you ain't got the guts to use it."

"One of you men take this boy home before he makes a statement he can't back up," said Stretch.

A couple of the more sober-looking Quarry men got up and started toward Chris. One was Charley Pratt.

Chris was not ready to go. "I ain't leaving here 'till I'm blamed good and ready." He pulled iron and waved it at the two approaching Quarry men.

"Come on now, Chris," said Charley Pratt. "Mr. Quarry will skin you alive if he finds out you been raisin' a ruckus in the saloon. Come on, go with us. I got a bottle in my room. We can keep on drinkin' there."

"Mr. Quarry," said Chris, in mocking tones. "He ain't nothing but a horse shooter. Yeah, a horse killer, that's all your Mr. Quarry is. Well, my name ain't Quarry. It's Armstrong, Chris Armstrong, and me and my daddy got the best ranch in the whole panhandle country. You can tell Mr. Horse Murderer that I'm going back where I belong, the Double-A-Slash Ranch. And Charley Pratt, you little weasel, you tell old horse killer that he ain't welcome on that ranch anymore. If I see him, I'll shoot him on sight."

Chris was still waving his pistol around and staggering all about. Stretch rolled his Greener over the bar top and pointed it at the drunken man. Chris caught the movement out of the corner of his eye and snapped a shot in that direction. The slug hit Cassidy high in the chest. He reeled against the back bar and dropped to the floor. His bartender rushed over and kneeled beside him.

"Somebody get Doc Whithers, quick! I think Stretch is dying."

"Oh, my Lord!" yelled Charley Pratt. "Some of you boys grab the kid and get him out of town."

"Where do we take him?"

"Take him to that line shack up in the hills. I'll get Mr. Quarry."

A dozen hands latched onto Chris Armstrong, who, in his drunken state, continued to protest. They hoisted him up on their shoulders and carried him out to the horses. In a flash they were gone.

Charley Pratt looked dazed as he stumbled out into the crisp night air. He mounted his horse and took off at a gallop to find his boss.

Chapter 8

Bam! Bam! Bam! The banging noise woke Mort Quarry up. He had snoozed off while reading the paper. "Just a minute, I'm coming. Hold your horses." He did not like to be disturbed at home. The squalid face of Charley Pratt met his gaze as he peered through the peephole. Quarry wrenched the door open. "Charley Pratt, this had better be important."

"Y-yes, sir, Mr. Quarry, it is real important. Chris Armstrong done got himself all liquored up and shot Stretch Cassidy down at his bar."

"What! How in the devil's name did that happen?"

Charley Pratt relayed the story while Mort Quarry listened in stoic silence. When Pratt finished, Quarry rubbed his chin and pursed his lips.

"Charley, you did the right thing getting that idiot out to the line shack. I want you to ride out there and assign two of the men to stay with Chris. They had better not let him out of their sight. If they do, it will be on *your* head."

"Yes, sir, I'll take care of it. What if Cassidy kicks off, boss? What'll we do then?"

"Leave that problem up to me. Now, you had better get out of here right away."

Charley started to go when Quarry grabbed his arm in a vice-like grip. Charley almost cried out in pain. Mort Quarry got right up in the small man's face.

"Charley, do you know where Dude is?"

"Yes, sir, I do."

"Before you leave for the shack, get one of the boys to round him up. Tell him to meet me in the Golden Ace. Understand?"

Charley nodded yes, and Quarry turned him loose.

Hack Bonner and the Irish Kid walked out of the Calico Kitchen cafe rubbing their full stomachs and moaning about how much they had eaten.

"Dang it, son," said Bonner. "Skinny as you are, I don't know where you put all them vittles. You got a hollow leg, Kid?"

"You know I don't eat real often, Hack, but when I do, I don't mess around." Both gunmen laughed and started in the direction of the saloon. They ambled along the dark wooden sidewalk talking and taking in the cool night air.

"Say, Kid, you ever seen anything as funny as Jim Butler tonight? I couldn't hardly keep from laughin' out loud."

"Yeah, me too. I believe that was the best job of crawfishin' I ever saw. He didn't say a word, just pulled in his feelers and slid out backwards. I thought I was gonna bust a gut."

"You boys think that was real funny, don't you?"

The voice came from the shadows of an alley on their right. The click of a revolver being cocked echoed off the dry boards of the buildings siding the alley. The two men froze in place.

"You two funny boys turn around and back over here into this alley. We got to have us a little palaver. I see your right hand twitchin', Cormac. A wise man never shoots at what he can't see. Be easy."

Careful to not make any false moves, the men eased their way backwards into the alley. They were ten paces in when the voice told them to stop and turn around.

"Howdy, fellers, how are y'all doin'?" It was Jim Butler.

"I knew it was you," said the Irish Kid. "You are the only person in the world, besides my sainted mother, who calls me by my real name."

"Dang, Jim, you sure had us buffaloed."

Hack Bonner had his hat off and was scratching his balding head. "Son, I'm gettin' way too old for these kinds of shenanigans."

"Sorry, Hack, but it just had to look real tonight. Hopefully, the Quarry bunch will be so confused about me that they'll lay off, and I can have time to find out where my dad and my brother stand in all this. Y'all got here quicker than I thought you would. Bartender said you rode in this afternoon."

"We been in that bar raisin' Old Ned since around three o'clock. We were gettin' hungry and thinkin' maybe you weren't comin'. We were about to head out for some grub when you showed up. What's so important that you had to call me and the Kid in on it?"

"It's a long story, Hack. So I'll just hit the high points."

Jim told his friends the story in as few words as possible. "So that's why I don't want anyone to know who I am, just yet," he said as he finished.

The Irish Kid whistled through his teeth. "You sure have you a mountain-sized problem there, Jim boy. That's for sure."

"Kid," said Hack Bonner, scowling at the Kid's last statement, "you've always had a way of statin' the obvious. Yeah, Jim's got a problem, and if he's got a problem, well then, we got a problem too."

"I know that," the Kid said, looking like he had just been scolded by his mama.

"You two cut it out," said Jim. "I knew you would help me, so I worked out a plan for when y'all showed up. Our little ruckus in the saloon tonight was the beginning of that plan."

He was about to explain his idea when they heard someone out on the street. The three men backed against a building and held their breaths. Two men walked by chattering like blue jays at a church picnic.

"I was there, I tell you." It was a short, dumpy hostler from the livery. "I saw it all. That Armstrong kid shot Stretch Cassidy in cold blood. Old Stretch never had a chance."

"Is he dead?" said the other man, whom Jim did not recognize.

"Lord knows. They carried him over to Doc Wither's place. I reckon he's still there. That is, unless the undertaker already has him."

"Stretch was a good man. They catch that kid, they'll hang him for sure."

The men disappeared down the street. Jim took off his hat and ran a hand through his hair. "Stretch is dead and Chris is on the run for his murder. Something isn't right. Did you boys see any of this?"

"No, Jimmy, we left right after you did."

"Your brother was sure snookered when we left the saloon. He was rantin' on about you bein' a coward and all. Said he knew that you wasn't no man. He said—"

"All right, Cormac, I get the idea," said Jim. "Be quiet while I think this out."

The Irish Kid started to say something else when Hack Bonner grabbed his shoulder and squeezed. Jim stood in silence for a long time before he spoke.

"Hack, I want you to ride out to the Double-A-Slash Ranch and tell my father you are an old saddle pal of mine looking for work. If he hasn't heard about Chris, tell him. There is an old friend of mine cowboyin' there named

Shank Halsey. He knows I'm alive. Get with him and anybody he can trust and y'all wait for word from me."

"Cormac, I want you to hire on with Mort Quarry's bunch. Tell him you and Hack split up. You'll think of a reason why. Try and find out where they are hiding Chris. I'm going to the doctor's place to check on Stretch. I'll be in touch."

Double-checking that the street was deserted, Hack and Cormac drifted out in five minute intervals. Jim edged down to the back of the alley and scooted along the shadows behind the buildings until he came to Doc Wither's place.

Jim crept up the side of the building and peered around the front. The street was empty. He could see lights coming from the saloon, and from the sound roaring out of the place, everything was going strong despite the earlier shooting. Stepping up onto the sidewalk he peeped through a window. Lights were on in the back room. Jim knocked on the doctor's front door. In a moment a shuffling noise brought someone to the door.

"What now?" said an old man in a night shirt, as he opened the door.

"I came to check on Mr. Cassidy," said Jim.

The doctor looked this stranger up and down. He moved the lamp he was carrying close to Jim's face. Jim raised his hand to shield the light from his eyes.

"Good Lord Almighty!' said Doc Withers. "You're Badger Armstrong."

———◆◆———

Chapter 9

oc Withers held the door open. "Come on in here, son. Stretch is in the back room. He's lost a lot of blood, but the bullet didn't hit any vital organs. He ought to be okay with some rest."

"Doc, they say Chris shot him in cold blood. Is that true?"

"That's what I was told, Badger, but I don't know for sure." Doc Withers pointed to a chair. "Sit down, son. I was just about to have a cup of coffee. I'll fix you one, too."

The doctor poured two cups of the steaming black liquid and handed one to Jim. He stepped around behind a worn maple desk and sat down with a groan.

"Bale Armstrong, Jr.," he said. "What in the world are you doing here? I see the rumors of your demise were premature, so I won't even get into that. You look a little different than the last time I saw you. What was it, twelve, fifteen years ago?"

Doc Withers took another sip of his coffee, and Jim got a chance to talk. "How did you recognize me, Doc?"

"When I flashed the lamplight on to your face I knew you looked familiar, a face from out of the past. I raised the light up to get a closer look and you shaded your face with your left hand. I recognized the barbwire scars across your palm; that's when it came to me. You were ten years old when that old mossy horn steer knocked your horse down and butted you into that barbwire fence around that pond up by Panther creek. You remember that? Boy, you were cut up all over the place. Thank God the only bad cuts were on your hand. It took a right smart of stitches to close that up if I recollect right."

"Yes, sir, it did. Are you sure Stretch is gonna be okay?"

"He's got the best doctor in these parts. 'Course, he's got the *only* doctor in these parts." Doc Withers chuckled at his attempt at humor.

Jim felt he could trust the old doctor; he really didn't have much choice since he had been recognized. He told Doc Withers what was happening to his father and how Mort Quarry was tied into it. Doc sat silent, cradling his cup and listening. When Jim finished, the sawbones got up and poured himself another shot of coffee. Jim declined.

"Badger," said Doc, his face grim, "I've been watching this problem develop for some time now. Your father is a tough man, but he's also an old man. He fought his wars forty years ago, and he shouldn't have to fight again.

"When the railroad bypassed us for Amarillo, the future of this county looked grim. Mort Quarry came to Two Bucks City, and we all hailed him as a savior of the town. He brought money, established a bank—as well as other businesses—and had some innovative ideas on how to put the town back on the map. He loaned ranchers money, renovated the local church out of his own pocket, brought in his daughter to teach school, and, most importantly, he gave the community hope."

"What changed everything?"

"Mort Quarry bought a couple hundred acres of land. He even paid cash. Said he wanted to start a small herd, and hired a bunch of men to work the place. After a while, ranchers started losing cattle; a few at first, then whole herds began to disappear into the night. Supposedly, Quarry even lost part of his herd. Before anybody realized what was happening, all of the ranchers in these parts that had notes at the bank got behind. Turns out the fine print in the loan contracts stated that if the note payment became three days late, the bank could foreclose. And that's just what happened."

This time Jim said yes to another cup of coffee. Stretch groaned in the back room and Doc Withers walked back to take a look. Jim mulled over what he had just been told. After a moment, Doc called him from the back room. Cassidy was awake.

"He heard your voice and wanted to talk to you, son. He's weak from the blood loss, so you can only talk a couple of minutes."

"Thanks, Doc." Jim knelt down by the bed and stared at the wounded man. He thought Stretch was asleep. Jim started to rise when the saloon owner spoke. His voice was shallow but clear.

"Jim, Jim, I've got to know. When you backed down from those two gunnies, were you scared or was it another reason? I can't believe you're yellow, Jim." Stretch struggled to finish what he had to say. "You've got something else in mind. Am I right?"

Jim wasn't sure what to say. He nodded his head. Stretch reached up and with a feeble grasp closed his massive hand around Jim's. Bony fingers dug into Jim's wrist, then the hand went limp and fell back to the bed. Jim looked up at the doctor, his eyes wide with apprehension.

"No, he's not dead, Badger, he just needs a lot of rest." Doc Withers sipped his ever-present cup of coffee. "You better get out of here, Badger, before someone else decides to check on Cassidy. Don't worry, he'll be safe here. I'm the only doctor for a hundred miles, and Mort Quarry knows it. He won't mess with me."

"Thanks, Doc, I appreciate your help. I will be going now."

"Badger, one more thing. Have you talked to your father? Because you two were estranged when we thought you had been killed, he took your death real hard. Never was the same after that. Now with Chris messed up, I don't know what will happen to him. Go to your dad, son. If not for you, then do it for him. He deserves to know you're alive."

Jim nodded and stepped out into the darkness. He was about to round the corner of the building when a voice stopped him in his tracks. He turned to see Melinda Quarry approaching from across the street.

"Mr. Butler—I mean, Jim. Hello. Remember me, Melinda from the bank?"

"Yes, ma'am, I remember you, Miss Quarry." Jim had drunk three cups of coffee, and, yet, his mouth was as dry as the Sonora desert.

"I saw the doctor's light on and thought I would check on poor Mr. Cassidy. How is he, Jim?"

Jim Butler shuddered every time Melinda Quarry spoke his name. He was experiencing a strange feeling that he had not felt before. Jim fought back the urge to stutter as his brain had difficulty forming words.

"Doc says he will live. He's a lucky man. If he hadn't have been so tall, the bullet would've hit him in the head."

"Oh, I am so glad to hear that. Mr. Cassidy seems like such a good man. It is so unfortunate that he was shot in his own place of business."

"Yes, ma'am." Jim struggled for words. He needed to get out of town to clear his head. "That was a terrible accident, Stretch getting shot like that. Liquor can do outlandish things to a man."

"My father said it wasn't an accident."

"What do you mean, Miss Quarry?"

"Call me Melinda, and I will tell you, Jim."

Jim took a deep breath and let it out slow. "Melinda," he said, trying to smile.

"My father says Chris Armstrong shot Mr. Cassidy because his father and Mr. Cassidy were having a feud. First thing in the morning the sheriff is going to put a posse together and search for Chris. When they find him they will hang him."

"Hang him without a trial? They can't do that."

"My father says it will send a message to Mr. Bale Armstrong and the other bad men in this county that we are tired of all the rustling and killing. In order to maintain law and order, sometimes you have to take the law into your own hands."

"That's what your father says, huh? You agree with him, Melinda?"

"My father is never wrong, Jim. But enough of this morbid talk. I am pleased that Mr. Cassidy is going to recover. Let's celebrate. The cafe is still open. I will let you buy me a cup of coffee and a piece of their wonderful pie." Melinda held out her hand.

"No, ma'am." The words surprised Jim as they came out. "I have something important to do. I will see you tomorrow, maybe." He reached out and shook Melinda's hand, and he was gone.

Jim walked back to his horse, mounted, and rode out of town. He let the mare have her head to run while his mind raced through the recent happenings. This night had succeeded only in muddying up the water. Jim did not believe the story about the feud between his father and the saloon keeper. Chris was a hot-headed kid, but he wasn't a murderer.

Melinda Quarry believed her father was perfect. How could a beautiful, intelligent girl be so naive? And those weird feelings... was he in love with her? He fought to clear his head as he rode toward the Double-A-Slash.

Chapter 10

Brilliant sunlight decorated the hillside as it filtered down in curious patterns through the broad blackjack leaves. The grass stood tall after a shower of morning dew. Jim Butler shivered from the early chill and rolled over in his blankets. As a rule, he was up well before dawn and off about his business. This night he had slept little, his mind churning thoughts concerning the coming day. He was anxious about the forthcoming meeting with his father. Fifteen years had been a long time. He had left as a headstrong boy. He returned as a man who had experienced both the good and the bad side of life. Now, he felt like he was somewhere in the middle with no direction to go.

Jim made a small, quick fire and boiled coffee. While the bitter black grounds rolled in the bubbling hot water, he tended to his horse's needs and struck camp. The coffee ready, Jim drank two steaming cups so fast he burned his mouth. Throwing out the remainder of his breakfast, Jim smothered the fire and secured his coffee pot and tin cup in his saddlebags. He threw a leg over the steel-dun mare and turned her in the direction of the Double-A-Slash ranch house.

The half-mile ride down a gentle slope took Jim past the edge of a corral. Three men were working there. Two replaced worn boards where the horses had eaten through them, while the third was whitewashing the new boards.

"Gosh durn it, Rusty, if you can't hold these boards straight, I'll get the new feller to help me, and you can do the paintin'."

"Well, Shank Halsey, my old granny is ninety-seven years old and she could hammer a nail better than you."

The third man, a new hire named Hack Bonner, looked at the men and shook his head. "Say, boys," he said, "we got company."

"You two ain't changed one bit when it comes to gettin' along. Folks that don't know y'all would think you two old boys don't much like each other."

Jim grinned down at his old friends. "Rusty Puckett, how in the world are you doin'?"

"My goodness gracious, son, look at you," said Rusty. "You done all growed up. I'm fine, Badger, now that you're here. I was in the saloon the other night when that ruckus broke out between you and Hack over there and your other *compadre*. You sure had us fooled, Badger."

Shank Halsey broke into the conversation. "Hack told us all about your plan, Badger. Me and Rusty are with you all the way. Most of the other hands will be too when they find out you're throwin' in with the Double-A-Slash. When are we gonna go and run that Quarry bunch out of the county for good?"

"Hold up there, Shank. We don't have any concrete proof that Quarry is running a crooked outfit. We've got to catch him or his men in action."

"Me and Rusty would've done called Quarry's hand, but Bale works us so dang hard, when we ain't workin', we're restin'."

"Boys, I'd like to jaw with you, but I have a chore I've got to get done."

"You goin' to see your daddy?" asked Hack.

"Yep, I am."

"He wasn't goin' to hire me, but the *señora* that takes care of him talked him into it. She said she had a vision about savin' the ranch and I was a part of it. I ain't afraid of no man, but she made my skin crawl. You be careful, Jim."

Jim nodded to his friends and rode up to the ranch house. He dismounted, tied his horse, and walked up to an ornate wooden door. Taking a deep breath, he knocked three times. In a moment, the massive door swung open. Maria stood in the doorway.

"*Buenos dias, Señor* Butler," she said, "please, come in. *Mi casa es su casa.*"

"Thank you, Maria. I need to speak with my fath... uh, Mr. Armstrong, please."

"Most certainly, *señor,* come and sit in the parlor. Mr. Armstrong is in the kitchen. I will get him. And, please, be gentle with him; he is not well. *Comprende, jefe?*"

Jim flinched, almost dropping the hat he held in his hands. "I understand, Maria, but why did you call me boss?"

"Are you not Bale Armstrong, Jr.?" Maria smiled, revealing perfect ivory white teeth. Then she was gone.

Jim stood stunned. How did this woman know his true identity? Was she a real *bruja,* a Spanish witch? He pondered what he was going to say to his father when the thump-thumping of a wooden cane announced Bale Armstrong's arrival.

The owner of the Double-A-Slash had once been a powerful man, both physically and politically. At one time he had controlled most of the land in Deaf Smith County and all of the politicians. Bale Armstrong had lived past his time. People had died; times had changed. Now he faced an uncertain future.

"I hired a man yesterday, and I don't need any more hands," he said, his voice still oak-strong. "I reckon you made the ride out to my ranch for the exercise, son. I thank you for coming. Goodbye." The old man started to turn toward the kitchen.

"I'm not here for a job." Jim fought to control his intense emotion. "Papa, it's me—Badger. I've come home."

Bale Armstrong's face turned to stone. He stared at Jim, eyes filled with hate and just a little sadness. "Maria!' he hollered. "Get Shank and that new man, Bonner, in here right now."

He hobbled closer to Jim, holding his cane like a club. "Mister, my son, Bale Armstrong Jr., has been dead and buried for a long time. He was killed in Arizona; I saw his grave. I don't know if Mort Quarry sent you or what, and I don't care. But if you don't get off of my property this minute, I swear to you, you will be buried here."

Bale Armstrong made a move like he was falling. Jim reached out to catch his father, but the old fox was faking. As soon as Jim's hands were in the air, Bale hit him across the face with his cane. Jim staggered backwards, tried to maintain his balance, and dropped to one knee. He looked up just in time to see the cane flailing at his head again. Blackness enveloped him and he was out.

———————

Dude Miller made his way through the briars and the creosote bushes up to the old line shack. He rode to within ten yards of the rickety tar paper hovel when a hail from the inside brought him to a halt.

"Who's out there?" The caller's voice was shrill and high-pitched.

"It's Dude. Charley Pratt, you idiot, I'm comin' in."

"Okay, okay, Dude. Come on." Charley turned to the other two men there. "It's okay, boys. It's my pardner, Dude Miller."

Dude stepped down from his saddle, loose-wrapped his horse's reins, and stomped inside the small one-room building. The place reeked of human filth and tobacco. Three bedrolls lay about in a haphazard manner. An old rickety table was pushed against one front corner. Two men sat on empty whiskey crates at the table. Chris Armstrong lay bound on the floor by the back wall. Charley Pratt stood in the middle of the room.

"What in the devil is that boy doin' tied up?" Dude had to do a little play acting.

"But, Dude," said Charley, "I thought Mr. Quarry wanted him tied 'til we decided what we was gonna do with him."

"Charley Pratt, you can't do anything right. You are the biggest foul-up I know. You other two boys are relieved. Go into town, have a couple of drinks on the boss, then get some rest. We got somethin' big comin' up, real soon."

The two waddies grabbed up their stuff and high-tailed it out of the shack. Charley Pratt hung his head and hurried over to untie Chris Armstrong.

Chris sat up and rubbed his wrists and ankles. He tried to stand, got his legs tangled up, and fell. On his hands and knees, Chris wretched his guts out.

Dude watched the boy puke and laughed. "Charley, pick up our hung-over friend here, and help him to the table. Then you clean up the mess he just made."

With Charley's help, Chris managed to stagger to a whiskey crate and sit down. "What's goin' on, Dude?" Chris's voice squeaked when he talked. "Why was I all trussed up like that? Somebody better be quick with some explaining."

"Charley made a mistake, Chris. Mr. Quarry told him to bring you up to this old line shack and keep you hid out until we see if Cassidy kicks the bucket or not. Heck, old Charley ain't all there sometimes. He just made the wrong decision, that's all."

"I'm plumb sorry, Chris," said Charley, sticking out his hand.

Chris glared at the little man but made no move to shake his hand. Charley shrugged and dropped it to his side. Dude patted Chris on the back while motioning with his head for Charley to go outside. Once the little gunman had gone, Dude sat down opposite Chris.

"Chris, the boss thinks a lot of you. We got a big deal comin' up and he wants you to ramrod the whole shootin' match."

"Why me?" Chris said. "What have I done to make him think I can run anything?"

"Aw, Chris, you know he's always liked you. He knows your old man never gave you a fair shake. How would you like to be runnin' the Double-A-Slash?"

"I will be someday." The bile-coated words escaped from the bitter young man's mouth like evil spirits. "My father's too old and feeble to run the ranch much longer. Soon it will be mine. Then, maybe I'll partner up with Mr. Quarry, and we can share the biggest spread in the panhandle."

"Yeah, yeah, now you're thinkin', Chris. That's just what Mr. Quarry wants, except he's not a patient man. He doesn't want you havin' to wait a year, maybe longer, for your ranch. He wants you to have it now. That's why he wants you to lead our next job. It'll be the biggest one yet."

Dude had the boy right where he wanted him and he knew it. The kid's greed would be his own downfall. "Charley!" Dude hollered. "Quit your eavesdroppin' and come in here and fix us a pot of coffee. Me and your new boss got a heap of talkin' to do."

Charley Pratt shuffled into the shack and started a pot of coffee, just like he was told to do.

Chapter 11

Jim groaned as he struggled back from the shadowy emptiness. He jerked his eyes open and, just as quick, closed them again. Light pierced his corneas like white-hot needles. For an instant, Jim thought he was blind. He raised his eyelids, slower this time. The brightness hurt, but his vision was creeping back. First he saw shadows, and then everything began to take shape. Maria was sitting beside him with a glass in her hand.

"Welcome back, *señor*. I have some water here. You must drink. Just a little bit, *por favor*."

She held the glass up to Jim's lips and he swallowed some of the water. "There, that is enough for now. I will give you more in a moment."

Maria sat the water down and adjusted a damp cloth on Jim's forehead. Her eyes transfixed upon Jim's head in an unworldly gaze, and her knobby hands moved over his aching skull, working to ease his pain.

Jim shut his eyes and kept them closed until a familiar voice caused him to rouse.

"For a little while, Badger, we thought the old rascal had punched your ticket." Shank leaned over and touched Jim's shoulder. "Whatever you said to him sure turned his mean light on. If me and the boys hadn't come in here quick when he hollered for us, he might have finished what he started. What got him goin', Badger?"

Jim's mouth was still full of cotton. He drank another sip of water and coughed. Even swallowing hurt. His head weighed two hundred pounds, but he managed to turn it far enough to see Shank, Rusty and Hack standing beside him.

"I told him who I was." The words came out soft and sounded strange to Jim, like he was talking using someone else's voice. "He told me to get out, and he started to fall. I reached out to help him and the rest is just a blur. Did he hit me?"

Shank told him what had taken place in as few words as possible. Jim was still a little groggy, but he understood what had happened. He stared up at Maria after Shank finished. He wanted to thank her for her kindness, but his voice was gone.

"You will be well soon, *señor*. Mr. Armstrong is angry and confused. He thinks his mind is playing tricks on him. He will accept you, but it will take time. He carries much fear and bitterness in his heart." Maria reached down and caressed Jim's cheek. "Do you not feel much better than you did moments ago, *señor?*"

"Yes. Yes, I do. What did you do that took away the pain, Maria?"

"I did little, *señor*. Perhaps your injuries were not as serious as first thought. I do not know. I am only an aged housekeeper, nothing more."

With Shank's help, Jim rolled over and sat up on the edge of the sofa. He stood up and found his legs shaky, but serviceable.

"Thanks for your help, Maria. I reckon I'd better be goin' before my father finds out I'm awake. I don't need another conk on the noggin today."

Maria nodded, and Jim and the other men walked through the hallway and out of the house. They were barely outside when a rider came in from the east. Jim mounted his horse as the rider pulled to a halt next to him.

"Hey, what's goin' on here?" said Valentine Rose. "That new waddy was supposed to relieve me up in the breaks an hour ago. I ain't had my breakfast, yet."

He glared over at Hack Bonner. Hack threw a look at Val Rose that could have withered a prickly pear. The puncher's eyes went to the ground like a whipped pup, and the corners of Hack Bonner's mouth crinkled up in a grin. He looked over at Shank.

"Go on out there, Hack," said Shank. "We wouldn't want Valentine to starve."

"Valentine," said Hack Bonner, looking perplexed, "ain't that a girl's name?" He stared back up at the new rider, an odd look on his face.

Val Rose snorted and dug heels in his horse's flanks. It just so happened, his mount had a sore rib from getting kicked inside the corral the night before. Val hit the horse right on top of that bruised rib and that hay burner broke loose bucking like his tail was on fire, jumping and hopping all over the place. Val was a fair to middlin' rider, but he wasn't any kind of bronc peeler. He made the first two jumps, but on the third one he blew both stirrups, and on the fourth, when the horse came down, Val stayed up in the air. When he hit the ground, he bounced and smacked down on his face. He didn't move.

Hack trotted over to check on him. He reported back that Valentine didn't look too good but he was still pumpin' air. Shank shook his head and sighed.

"I don't like that man," Shank said. "There's somethin' about the chowder head that don't smell right, and I ain't talkin' about his bathin' habits, neither."

"Shank," said Jim, "I think that man works for Mort Quarry." He told Shank and the others what he had seen take place at the message tree.

"I'll be dipped," said Shank. "I know just which pecan tree you're talkin' about, too. We been gettin' good papershells off that tree for twenty years. It's down in a little sink hole with half a dozen other old pecan trees."

"Let's go tear down his meat house," said Rusty. "I get first turn."

"Wait a minute, boys. Let's think about this situation," said Jim. "We know who he is workin' for, but we don't know his real purpose here. Rusty, I think you need to keep an eye on our friend Valentine and see what he is up to."

"I'll start right now." Rusty Puckett wallowed his hat down over his ears like he was getting ready to bust a bad bronco, and stomped off toward the cook shack.

Watching him go, Shank said, "Who's gonna watch *that* wall-eyed cuss?"

Jim, still astride his mount, nodded goodbye and rode off toward Two Bucks City. He was more confused about what to do now than he was before his abortive meeting with his father. Jim hadn't expected to be embraced with open arms, but he sure hadn't planned for the caning he had received at his dad's hands. He was hurting, inside and out. As he rode up into the trees, he wondered where they had stashed his brother. He hoped Cormac had been able to join the gang. Maybe he would have some answers.

———

"Yes, sir, Mr. Quarry. That Armstrong boy fell for the whole thing. He thinks I came into town to get the final orders from you."

"Outstanding, Dude, this calls for a drink."

Mort Quarry reached into a burled oak liquor cabinet and drew out a bottle of ancient Scotch whiskey. He put two short glasses on the table; half-filling one glass, he handed it to his *segundo*. Leaving the other glass empty, he raised it in the air.

"To our complete control of Deaf Smith County," he said.

"But, boss. Your glass ain't got nothin' in it."

"I am well aware of that fact, Dude. But unfortunately, I promised Melinda I would stop drinking. If she caught me, she would raise Old Ned."

Dude smiled and turned up his glass, sucking down the expensive double malt beverage. He was about to ask for another when Melinda sashayed into the office.

She went straight to her father's side. "Father, do I smell alcohol?" Her tone bordered on indignant. "Are you breaking your promise to me?"

"No, my nosey daughter, I am not. I gave Dude a drink in celebration of a business deal, and now he is leaving." Dude took the hint and backed out of the office, closing the door behind him.

"A business deal, Daddy? Is it a good one?"

"Melinda, by this time next week we will be the sole owners of the Double-A-Slash ranch."

"Oh, Daddy! That is the best news, and without a fight. I am so pleased, and, of course, relieved. How did you get that stubborn Mr. Bale Armstrong to agree to sell without a struggle? No fighting, right, Father?"

"Why, Melinda, you hurt me to the quick. I would never do a thing to force Mr. Armstrong off of his land. You listen to too much gossip. Now go home early today and get all dressed up. We will go to the hotel dining room and celebrate with a fancy dinner."

"Wonderful, Father. I will finish up and go right away." Melinda Quarry flew from the office.

Mort Quarry looked at his empty glass and sighed. He put it and the bottle of Scotch back into the cabinet and locked the small door. "No warm Scotch today, perhaps," he said, rubbing his lips, "but we will have chilled champagne tonight."

Chapter 12

As Jim rode into Two Bucks City for the night, he tried to think about what he would do tomorrow, but his mind wouldn't cooperate. The bonk on the skull had caused his head to hurt all day, tiring him out quicker than usual. He decided to grab a quick bite at the hotel restaurant and then go to bed.

Jim trotted his mare into town and set her up at the livery. He walked to the hotel, going to his room just long enough to wash up and put on a clean shirt for supper. Most of the time it made little difference to Jim how he looked when it came time to eat. Tonight for some reason he felt like he ought to look a little bit more presentable than normal. He pulled on a sky-blue shirt with black buttons in a horseshoe shape on the front. He extra-washed his face and ears and slicked down his long black hair with his fingers. Ready, he stepped out into the hallway and headed for the stairs.

Jim followed the aroma of food into the bustling dining room. Waiters in white shirts scurried about the place. Jim chose a table that sat out of the way in a front corner. He straddled a chair, facing his back to the wall. The waiter brought a menu, but Jim didn't look at it. He ordered beefsteak rare, beans, potatoes and coffee, the blacker the better. The waiter was right back with the coffee. Jim thanked him and sat back in his chair to sip the burning brew and watch the other diners.

The Quarry Hotel dining room had a far-reaching reputation for good food and immaculate service. People from six counties came to town just to dine at the prestigious restaurant. Jim had to admit that whatever Quarry was, he did go first class. Too bad he was a low-down thief. He sat back and as the coffee and the nice soft chair began to take effect, Jim felt the knots and kinks in his muscles begin to melt away. In spite of the bad day he had experienced, he was beginning to feel pretty good. His eyes were almost closed when he heard the voice of an angel. He jerked his eyelids open and realized the golden voice was standing beside his table and was directed toward him.

"Father," said Melissa, "This is Jim, er, Mr. Butler, our new depositor."

Jim jumped up from his seat like he had been hotfooted.

"Mr. Butler, this is my father, Morton Quarry."

"Pleased to meet you, Mr. Butler."

Jim reached out and shook the gargantuan paw that was extended to him. His hand disappeared up to the wrist inside the large man's hand. "Howdy," Jim managed to squeak out.

"Mr. Butler, if you are dining alone, we would be pleased if you would join us for dinner," said the angel. "We are celebrating an important acquisition to our family of businesses."

Mort Quarry's eyes betrayed his surprise at his daughter's invitation to this stranger, but his attitude remained cordial. "Melissa, forgive me for saying this, but I believe Mr. Butler has had a long hard day and might prefer to dine alone tonight. Isn't that so, Mr. Butler?"

Jim nodded in agreement, excusing himself from their celebration for the exact reasons Mort Quarry had stated. Melissa expressed mild disappointment, and she and her father went off to a private room in the back of the restaurant.

Jim wondered offhand how Quarry knew so much about his hard day, then it came to him. Val Rose must have already told him about the incident at the Double-A-Slash. How much did Quarry really know? He had no way of knowing Jim was Bale Armstrong, Jr. Or did he? Jim's thoughts were interrupted by the waiter bringing his food. With no more thought of his problems, Jim attacked the steak and fixings like he had never eaten before.

He was halfway through wolfing the meal down when Mort Quarry approached his table. Dude Miller and two other men stood around the giant banker looking like they were guarding some sort of valuable treasure. As the men spread loosely away from Quarry, Jim realized that the one in the back was Cormac McCafferty, the Irish Kid. The Kid stood stone-faced and evil looking, and Jim grinned inside as he thought how two could play the game of spying.

He looked up at Mort Quarry with a puzzled look on his face. "What can I do for you, Mr. Quarry?"

Both of Jim's hands were under the table, a fact that did not go unnoticed by Dude Miller. He fidgeted around and his fingers twitched as his boss spoke.

"Mr. Butler, I know who you are, and I know why you are here."

Jim swallowed, involuntarily, but otherwise showed no reaction to Mort Quarry's statement.

"I know you are supposed to be a quick man with a gun, but I also know you crawfished the other night rather than face Mr. McCafferty here. Well, Mr. Butler, the Irish Kid is in my employ now, and he will be more than willing to meet you at your convenience to determine who is the faster gun. If that is too much for you, sir, then let me suggest an alternative. You ride out of Two Bucks City first thing in the morning and don't look back. Your job is finished with Bale Armstrong. You have failed at your task. Within the week, I will be the sole proprietor of the Double-A-Slash ranch. Bale Armstrong is a beaten man."

Jim's insides churned to the boiling point. He was ready to face up to who he was and to let it be known what would happen to Mr. Mort Quarry and his gunslicks if they even set foot on his father's ranch. His hand closed on the pistol at his side. He glanced at the Irish Kid. The Kid moved into position to help his partner clean house. Jim started to speak when an intruder changed his plan.

"Daddy, the champagne is ready. The sommelier is waiting to remove the cork as we speak." She looked down at Jim, who struggled to soften his features. He only managed a partial success. "Mr. Butler, are you sure you won't join us? The invitation is still open."

"I'm sorry, my dear. Mr. Butler has made other arrangements for the rest of the evening. Please allow me to pay for your meal. It is the least I can do for our newest depositor. Come, Melissa. It is time to toast our great fortune. Dude, Hank, join us. Mr. McCafferty, why don't you accompany Mr. Butler and see that he gets his little chore taken care of."

Quarry hooked Melissa's arm and they strolled back to their party. Melissa tried to look back, but her father's firm grasp prevented her from doing so. At the same time, the two bodyguards blocked her vision.

"All right, Butler. You heard the boss—let's skedaddle on up to that room of yours and get you squared away. We wouldn't want you to have to be gettin' ready in the mornin' and be dallyin' too long for your own good." The Irish Kid's smile was pure malevolence. "Of course, if you want to do it the other way and face me like a man..."

The Kid said the last part way louder than he had to. People close to the two men stopped their conversations to see what might happen next. Jim scowled at the Kid, but did nothing. He rose from his seat and, with the Irish Kid dogging his every step, trudged up to his room.

Jim unlocked the door and stepped inside his room. Cormac followed him in and closed the door. Jim walked over to the bed and removed his gun belt. He motioned the grinning Kid to step over to him. The Kid obliged. Jim stuck out his right hand, and the Kid reached to shake it. Jim clamped his fingers around Cormac's hand and with a lightning move jerked the Kid off balance. Jim's left hand shot around and connected to the unsuspecting man's jaw. The Irish Kid dropped like a horse apple.

Shaking his head to clear the cobwebs, Cormac peered up at Jim from a bulging right eye and a bloodshot left one.

"Cormac, you ever embarrass me again around a bunch of respectable people, we will go out behind a barn, and I will show you who the best *pistolero* is."

Cormac McCarty looked up at Jim with innocent green eyes. "Shucks, Jimmy," he said, "I expect that feller would be Wild Bill Hickok, wouldn't it?"

Jim Butler stared down at his *compadre* for a moment, and then both broke into raucous laughter.

Chapter 13

The Irish Kid got up slowly from the floor. "It wasn't a problem at all gettin' hired on with that bunch of polecats," he said. "I just charmed 'em with a little of the old Irish blarney, and they just naturally couldn't stand to do without me." He dug a finger in his teeth, moseyed over to the window, and spat out a tiny piece of beef. "Old Mr. Quarry, he lays out a doggone tasty spread of vittles for us workin' cowhands. It's gonna bother me a right smart to have to be shootin' some of them boys pretty soon." He peered at Jim out of the corner of his eye.

"If you're through spouting off the wonderful qualities of your new boss, Cormac, maybe now we can get down to business. If you don't show back up at the party pretty soon, Quarry might send someone up to check on you."

The Kid nodded and grabbed the one chair in the room, spun it around backwards, and sat down straddlelegged.

"So far, Jimmy, all I know is that they're plannin' somethin' real big, real soon. Bein' new, I ain't been privy to no inside information."

"Did you find out where they're keeping my brother?"

"Yep, that I did find out. They got him up at an old line shack way back in the hills, deep inside Quarry's ranch. That's somethin' else I was goin' to tell you. I got me a strong hunch that whatever it is they're gonna do, it involves your brother."

Jim got up, walked to the window, and stared out. The night was as black as the devil's heart. A breeze drifted in from the north, cooling the dry air. The evening cacophony of street sounds was dying down. Two Bucks City was rolling up its sidewalks, ending another day.

Midnight had passed and the moonless night shrouded the country in cavernous shadows. Dude Miller and four other men rode up to the line shack where Chris Armstrong and Charley Pratt awaited the big orders from the boss. Dude was in charge, but all of the Quarry men had been instructed to act as if Chris were the head honcho. The five made their way to the dilapidated old cabin, dismounted, and went inside.

All the men said their howdys to Charley and Chris, some even calling Chris 'boss'. The young man enjoyed the attention. He was ready for bigger things and he didn't intend to let Mr. Quarry down. When his boss found out he could get the job done, Chris thought he might just set his eyes on that good-looking Melissa Quarry. A man could do a lot worse than marry the beautiful daughter of the richest man in the panhandle. Chris couldn't help but smile.

"Looks like you're feelin' a heap better, Chris." Dude strolled over and patted the boy on the back. "You up to some hard ridin' tonight? When we pull this deal off, it will only be a matter of time before you're sittin' in your daddy's big old easy chair out at the Double-A-Slash."

"What's the plan, Dude?"

"No time to talk now, I'll fill you in on the way. Pete's got your horse saddled and ready to go, so let's vamoose."

Dude took off leading the six men down a faint trail, headed in the direction of the Armstrong ranch. Despite the lack of light, the seven riders made good time in getting to where the Double-A-Slash herd was bedded down. Upon reaching the herd, Charley rode ahead while the remaining men stayed back in the trees. He cupped his hands and let out a long, low whistle.

Val Rose, riding night guard, heard the whistle coming from the trees. He nudged his pony's sides and walked him in the direction of the sound. As he neared the trees, Charley called out to him.

"Val, it's me, Charley Pratt. Is everything hunky-dory?"

"As well as it's gonna be," answered Val. "There's a new man on the other side of the herd named Bonner. He looks like a tough *hombre,* might cause us some trouble."

"If he tries anything we'll make him wish he stayed on the farm," said Charley.

"Now, Charley. Dude gave me his word there wouldn't be no killin' done here tonight. I can't be no part of somebody's death."

"Gave you his word, huh? Well, I reckon that's about as good as gold... fool's gold."

At that moment, Dude and Chris rode up to the two men. Dude had informed Chris of the plan along the way. They were to stampede the big herd of his father's cattle that were grazing down closest to the ranch house. The plan wasn't to steal the cattle, but to spook them enough to wake up the Double-A-Slash crew and get them out on the range. Mr. Quarry figured that if they did something every night, always at different times, the Armstrong punchers would eventually give up and leave the old man in a position where he had to sell because no one would ride for him.

The plan sort of made sense to Chris, but he knew all of those punchers. Most had been there a long time; they had watched him grow up. These men were all friends, and he knew they wouldn't quit and leave his father high and dry. All at once, Chris knew what he had to do. He was angry with his father, but they were still blood. He was an Armstrong and this was his home. He could not let Mort Quarry, Dude Miller, or anyone stampede this herd. When his brother had left so long ago, the last thing he told Chris was to take care of the old man. He had to act and he had to do it now. Chris urged his horse up to where Dude, Charley, and Val Rose were talking.

"Dude," said Chris, "I need to talk to you."

"Sure, Chris, you ready to get this *fandango* goin'?"

"No, Dude, I'm not." Chris pulled his pistol and pointed it at Dude.

"Hey kid—what gives here? You changin' sides?"

"No, I'm just staying on the side I was always on. It just took me awhile to realize it, Dude. You and Charley and that other fella bunch up here where I can see all of you. Come on, do it. I will shoot the first one who even looks at me funny."

The three men moved their horses close together.

"Chris, thank God, you're here," said Val. "I was out here ridin' night herd when these fellers rode up on me. They was tryin' to persuade me to join in with 'em when you showed up just in time. They might've killed me."

"Val Rose, is that you?"

"Yes, sir, boss. In the flesh. What are we gonna do with these here cattle rustlers?"

Chris was confused. He had known and trusted Valentine Rose for over five years, and had considered the man his best friend. He had to be telling the truth. Chris wasn't sure what to do, and he made a snap decision.

"Okay, Val, I believe you," said Chris. "You gather up these two galoot's guns, right now. Dude, you tell the rest of the boys to just stay put back in the trees. Tell them we are working this thing out and it will take a little while. Do it now."

Chris rode up next to Dude and jabbed his pistol in the man's side. Dude did as he was told, and Val rounded up Dude and Charley's guns.

"Val, keep a sharp eye on these boys. I'm going to ride to the bunkhouse and roust out some men. On my way, I will tell the other night guard to ride over and help you. Can I trust you to do that?"

"Yes, sir, boss. Why, I can't hardly wait to watch these hardcases kicking and choking on the end of a rope."

Chris nodded and started to ride in the direction of Hack Bonner. As soon as Chris turned his back, Dude Miller's hand shot out and grabbed his six-gun from the loose fingers of Val Rose. Before Val could shout a warning, Dude raised the pistol and fired one shot. The back of Chris Armstrong's head burst open like a dropped watermelon. His startled horse jumped and Chris's lifeless body leaned over sideways and slid to the ground. Val Rose came out of his stupor and tried to lift one of the guns in his hand. Another loud pop rang out. Val leaned back, and then fell forward, slumped over his saddle. Charley Pratt rode over and grasped his pistol from the dead puncher's hand. The shots had upset the cattle and they were getting ready to run. The sound of gunfire brought the rest of the Quarry men out of the trees.

"Quick, Pete, you and Cavanaugh pick up the kid's body and tie it to his horse. We'll run the cayuse with the boy's body on its back into the cattle when they stampede."

The two men did as they were told and within minutes Chris's corpse was sitting more or less upright on his frightened mount.

"Yeehaw!' yelled Dude Miller. "Turn 'em loose, boys, and let's get the heck out of here." He whipped his hat into the rump of the horse carrying Chris's body. The animal took off like a scalded hog straight in amongst the jittery livestock. The rest of the Quarry bunch emptied their pistols into the air with whoops and hollers. Some of the cattle started to bolt and, within seconds, the whole herd was running blindly into the darkness.

"This ought to stir the old man up!' Dude yelled above the thunderous sound of thousands of hoofs pounding into the hard pack prairie soil. "Come on, boys! Let's make tracks. The whiskey's on Mort Quarry."

Chapter 14

Shank Halsey wiped the sweat off his brow, shaking his head. "Sweet Mary and Joseph," he said. "I ain't never been a part of somethin' like that. How many of them chowder-headed cows did we lose?"

"Rusty and a couple of the boys are still out checking." It was Hack Bonner, who had just ridden up with a bunch of the hands. "They ought to be in shortly."

"Well, daylight ain't too far away," said Shank. "You fellers go on over to the cook shack. I'm sure Cookie has got the coffee goin'. Hack, what happened out there?"

"I heard two shots, right together. The beeves started milling, and I had my hands full tryin' to calm 'em down. Then, all of a sudden you'd a thought there was a war goin' on. Somebody started shootin' and yellin' to beat the band. Them jughead cows took off and I was ridin' for my life. The shots were echoin', but they sounded like they came from Valentine's side of the herd. Say, have you seen that runt since this all started?"

"Naw, come to think of it, I haven't. Let's ride out and see what Rusty's found."

In ten minutes the two men were at the site where the stampede had begun. Rusty was on his knees in the scrambled dirt. Something lay on the ground in front of him, but Hack and Shank couldn't make out what it was.

"What in tarnation is that thing you got there, Rusty?" said Shank, squinting to try and make out the mess on the ground. It looked like a pile of old dirty rags. As he moved closer, he realized the rags were covered in blood. "What is it, Rusty?" he said again.

Rusty Puckett raised his head. Tears cascaded down his cheeks and splattered onto the dirt. "It's Chris. This pile of rags is Chris Armstrong."

"Naw, that can't be. Quarry's got Chris hid out up in the hills. Rusty, you're wrong." Even as he said it, Shank knew Rusty was right. Although it was almost stomped to pieces by the rampaging cows, he could still recognize the hand-tooled English leather gun belt lying in the pile before him. Bale Armstrong had given the rig to his son on the boy's eighteenth birthday, and Chris never let the holster out of his sight. The pile on the ground had been a man, but now his own mother wouldn't recognize him.

Hack Bonner sat astride his horse, his jaw muscles clenched tight. He never knew this boy—only saw him once, and didn't like what he saw. But nobody deserved to die like this. When Jim found out, there wouldn't be a rock in Texas big enough to hide the snake that did this. Hack rolled his neck to loosen the fatigue he felt. He hadn't gotten any sleep last night, and he didn't expect to get any more for a long time. Turning his horse, he patted the animal on the neck and nudged his heels into the big bay's ribs.

———•——

"That wasn't the plan, but as long as it worked, I'll take the results." Mort Quarry was enjoying a rasher of bacon with scrambled eggs and potatoes. He usually took breakfast at home, but this morning he ate in the hotel restaurant. Pleased with the report Dude had delivered, he dismissed his *segundo*, and leaned back to enjoy his second cup of coffee. In a few minutes he would stroll down to his office and put the final touches on the last proposal he would present to Bale Armstrong for purchase of the Double-A-Slash ranch. With his son dead, his hands spooked, and his gunfighter run out of town, even a stubborn old fool like Armstrong would see that it was futile to continue fighting.

Quarry wiped his lips and rose from his table. He felt better today than he had felt in a long time. As he stepped onto the sidewalk, his thoughts turned to Melissa and how he would explain why Mr. Jim Butler had to leave Two Bucks City in such a hurry. He smiled at the thought of his child falling for a two-bit gunfighter, and a yellow one at that. "No, my dear, I have much bigger plans for you," he said, "whether you like it or not."

Stepping into his office, he watched Hack Bonner ride up to the hotel. "I may have to turn the Irish Kid loose on that one, too," he said to himself, a little too loud.

"What did you say, Father?"

"Melissa, what are you doing in my office, so early?" She had caught him by surprise, so much like her mother used to. He regained his composure and smiled at his daughter. "Melissa, I have something to tell you. Please, sit down."

———•——

Jim Butler sat on the edge of the bed and pulled on his boots. He needed to get to the ranch and try talking to his father again. This time he would have Rusty and Shank to vouch for him. He stood up and had just buckled on his gun belt when someone began banging on his door. His .44 Colt jumped into his hand. "Who is it?" he said, eyes narrowed on the door.

"It's me, Hack. Let me in, Jimmy." Jim crossed the room and, gun in hand, opened the door. Hack hurried inside. Jim locked the door behind the huge gunfighter. Something in Jim's boot hurt his foot. He motioned Hack to the chair, and he sat back down onto the bed and began removing the boot. Hack stood in the middle of the room, not moving toward the offered chair.

"Jimmy," he said, as he removed his hat, "there ain't no easy way to tell you this, but your brother has been killed."

Jim dropped the boot he had been fiddling with. Mouth agape, his eyes rose to meet Hack's. He read the pain there and knew Hack was telling the truth. Jim closed his eyes and took a deep breath. "What happened, Hack?"

While Hack Bonner told him the story, Jim sat and looked at the floor. The part about how they recognized Chris caused Jim to drop his head to his hands and weep. When Hack finished, Jim stood and wobbled over to the wash stand. Hands shaking, he poured some tepid water into the basin. He lowered his head and splashed his face. Done, he toweled off and faced Hack. His eyes were red and bloodshot, but his tears were gone.

"The last time I cried was when mama died. I cried today, but I'm not gonna shed another tear as long as Mort Quarry and his bunch walk the earth."

Hack nodded his head.

"Hack, did they find Chris's horse?" It hurt him to even say his brother's name.

"Nobody had found it when I left to ride into here."

"Hack, one thing Chris could do better than any man I ever saw, even when he was a kid: that rascal could ride like he was stuck to the horse. I never saw him fall off. He was dead when that herd started, or they killed him while the cows were stampeded."

"Let's go get them Quarry men right now, Jimmy."

"No, Hack. As much as I would like to do that, we can't. I don't want to kill Quarry. I want to break him, take away everything he has worked for and stolen. I want him to see it coming and know in his heart that he is powerless to do anything about it. Hack, I want you to go get Chris's remains and take them to Doc Withers. Tell Doc to see if he can find anything that would prove Chris was dead before the stampede. I was goin' to the ranch, but I believe I will stay in town for a while. Maybe I can learn something. Let me know as soon as the doc finds anything. I'll be around town."

Hack nodded and was out the door. Jim walked out right behind him. He had to keep a poker face. He didn't want anyone to know that he knew about Chris's death. He wasn't hungry but he went downstairs into the hotel dining room anyway.

Sitting at his usual table, his back against the corner wall, Jim ordered bacon, eggs, and coffee. When the food came he tried to eat, but couldn't. He drank the coffee, though, four cups: hot, black, and strong. His thoughts centered on his dead brother. Why would anyone want Chris dead? He was brash and wild, but he was harmless, just an overgrown kid trying to be a man and not knowing how to do it. The only thing Jim could come up with was that Mort Quarry must have wanted Chris dead. He didn't do the deed, but he gave the order. An idea popped into Jim's head and he sprang up, laid some money on the table, and stepped outside.

Jim pushed his hat back on his head and strolled across the street to the bank like he didn't have a care in the world. When he got there he hopped up onto the plank sidewalk and stepped inside. Melissa Quarry was alone at the teller's cage. When Jim walked in, she looked up to issue a greeting. Upon recognizing who it was, she dropped her head and went back to her counting. Jim thought it strange that her attitude toward him had changed overnight.

"Howdy, Miss Melissa," said Jim, smiling. "How are you today?"

"I am fine, under the circumstances, Mr. Butler. I assume you are here to withdraw your money. I will get the form for you to sign. It will only take a moment, and then you can be on your way."

"On my way? Just where am I going, Melissa?"

"Why back to New Mexico, or Arizona, or wherever it is you come from, Mr. Butler. My father said—"

Jim interrupted her in mid-sentence. "Oh, that thing with your father and the Irish Kid, why, that was all just a big misunderstanding. Heck, Cormac, uh, that's the Kid's name, Cormac McCafferty, and I have been saddle pals for a coon's age. We was just sort of play actin' last night. All that stuff don't amount to a hill of beans."

Melissa looked dazed. "Well, Mr. Butler." She smiled up at him. "In that case, I am glad that you decided to stay."

"Yes, ma'am, me too, I kinda like it here. I might even decide to settle around these parts. There are an awful lot of pretty things to look at here in this country, and I reckon I'm lookin' at the most beautiful one of all right now."

Melissa slapped her hand to her bosom. Her face glowed a striking crimson.

"As a matter of fact, Melissa, the reason I stopped by was to ask you if you would take a buckboard ride with me this evening. I thought we might drive up on one of these hills around here and watch the sunset. Will you go with me?"

"Yes, I will! I mean, of course. I have to work in the bank until four o'clock. After that I will be free for the rest of the evening."

"Good," Jim said, putting his hat back on his head. "I will pick you up at seven. I'm looking forward to our evening together." He turned and headed toward the door.

"I'll see you later... Jim," said Melissa.

Chapter 15

Doc Withers drained the lukewarm coffee from his cup, and poured himself a fresh one. "In all my years of practice, I've never seen a body so torn up. Hold out your hand, son."

Hack Bonner offered his left hand. The doctor dropped a small chunk of lead into Hack's open palm. The gunfighter gazed down at the bullet, and squeezed it.

"Found it lodged in the boy's lower jaw. Someone shot him in the back of the head. It must have exploded his brain. He had to have died instantly—never knew what hit him."

"At least that's something," said Stretch Cassidy from the next room. He had one more day and the Doc was going to let him go back home.

"Yeah, ain't it, though?" Hack opened his palm and stared down at the slug.

He stuck it in his shirt pocket and started for the door. "Doc," he said, "Jimmy asked if you would take care that his brother's body gets to the mortician. He'll get with the man to make arrangements later." The doctor nodded his head and Hack exited the building.

Melissa Quarry had closed the bank right on time. She hurried home, went straight to her room, and spent the next three hours preparing for her sunset ride. She changed clothes three times and combed her hair twice before she was happy with the way she looked. At seven o'clock on the dot she skipped down the stairs, hitting every other step, and sat down in the parlor to wait. Her father had not come home yet, but that was not unusual. He was often late and sometimes stayed at the hotel. Since her mother died, he had begun to spend more and more time away from home.

A soft knock at the door announced the arrival of her riding partner. Satisfied with her reflection in the hall mirror, she opened the door. Jim Butler stood on the porch, hat in hand. He gulped a mouthful of the warm evening air, coughed, and sputtered.

"Jim, are you okay?" said Melissa. "May I get you a glass of water?"

"No, no," he said, waving that he was all right. "It's just that I have never seen anything as beautiful as you are tonight. Melissa Quarry, you are stunning."

Melissa beamed at Jim's compliments. "Oh, Jim Butler, you are such a flatterer. I haven't done anything special tonight."

"Whatever the case, you are the finest looking lady I have seen in a long time."

"Just the finest in a long time?" she teased. "Not the finest ever?"

Jim blushed. "Are you ready to go, Melissa?"

"Let me get my wrap. It gets cooler as the sun goes down." She retrieved her shawl hanging on the hatrack by the door and joined Jim on the front porch. They boarded the buggy Jim had rented, he shook the reins, and the horse took off at a trot.

Jim and Melissa sat on opposite sides of the buggy seat all the way to the hill Jim had picked out to watch the sunset. He found a spot he liked and guided the horse over to it. Bunch grass grew in abundance in the area, so the animal had plenty to graze on. Jim jumped from the buggy seat and walked behind the rig. Rummaging around, he found a large wool blanket and spread the covering on a flat spot on the hillside. He then reached up and took Melissa's hand to help her to the ground. Jim wasn't sure, but for a moment he thought he felt Melissa squeeze his hand a bit harder than she had to. The time was around eight-thirty, so the couple had an hour before the sun started going down.

"Jim, we have been sitting here for five minutes now, and all you are doing is staring at me. I am doing all the talking. Jim? Jim, do you hear me?" She reached over and squeezed his arm hard.

"Hey," he responded, "What's that for?"

'Jim Butler, I declare, you haven't heard a word I said."

"Sorry, Melissa." Jim stroked his mustache. "I was just wonderin' how a plug ugly like Mort Quarry could end up with the most beautiful girl in Texas as his daughter."

"Oh, Jim! My goodness, can't you think of anything but how I look? I have brains, too. I can run Daddy's bank as well as he can—maybe better."

"Oh, I'm sure of that, Melissa, and you're right, I need to think about something else besides your incredible beauty."

"Good, what would like to talk about? I am well versed in the arts. What do you think of William Shakespeare?"

"What do I think?" Jim smiled. "Why, I think your mother must have been a beauty, too."

Melissa elbowed Jim in the ribs, pushed him over on his side, and pummeled him with her fists. He lay on his side protesting the mock beating he was receiving. Finished with the playful punching of her beaten adversary, Melissa offered him her hand in assistance. As he was being pulled up, Jim felt, for sure this time, an extra strong squeeze from Melissa. This time he squeezed back.

They sat close to each other and talked as the west Texas sky turned into a kaleidoscope of ever-changing colors. The sun dipped below the horizon, turning the sky silvery indigo. A hint of the coming spectacular show of stars began as random twinkling filled the heavens. Jim stared deep into Melissa's eyes. He reached out and took her into his arms. Her eyes were closed and her lips were wet and inviting. She raised her mouth to his and he turned away.

"What's the matter, Jim?" Her eyes were open and questioning. "I thought—"

"I'm sorry, sweetheart. If I had my way I would take you in my arms and never let you go. I have never felt about a woman the way I feel about you. Melissa Quarry, I love you."

"Why, Jim. Jim, darling—I love you, too. I wasn't sure until tonight, but now I have no doubt about my love for you. If you feel the same way, why did you turn away?"

"Melissa, I haven't been exactly truthful with you. I said that incident with your father wasn't real, but it was. Your father was trying to run me out of town. He threatened to have me killed if I didn't go."

"What! But why?"

"Your father wants the Double-A-Slash Ranch and Bale Armstrong won't sell it to him. I'm determined not to let that happen."

"Oh, Jim, you must be wrong. My father told me yesterday that Mr. Armstrong had decided to sell the ranch to him. That's what we were celebrating last night."

"Melissa, do you know why your father said that? It's because only two people stood between him and his taking Bale Armstrong's ranch away, Chris

Armstrong and me. Your father thought he had me buffaloed, and Chris... Chris is dead."

Melissa gasped and twisted her hand over her mouth. "Chris, that sweet boy, is dead?"

"Somebody shot him in the back and threw his body into a herd of stampeding cows. The only way we recognized him was by his gun belt." Jim choked up.

Melissa sobbed and put her head against Jim's chest. She cried for a long time, not noticing the tears falling into her hair from Jim's eyes. He gently stroked her neck and tried to soothe her.

"Jim," she said, her voice on the verge of breaking. "Who could have done such an evil thing?"

Jim yearned to tell her the truth about her father. He wanted to tell her who he really was, and that everything was going to be fine. But he couldn't tell her anything more without jeopardizing the whole plan. He loved this woman more than anyone he had ever known, but he despised her father and what the man was trying to do to his family. His blood was Armstrong blood. The same blood as his brother's that now soaked the ground of the Armstrong ranch. If Jim did not succeed, the blood of his father and his own blood would join that of his brother. He had made a lot of tough decisions in his life, most of them affecting only him. What he did now would affect many people; some he despised, and some he loved.

"Jim," said Melissa, her voice a whisper, "You don't think my father was responsible for Chris Armstrong's death, do you?"

Jim was ready to burst inside. "Sweetheart, I don't know for sure who was responsible. I know your father didn't kill Chris." Jim hesitated too long before he spoke again.

"Jim Butler, you *do* think my father was involved. I can't believe this! I confessed my love to you, and now you are calling my father a murderer. Oh, my goodness." The distraught young woman raised her hands to her face and began to cry again.

Jim reached out and touched her arm. She jerked the arm away, and then swung it forward, slapping Jim hard across his left cheek. Just as quick as the crying began, it stopped. Melissa Quarry sprang to her feet.

"Jim Butler, take me home this instant. I will not stand here and let you accuse my father of some heinous crime. If you do not leave Two Bucks City tomorrow morning, I will tell my father what you have said tonight. And I promise you he will not be generous as to your fate."

Jim was stunned by Melissa's behavior. Without thinking, he reached for her hand to help her back into the buggy. She slapped his hand away and scrambled up by herself. Jim walked around the rig and climbed up beside her. He shook the reins, and the horse started for home.

Fresh meat would have frozen solid had it rested between Jim and Melissa on the ride back into town. When Jim stopped the buggy in front of the Quarry home, he made no attempt to help Melissa down from the seat. She jumped off the buckboard and ran into the house. Jim sat like a statue, not watching her go. The slamming of the house's front door signaled him she was safe inside, safe from all the bad things that could happen to a body late on a dark west Texas night. She was safe from the knowledge that her father was the most evil man in the panhandle. But most of all, she was safe from her father's worst enemy—an enemy who loved her very much.

Chapter 16

Jim had ridden out of Two Bucks City well before dawn. He sat astride the big steel-dun mare on top of the knoll overlooking the ranch house and watched the first rays of the sun climb the horizon. He squinted as the bright ball of fire and gas rose above the far hills. Little sleep had come the night before and Jim was restless. Today he had to convince his father that his intentions were good. If the old man hated him, there was nothing he could do about it, but, for the Double-A-Slash to remain in Armstrong hands, his father had to listen to what Jim had to say. He rode down the knoll, but instead of going to the main house, he headed for the bunk house. This time he would take his friends with him.

Jim dismounted and stepped through the only door of the rough-hewn log building. The men were awake and shuffling around the room. Most were dressed and ready to head for the cook shack and breakfast. Jim spied Shank and strolled over to him.

"Rusty, I know you didn't like that cuss," Shank was holding forth on the subject of Val Rose, "but he's dead and gone now, and it ain't polite to speak bad about the dead."

"All I said, Mr. Shank Halsey, was that the galoot was a no-good polecat, and I, for one, don't miss his lyin' carcass one little bit."

"Excuse me, boys, but what are you talkin' about?"

Shank and Rusty looked up to see Jim grinning down at them.

"Why, howdy, Badger," said Shank. "We didn't see you come in."

"No, you two were jawin' so loud, it's a wonder anybody else in here could think."

Both men looked at each other. His two oldest friends had been partners for over twenty years, and they couldn't have argued more if they had been married that long. Rusty started to protest, but Jim stopped him short.

"Boys," said Jim, serious now, "I want to try and get through to my daddy again. This time I want you two to go with me and vouch that I am Bale Armstrong, Jr."

Jocko Lunt, who was another old-time Double-A-Slash hand, was eavesdropping on the conversation and jumped a foot in the air when Jim said he was Bale, Jr. The old puncher ambled over to Jim, scratching the three-day growth of gray whiskers scattered about his face. He walked up next to Jim and stared.

"Well, I'll be a prairie dog's uncle, you are Bale Armstrong, Jr." Jocko said. "Howdy, Badger. We thought you were dead a long time ago." He stuck out his hand. "Remember me, Jocko Lunt?"

Jim gave the old timer's hand a vigorous shake. "Howdy, Jocko. How are you?"

"Mighty fine, now that you're here, son, mighty fine."

Before anyone else could speak, Jocko started yelling to the other cowboys about who was in the bunkhouse. "Say, all you ne'er-do-wells, come on over here and meet a real wampus cat on two legs, Bale Armstrong, Jr. We always called him Badger because he was so tough, and he wouldn't never give up on nothin' if he thought he was right."

Shank Halsey tried to stop Jocko from letting the cat out of the bag, but Jim seized his arm and held him back.

"It's okay," said Jim. "The time has come for everyone to know who I am." He faced the men who had become quiet at Jocko's announcement. "Boys, I have gone by the name Jim Butler for more years than I care to talk about. Whatever you might have heard about me is only half true, but I ain't gonna tell which half that is."

The bunkhouse erupted with laughter. The crew of the Double-A-Slash needed someone with the brains to formulate a plan to save the ranch and the guts to get the job done. It didn't take a bunch of book learning to see that Jim Butler was that man.

"My real name is Bale Armstrong, Jr. Those of you that were here when I left called me Badger. Now I answer to Jim, but Jim or Badger, either one is okay with me. Boys, I'll make this speech short and sweet. I have come home to help save this ranch from that thieving varmint Mort Quarry and his gang of cutthroats. There is no doubt in my mind that they are responsible for my brother's death. Now, I know some of you hands aren't experienced fighters, and that's okay. I'm not asking you to shoot anybody. Just keep your eyes and ears open. If you notice anything irregular, find me or Shank or Rusty or Hack over there and let us know what you saw. This is war. I don't intend for it to last too long, and I don't intend to lose. If you don't like what I'm saying you can draw your pay, no questions asked. Anybody got anything to say?"

Jocko raised his hand. "Shucks, Badger," he said, his grin revealing just six tobacco-stained teeth in his whole mouth. "We was with you when you told the boys who you were."

Jim turned to Shank. "Well, old son, I guess it's about time we went to see my daddy. You boys stand around me so he doesn't cold cock me again."

He wasn't smiling when he said it, either. Bale Armstrong, Sr., was about as predictable as Texas weather—which wasn't predictable at all.

―――・―――

Melissa Quarry yawned and stretched her sore body. She wasn't used to sitting on the ground for such a long time as she had the previous night. She stood at the kitchen stove making toast on a newfangled toast-making machine that had recently arrived from St. Louis.

When the bread reached the desired shade of brown, Melissa opened the hinged wires with a pot holder and placed the two slices of bread on a plate. She was looking for the butter when she noticed her father outside the back door. He was in heated conversation with Dude Miller.

"Dude, are you absolutely positive about this?" Her daddy looked upset.

"Yes, sir, ain't no doubt about it. I seen the Armstrong boy's body with my own eyes. Mordecai Burns, the undertaker, showed it to me. He said Doc Withers told him he pulled a .45 slug out of the boy's head."

"Somebody was smart enough to get the doctor to do an autopsy on the body. Now they know he didn't die in the stampede."

"What are we gonna do, boss?"

Mort Quarry ran his thumb and index finger down his chin. "Dude, I want you to round up the Irish Kid and a couple of the other boys. After dark tonight, send them over to Doc Withers' office. I don't want the good doctor flapping his gums anymore about how the Armstrong boy died. Tell the Kid to silence the doctor for good."

"What about old Mordecai? You want us to clean his plow, too?"

Mort thought for a minute. "No, just put the fear of the devil in him." He smiled. "Doctors come a dime a dozen, but good morticians are hard to come by. And, besides, I believe the Armstrong bunch will be needing his services right soon."

Dude nodded his head and sauntered away. Mort Quarry started to head for his office but changed his mind and reached for the knob to the kitchen door. His abrupt change of direction startled Melissa and she dropped the bowl of butter she held in her hand. The crockery bowl clattered to the floor, shattering into a dozen pieces; butter flew everywhere.

"Oh, my!' she said.

Quarry opened the door just in time to see the bowl hit the hardwood floor. He jumped back, barely missing being hit with flying butter. Melissa was on her knees picking up pieces of the bowl before he could speak.

"What on earth, child?" he said. "How did this happen?" He wondered if his daughter had heard the conversation with his *segundo*. If she was eavesdropping, he would find out.

"Oh, Father! I was getting ready to butter my toast and it slipped from my hand. When I grabbed for it, I dropped the butter. I am so sorry." Melissa scrambled around on her knees picking up the crockery shards.

Mort Quarry reached down and grasped his daughter's arm. His grip was firmer than it had to be as he lifted her to her feet. He held her by both arms and lowered his head until they were eye to eye.

"Melissa, I have a feeling you overheard my conversation with Dude."

The frightened girl tried to protest, but Mort Quarry's grip was like iron.

"I will tell you this one time, young lady. Whatever I do, I do it for you. Do you understand me?"

She nodded her head in silence.

"Good. Now someday you will own the largest land and cattle empire in West Texas. That will be my legacy to you. I will do whatever it takes to make this happen. Some of the things I do, you may not comprehend for a while, but someday when you reap the rewards of my efforts you will understand. All I ask of you is your trust. Do you trust me to do the right thing?"

She nodded again.

"Sweetheart, do not speak to anyone about what you heard today. Is that clear?"

"Yes, Father."

Mort Quarry released his grip on Melissa's arms and hugged her to his body. "Oh, my darling, I knew you would understand. I love you very much."

"I love you, Father," she said.

Chapter 17

Maria opened the door to find Jim Butler and his friends standing there. "*Señor* Armstrong," she said, bowing her head. "I have been expecting you."

"How did you know I would be here today, Maria?" asked Jim.

"Shoot fire, Badger," said Rusty. "Ain't much this lady don't know about. She's one of them *curanderas*. They say they talk to spirits, got the evil eye, and such like that."

Maria's brow furrowed as she cut her eyes toward the red-headed cowboy, who ducked his head and averted his eyes. She winked at Jim, reached out, and took his hand. Her flesh was so warm that Jim flinched from the touch. She led him and his men into the big, sprawling kitchen. Bale Armstrong sat with his back to them, drinking coffee.

"*Señor*, we have visitors," said Maria, pausing for a moment. "Your son is here to see you again."

Bale Armstrong whipped around and leaped to his feet. He was face to face with Jim before it sunk in, what Maria had meant. "I thought I told you lyin' piece of trash to get off of my property." The old man began a frantic search for his cane. Maria, still grasping Jim's hand, reached out with her other hand and grabbed hold of Jim's father's hand.

Bale, Sr., started to protest, but Maria held on tight. She took both of the men's hands and placed them one upon the other. Jim stood still. Bale, Sr., continued to struggle, but couldn't shake loose from the Mexican woman's grip. Gradually his opposition to Maria's hold lessened. Bale Armstrong looked into the eyes of the man whose hand was touching his, and found Jim's gaze fixed upon him. All at once, he stopped struggling.

"Badger," he said. "Bale, Jr.—you're alive."

Then he fainted.

Rusty and Hack lifted Bale, Sr., and carried him to his bed. The rest followed, with Maria fetching water and some clean cloths.

"Your father must rest, *Señor* Bale. He is not a well man and the truth that you are alive and here at home has been a great shock to him. Even a *curandera* would need all of her powers to heal such a sick man."

Jim squinted as he stepped outside into the bright sunlight. "Boys," he said to his three friends. "We got us some hard riding to do. I'll tell you on the way what the plan is."

Mort Quarry was concerned about how much Melissa might have heard of his conversation with Dude. He knew she wouldn't break his trust, but still it troubled him. He decided to take a ride up into the hills. Long rides alone always cleared his mind and helped him to think straight. Without telling anyone, he went down to the livery, saddled his favorite horse, and took off for the countryside.

Many hours later, Mort stood under a thick, leafy cottonwood tree and watched a storm roll in from the north. He had ridden all day, enjoying being outdoors. It had been a long time since he had ridden on his ranch property. He was proud of his land, his cattle, and the mansion he had built for his wife.

Sarah had been such a simple person. She had never liked the house; she said it was too big and a waste of money. Mort smiled at the thought of Sarah and money. Frugality was a way of life for her, while Mort liked to spend freely. In their last argument, she had said that she was sick and tired of his grandiose ways. *Grandiose,* her exact words. Mort hadn't realized she even knew what the word meant. That had been the last straw. Mort had known it was time to terminate his relationship with his wife. It had been easier than he expected, and now Melissa was the apple of his eye.

He looked up at the darkening sky. The leaves in the cottonwood above him had begun to whip like thousands of miniature green flags. The roar of the wind whistling through his ears invigorated him. He turned his face to the heavens and yelled out like he was speaking to God Almighty himself. "I did it all for you, Melissa, I did it all for you!"

The riders had been on Quarry land for about fifteen minutes when Jim raised his hand for them to halt. They sat four abreast staring down at the Rancho Bonita complex. There was still enough daylight to make out the buildings. The main house was massive. It was built in the majestic style of the Old South. Four white pillars stood on the porch that ran the width of the house. Three bedrooms crossed the front of the second story, each with its own private balcony. Hanging baskets of multi-colored flowers, sea-green ivies, and delicate-looking ferns decorated the front porch.

The rest of the buildings consisted of a barn, bunkhouse, blacksmith's shop, and a smokehouse. Every building was painted bright white, even the pump house. The buildings were unusually close together.

"Whoo-ee, I ain't ever seen a place this fancy before," said Rusty.

"Yeah," said Shank, "and don't nobody live in that big house anymore, either. Ever since Quarry's wife passed, him and his daughter have stayed in town."

"How did his wife die?" asked Jim.

"She fell out of a carriage and broke her neck," said Shank. "It was an odd thing. No one was with her when it happened. Quarry had expected her in town, and when she didn't show up, he rode out to check on her. He's the one who found her dead."

Jim took off his hat and ran his fingers through his hair. "So boys, do you think we can do this? That storm yonder is gonna be right on top of us when we stampede those Quarry beeves across the ranch headquarters. It's not gonna be a picnic."

"Aw, Badger, we can do this with our eyes closed, but there's somethin' I need to ask you." Shank Halsey had ridden with a burr under his saddle ever since he learned of the plan. "Badger, I know most of them punchers down there in the bunkhouse; shucks, I've even rode with one or another of 'em in the past. For the most part they're good men. They work Quarry's cattle, and they ride for the brand, but they ain't gunmen. They don't get involved with what goes on in Two Bucks City. They don't have no doin's with Quarry's bunch of gunnies. Son, will you let me ride down there and warn 'em to get out or face the consequences?"

Jim thought about it for a moment. "Shank, you've got fifteen minutes before we start those beeves to running. That doesn't give you much time, but that's all you're gonna get. Tonight I'm sending Mort Quarry a message he won't soon forget."

Shank nodded and took off toward the bunkhouse at a gallop. Jim and the others started east toward Quarry's largest herd of cattle.

Chapter 18

The Irish Kid knew he wasn't going to kill Doc Withers, but he was unsure about how he was going to get out of it. One thing he did not want was a bunch of Quarry's men with him when he went to the doctor's office. "Shucks, Dude," he said. "I don't need no help takin' care of one old man. It'll be quieter and cause less of a ruckus if I go by myself."

"Come on, Kid," said Pete Allday. "We just want to see you work. It would sort of be an honor to watch a shootist like you take care of business. Right, boys?" The few men listening to the conversation voiced their agreement. Some of them, however, believed the Kid wasn't all he was cracked up to be. They hadn't seen him do anything since the boss hired him but strut around and brag about his prowess with a gun or with the ladies. Some of them hoped he would fail at this task.

"We'll go and clean up after this one-man cyclone, Dude." This came from a man named Quint Mullins, who had been a part of the Quarry bunch for almost a year. Most of the men considered him to be the best man with a gun in the gang, even quicker than Dude. Then the Irish Kid came along and stole his thunder. Mullins was ripe to see the Kid shown up as the four-flusher he was.

"I don't see a problem with a few of the boys going along to watch the fun," said Dude Miller. "Maybe, it'll stop some of the grumblin' about who is and who ain't a master gunfighter." He stared at Quint Mullins the whole time he was speaking.

"Mullins, you go with the Kid. Pete, Andy, Carlos, you boys tag along, too. But there is one thing I will make doggone clear. The Kid does the killin'. After that, you boys can get rid of the body, and while you're at it, trash the place real good. Make it look like somebody was tryin' to rob the doc. Now, Kid—go on and get it over with."

The Irish Kid sighed and headed out of the saloon in the direction of Doc Wither's office. His entourage followed close behind. He had no idea what he was going to do, but he knew, somehow, that these men with him could not leave the doctor's office alive.

The wind was picking up and blowing out of the north as the five men ambled down the street. Dust devils swirled about, and tumbleweeds bounded through the air like giant hollow balls of twine. A Blue Norther was coming, bringing hammering rains with it. Great frosty globules of water splattered onto the dust-blown street as the Kid and his followers reached the doctor's office.

Doc Withers arose with a start when the bunch of disheveled men tromped into his office. Just as quick, he sat back down and placed his hands on his desk.

"What brings you boys in here on such a stormy night?" he said. "If you're looking for shelter from the storm, I have a pot of coffee on the stove. You're sure welcome to some. Here, I'll get up and find you fellas some cups."

"Shut up and stay sittin' down, old man," said Quint Mullins. "We might have us some of that coffee after we take care of your lyin' hide."

"What are you talking about, young man? I am not a liar."

"You was the one that told the undertaker Chris Armstrong was killed by a bullet to the head, not by them stampedin' cattle. Well, old timer, that was just a flat out lie, and we've come here to make sure you tell no more filthy stories about Mr. Quarry."

"Mr. Quarry!" The doctor was looking straight at his mortality, and the odds weren't in his favor. "Why, I never said a thing about who was responsible for that boy's death. I haven't a clue who shot him. Now you ruffians get out of here while you can, and I won't report this to the authorities."

"We're Quarry men, Doc," said Pete Allday. "We *are* the authorities."

The obscene laughter of the gunmen put Doc Withers on edge, but he was a long way from being afraid. He had been through the War Between the States, and there wasn't much he hadn't seen.

The Kid took advantage of the jawing to edge closer to the doctor. By the time the conversation had just about played out, he was almost parallel to the seated man and facing the four gun hands.

"Okay," said the Kid, "that's enough rattlin'. It's time to take care of business. I told you boys I didn't want you comin' with me, but y'all were too stupid to listen. Now, I'm gonna have to kill you."

Doc Wither's head jerked up like it was spring loaded.

"Dang it," said Quint Mullins, "I told you knuckleheads he wasn't with us. There was somethin' fishy about him from the start. You're with that Butler feller, ain't you, Kid?"

"Me and him are like brothers," said the Irish Kid. "You know, Mullins, you're not as dumb as you look. You might've had a pretty good future ahead of you. It's a shame I'm gonna have to end it tonight."

"They's four of us, Kid, give it up," said Pete. "Quint's as fast as you, and me and Carlos are almost as fast as him. Andy ain't no slouch, either. You've got one chance, Kid. Why don't you walk out of here and ride while you still got time? Ain't no man alive that could beat four to one odds when it comes to gunplay."

"How about four to two?"

The Quarry men looked up to see a sawed-off ten gauge Greener shotgun staring them in the faces. Stretch Cassidy had been asleep in the back when the men had barged in. He had quietly dressed and waited for the right moment to appear. No man likes to look down the barrel of a loaded shotgun. The four Quarry men began to squirm around like they were standing in the middle of a red ant bed.

"Hey, now, Stretch," said Pete. "You just be careful with that Greener. We ain't fools. We'll back on out of here and let this sleepin' dog lie."

"The devil we will," said Quint Mullins under his breath, and he clawed for his six-shooter.

By the time Mullins cleared leather, the Irish Kid's pistol was spitting flame and death. Two holes popped open in Quint's chest. He stumbled backwards until he hit a wall, sliding down to the floor in a sitting position. At the same instant, Stretch triggered both barrels of the Greener. Pete Allday took the full force of the shotgun in his middle. There wasn't much left between his chest and his knees but a whole lot of daylight. Part of the shotgun blast tore into Andy's right arm, blowing his six-gun out of his hand. He screamed in pain and fell to his knees. Carlos managed to snap off a shot in the Kid's direction, but the slug flew high. The Irish Kid's next bullet blew out Carlos' heart. The Mexican gunman was dead before he hit the floor. In less than a minute, two men were dead, two were dying, and one more was wounded.

Cormac ejected the spent cartridges and reloaded fresh ones as he walked over to what was left of Quint Mullins. Mullins was looking at the tiny holes in the middle of his chest. He raised his head and stared into the Kid's eyes.

"I thought I could beat you," Quint said. "You really was as good as you said."

Cormac shook his head. "Some people got to learn things the hard way, Mullins."

———•———

The doctor's office was a mess. It stank of gunpowder, blood, and human waste. Carlos and Quint were dead, Pete was blown to pieces. Andy had stopped screaming. He lay on the floor shivering like he was freezing. He was in shock and he was bleeding to death from his shredded arm. Doc Withers had seen Stretch go down, and he was in the bedroom tending to the man's wounds. Stretch was cussing a blue streak.

"By durn, if that don't beat all," said the wounded saloon owner. "I got shot in the same place as before. I'll be a dad gum prairie dog's uncle if this ain't the dangdest thing that's ever happened to me. I'll swear."

"Sounds like you've said about every swear word there is already, Stretch." Doc Withers was smiling. "Now be still and let me clean this bullet hole. The slug went all the way through, so I don't think I'll have a problem patching you up again. But, son, you have got to stop getting shot."

Stretch launched again into another cussing tirade, but he sat still enough to let the doctor work.

The Irish Kid looked Andy over to see if he had a chance to survive. If he did, there wasn't much a one-armed man could do.

Andy had quit shivering and lay still. The Kid figured the man was almost gone. "So long, *amigo*," he said. He had liked Andy. "You were a good cowboy in the wrong place at the wrong time."

Chapter 19

The Irish Kid helped Doc Withers get Stretch back into bed. The lofty man protested some, but the adrenalin from the shootout had begun to wear off, and he was feeling the effects of his new wound. After Stretch was made comfortable, the two men walked back into the doctor's office.

"Care for some coffee, son?" said Doc, seeming oblivious to the ordeal that had just taken place.

"Uh, yeah. Sure, Doc," answered the Kid, surprised at the casual tone of the medico's voice. "What about these dead men? You want me to take care of the bodies?"

"No, sir. You leave 'em be, right where they are. After I drink me some of this black magic elixir I'm brewing, I will stroll on down to Mordecai Burns' house and tell him what happened. He's the mortician, and he'll take care of removing the bodies."

That sounded good to Cormac. He didn't like to kill unless he had to, and he sure didn't have any taste for taking care of the corpses afterwards. He accepted the hot black liquid from the doctor and raised the cup to his lips.

Mort Quarry had made it to Rancho Bonito in time to beat the storm. He sat in his expansive study and gazed down at the twelve-year-old bottle of Scotch whiskey that rested on a table beside him. He reached for the bottle, handling it as one would handle a newborn child. He put the crown of the whiskey bottle against the lip of a tall crystal goblet and poured the pale amber liquid down the side of the glass. He had sworn to his daughter that he wouldn't drink anymore, but he felt like having just one. It wouldn't hurt him to have a small glass of the Scotch nectar.

He raised the glass to his lips. "Here's to you, Bale Armstrong, you old codger. Within a fortnight, I will have your land and all that comes with it."

Jim reckoned Shank's fifteen minutes were up. He and his *compadres* raised their six-guns and fired into the air at the same time. The herd, already skittish from the approaching storm, took off at a dead run in the direction of the Quarry compound. The storm broke loose before the cattle had gotten a hundred yards.

The rain was coming down in sheets, and Jim Butler had lost sight of his companions. They had become separated right after the Norther hit. Jim was on the right flank of the herd riding for all he was worth. Visibility had been reduced to only a few yards, and Jim wanted to stop, but he feared the cattle would trample him and his horse. He kept riding and hoped for a break in the storm. All of a sudden, a rare bolt of ball lightning charged across the sky illuminating the whole horizon. The flash only lasted for an instant, but Jim could see a group of white structures a short distance ahead.

He dug his heels deep into his horse's sides, and leaned forward in the saddle. The blue mare reacted with a sudden burst of speed. The big horse was gaining ground on the herd's frantic leaders when a slingshot stab of lightning struck a giant blackjack tree directly in her path. The ancient oak splintered into a dozen airborne pieces. Jim stood up in his stirrups and yanked back hard on the reins. The mare was running flat out when Jim jerked her head back. She reared straight up in the air, her hoofs flailing at the black void in front of them. The panicking horse lost her balance and tumbled over backwards. Jim went flying through the air straight into the path of the storm-maddened cattle. He hit the ground hard but rolled to his feet and came up running in the direction of his horse. The crazed beast had regained her footing and, before Jim could reach her, she took off into the night.

Jim almost panicked for a moment, but he didn't stop running. Regaining his wits, he began to frantically look about him, searching for a safe haven from the charging herd. A large chunk of the lightning-split tree lay right in his path. He leaped over the massive slab of wood and squirreled himself down behind it. The maddened cattle tramped around and over the log, showering him with dirt and rocks. Jim Butler squeezed his eyes shut, and for the first time in a long time, he prayed.

As the violent thunderstorm intensified, Mort Quarry thought he was having a nightmare from which he couldn't awaken. He felt like he was in the middle of a raging tornado. His house began to vibrate; a plate glass window in the front living room shuddered and popped out of its frame like an overripe boil, shooting shards of glass in every direction. One of the flying shards hit Mort in the face, tearing a jagged three-inch hole in his right cheek. Raising his hand to the gash in his face, he realized this was no bad dream.

Mort sprinted to the door just in time to see a thousand-pound steer run headfirst into one of the thick oak columns that held up the massive balcony. The column held and the steer went down, disappearing beneath an enraged mass of hide and hoofs. Abject alarm masked the man's features as he realized that his cattle were stampeding through the Rancho Bonito compound. He knelt by the blown-out window and watched in awe as the livestock rushed by his home.

As soon as the last bawling cow passed, Mort Quarry ran to his barn and saddled his horse. His world was unraveling, and if he didn't do something quick to stop the decay, all of his hard-earned gains would crumble around his feet.

———————

"Hack! Shank! I found him!" hollered Rusty. The little puncher had dropped to his knees and was digging like an armadillo, trying to extract Jim Butler out from beneath a thick pile of rubble. "Oh, my Lord," he said, "I think he's still alive."

Both men jumped down and began to help with the excavation. Struggling, they pulled Jim from his hidey hole. Hack had grabbed his canteen as he dismounted and as Shank elevated Jim's head, he poured a tiny amount of clean water into Jim's mouth.

Jim sputtered and choked on the liquid. He shook his head and squinted his eyes, staring up at his rescuers. "You boys tryin' to drown me?" he said.

Tears ran down Rusty's cheeks, balling up in the dirt that caked his face, forming tiny streaks of mud.

Shank looked over at his old saddle mate and grimaced. "Dang it, Rusty, I think you would bawl at your own funeral. Can you walk, Badger?"

"Yeah, I think I'm okay." With Hack and Rusty's assistance, Jim struggled to his feet. He was covered in dirt and cow manure from head to toe, but everything seemed to be working okay. He was hurting, but he figured that came from being scrunched up under the fallen tree for too long.

"Shank," said Jim, "you and Rusty better hightail it on back to the Double-A-Slash before you're missed. I'm goin' to the hotel and get a bath.

Hack, you ride into town and camp out at the saloon. Keep your ears open and your mind clear."

"No whiskey?" Hack screwed his face up like he had just bitten into a sour apple.

"No more than two beers, either, Hack. We've all got be on the alert and ready for anything."

The massive gunfighter shrugged his shoulders and stepped into the saddle. He dug heels into his horse and was gone.

———•———

The drovers found Jim's horse wandering not too far from where they had dug their friend out from under the lightning-scarred tree. Rusty handed the mare's reins to Jim, and he and Shank headed for the Double-A-Slash.

Jim rode down to the Rancho Bonito complex to check out the results of the stampede. All of the outbuildings were damaged but still standing. The front windows had been blown out of the main ranch house and manure covered almost everything. Half a dozen dead cows lay about, trampled during the mad rush.

Jim searched the bunkhouse and the ranch house but found no sign of human injury. Satisfied that no one was hurt during the stampede, Jim turned the mare toward town. He was anxious to get out of his nasty clothes and into a tub full of hot, soapy water.

Chapter 20

Jim arrived at the hotel and headed around back to the public bath house. In a flash he was stripped and into a tub of clean, hot water. It took a second tub of water before Jim got all of the dirt and manure scrubbed off of his body. Finally, dressed in clean clothes and revived from his ordeal, Jim felt pretty good as he started toward the bank.

He was in the middle of the street when he heard a man call out his name. He looked up to see a rider making a mad dash in his direction. Jim loosened the thong over his six-gun and crouched in anticipation. Relieved to see it was Cormac McCafferty, he relaxed and waited for his friend to reach him.

"Jim, you've got to get down to the doc's office." The Irish Kid had a grave look on his face.

"Why? What's the matter Cormac?"

"Hop on behind me, Jim. There's someone there who can explain it better than me."

Jim grabbed the Kid's arm and swung up behind him. Before he could ask Cormac any more, the Kid jerked his horse around and took off in the direction of Doc Wither's place.

Mordecai Burns had taken the dead outlaws' bodies to the mortuary, and the saloon swamper had just finished cleaning the blood off of the floor. The doctor was in the back room with Stretch Cassidy when Jim came rushing in the front door. Seeing Jim, both men walked into the front room. Hack and Melissa Quarry were already in the room.

"Melissa?" said Jim. "What are you doing here?"

"Oh, Jim," she cried as she rushed into his arms. "Darling, I am so sorry. I have been a blind fool."

Jim looked down at the young woman, dismay masking his features. "What are you talking about, Melissa?"

She told him about overhearing the conversation between her father and Dude Miller. When she finished, Cormac filled Jim in with the details of the previous night's gun trouble. Jim listened in silence, his placid features failing to reveal the tempest tearing at his heart.

When Cormac was done, Jim turned and stared out the window for a long time. Suddenly a voice appeared in his head. He felt it rather than heard it, but somehow he knew it was real. The voice told him to get off of his backside and start acting like the man he was, Bale Armstrong, Jr.

Jim shook his head and looked around to see if anyone else had heard the voice. Hack was talking and the others were listening to him.

"I'm Bale Armstrong, Jr.," Jim said.

"Why, sure you are," said the Irish Kid. "Who says different?"

Jim ignored the Kid's response. He stood up and stretched his sore, aching body. The physical pain he had been enduring just moments before was forgotten. It had been pushed away to some remote part of Jim's brain, stored away until the job he was compelled to do was finished. Walking over to Melissa, Jim bent down and kissed her cheek.

Turning back to face his friends, a look of total determination cloaked his face. "Boys," he said, "Jim Butler died in a cattle stampede last night. He lived a rough life and he's gone. Bale Armstrong, Jr., is back to stay, and I'm here to protect my birthright. Anyone who gets in my way will go down."

Badger looked at his friends, and his lips parted into a thin, mirthless smile.

Mort Quarry had arrived at his office before sunup and locked himself inside. He sat in the darkness and drank Scotch whiskey straight from the bottle. The fiery pale liquid helped to soothe his nerves and calm down the torrent of self-doubt that churned inside him.

Rancho Bonita, his shrine to his late wife, had almost been destroyed. Sheer dumb luck had caused him to escape death. Someone had to pay, and pay they would. He would get Dude Miller to round up all of his gun hands and blow Deaf Smith County apart if that's what it took. He would put out a bounty on Jim Butler, Hack Bonner, Bale Armstrong and the whole Double-A-Slash crew, even that Mexican witch. Soon, all of Deaf Smith County, Texas would belong to him.

He had sat alone in his office and drank half of the bottle, when he heard someone come in the front. *My Melissa,* he thought. *Always on time.*

He reached over and clicked on his lamp. "Come in, Melissa," he said. "I am in the back room. I worked all night on the Double-A-Slash proposition."

"Boss, it's me. Dude Miller. Are you okay?"

"Oh, uh, Dude. Why, of course I'm okay. Why shouldn't I be?"

"You sounded strange and you were calling me Melissa like you thought she was comin' in the door. You knew she was over at the doc's, didn't you?"

"Good Lord, Dude, are you sure about that? I saw her just this morning, and she was fine." The alcohol clouded Mort's mind and caused his thoughts to be sluggish. "No, I guess it was yesterday when I last saw my daughter." He hesitated as he spoke.

"She ain't the only one at the doc's, boss. Butler, Stretch Cassidy, Bonner and the Irish Kid are there, too."

"I thought we sent the Irish Kid to kill the doctor?"

"Yeah, we did, but he double-crossed us and killed some of the boys."

Dude told Mort Quarry the story of the gun battle as he had heard it third hand from Mordecai Burns. Quarry showed no emotion as he listened to the bad news.

When Dude finished, Mort Quarry erupted in a torrent of profanity, slamming a beefy fist on his desk top. "No doubt Melissa has told the doctor and her new friends that I was the one who ordered the Armstrong boy's death. So be it. Dude, I want you to round up as many of the men as you can find and meet me here. We ride in one hour. Bale Armstrong and anyone else who gets in my way are dead."

Badger Armstrong stepped out of the relative comfort of the doctor's office into the blistering Texas heat. He did not feel the sun burning his skin, nor the sweat that soaked his clothing. He felt only one thing. Rage. Not wild, unrestrained, seething fury, but rigid controlled anger.

One man was responsible for the way Badger felt. Mort Quarry had tried to take everything from Badger that he cared about. Now, he was going to take away all that Quarry held dear.

The Double-A-Slash ranch had belonged to the Armstrong family ever since Bale Armstrong, Shank Halsey, and a handful of other pioneers had ridden into Deaf Smith County and made the land theirs. Badger intended to keep what was his.

He looked up and down the main street of Two Bucks City and read the name of each business: Quarry Land and Cattle Company, Deaf Smith County Bank, proprietor, Mort Quarry, Two Bucks Mercantile, Mort Quarry, owner. The names on the signs made Badger's skin crawl. His shoulder muscles bunched up like knotted rope, and he moved his head in a circular motion, trying to relieve some of the tension in his neck. Badger planned to end Mort Quarry's stranglehold on Deaf Smith County and, by all that was sacred, he swore he would end it today.

Chapter 21

Against the protests of Doc Withers, Stretch Cassidy left the doctor's office and walked over to check on his business. The Golden Ace was half full, a considerable-sized crowd for the time of day. Most of the Rancho Bonito cowboys were in the place. Half a dozen of Quarry's gun hands were there, too, lounging around at tables, playing cards, and drinking. Stretch walked behind the counter and felt around under the bar top. A smile traversed his features as his hand found the back-up shotgun he always kept there.

Stretch spoke to his bartender, Max O'Hara, and the man left the saloon in a hurry. Stretch settled in behind the bar. As he began to wipe down the bar top, he noticed a stranger at the far end.

The stranger stood with his back to the crowd; whiskey, the good stuff, and a shot glass stood before him. He had an unkempt look about him. His clothes were dusty and ragged, and his hat was pulled down low in front, hiding his eyes. His right arm hung limp at his side. He wore a .36 Navy revolver belted horizontal, handle to the left, across his middle, and a .45 Colt Peacemaker slung low on his left side. When he took a drink, he would fill the shot glass, set the bottle down, and gulp the whiskey all in one swift movement.

Hack Bonner and the Irish Kid decided to stop at the Golden Ace to wet their whistles before Hack rode to the ranch to round up the Armstrong hands and bring them to town. They stepped through the swinging doors and looked around. The place turned quiet as a mausoleum. Hack cursed under his breath.

The Kid smiled and whispered to his *compadre*. "Well, it's sure been nice knowin' you, *boyo*."

Hack Bonner answered the Kid in a voice loud enough for all in the saloon to hear. "I'll most likely die someday with my boots on, Kid, but today ain't that day." He strode up to Stretch and ordered a cold beer.

Cormac McCafferty snickered and sauntered up beside his trail mate. The noise in the place began to grow in bits and pieces, and you could have bet money on the subject every conversation had turned to. Hack glanced at the man at the other end of the bar. There was a hint of recognition in his eyes.

"Kid," said Hack, "Put an eye on that dried-up lookin' *hombre* down yonder at the end of the bar. You ever seen him before?"

The Irish Kid looked up from his beer and stared at the stranger, who stared right back at him. "I don't recognize that bone bag directly, but I seen him plenty of times before."

"How's that, Kid?"

"Not him, but his kind. He's got the mark of Cain on him. He's walkin' around, but he's more dead than alive. He's lookin' for somebody in particular to kill."

"Look at him, Kid, see how he don't use but one arm. By gosh, that's Ott Carlyle."

"Dang, Hack, do you think so?"

"Yeah, it's him all right. I heard Jimmy speak of him plenty of times. The man wants one thing, and that's to kill Jim Butler."

"I believe I'll waltz on down there and put the fear of God into him, Hack." The Irish Kid finished his beer and hitched up his gun belt.

"Wait a minute," said Hack. "I got an idea. Stay here and back my play. We might just get out of here today in one piece, yet." He stepped away from the bar and moseyed down in the direction of Ott Carlyle.

"Howdy, Carlyle," said Hack.

Ott Carlyle's good hand dropped like a guillotine blade to rest on his Peacemaker. Without looking at Hack he spoke, his voice a rasping monotone.

"You seem to know me. How is it that I don't know you?" His head swiveled to meet Hack, eye to eye. Dark bloodshot orbs peered from under half-closed eyelids.

"We've never met, but I know you by reputation. My name's Hack Bonner and I ride with Jim Butler."

Ott Carlyle turned his attention to his whiskey. "I suppose you intend to kill me, Mr. Bonner. If you know my story, then you know I can't be killed. Least ways, not by the likes of you." He turned to face Hack again and took a long step backwards, his hand resting easy on the butt of the .45.

"That day may well come, Carlyle, but today I have a proposition for you." Ott Carlyle took in a long, slow lungful of air, like a man swigging water after a hard day's work. He pursed his gray, cracked lips and nodded one time.

"Practically all of these *hombres* in here work for Mort Quarry. Now Quarry don't like Jim Butler or anybody who rides with him. Most of these fellers are cowboys who ain't interested in a fight, but six or eight of 'em are hardcases on Quarry's payroll. Me and my friend over there," Hack leaned his head in the direction of the Irish Kid, "when we get ready to leave this saloon, those men are gonna call us out. If you throw in with us when we get ready to go, we just all might make it out of here alive."

"What if I just stand over here and let all you bad men shoot each other to dog meat?"

"Well, Mr. Carlyle. Then my friend and I will have to kill you, and you won't ever get that chance at Jim Butler. You might shoot me, but my *compadre* there is the Irish Kid, and you ain't got a worm's chance on a fish hook of killin' him."

Ott Carlyle shook his head and looked up at Hack Bonner. "You boys about ready to vacate this place?"

"Yeah," said Hack. "I think our business is finished here." He turned and started walking back to where Cormac McCafferty stood.

Ott Carlyle corked the bottle of whiskey and stuck it in his vest pocket. He scowled and fell into step behind Hack. When the two men reached the Irish Kid, all three of them spread out a few feet apart and turned to face the Quarry crew.

A hard expression swathed Hack's features as he glared at the group of men. "My name's Hack Bonner and I ride for the Armstrong brand." His voice carried the entire length of the saloon. All eyes turned to him. "I reckon most of you boys know who this ring-tailed wampus cat on my left is, since he done killed some of your best gunnies."

"Howdy, y'all," said the Irish Kid, grinning like a kid skinny dipping in the old swimming hole.

"This pile of bones and skin on my right is Ott Carlyle, and he says he can't be killed. Now, I know most of you boys ain't gun handy; you just punch cows and ride for the brand. Well, if any of you got a hankerin' to head for healthier pastures, I believe this is the time to fork your bronc and ride."

For a long moment nothing happened. A few heads began turning, followed by a smattering of nods. All at once, men started jumping up and a grand exodus of cowboys took place. Within seconds the Quarry outfit was down to eight men.

Charley Pratt was one of the Quarry bunch that was still around. He whispered in the ear of the man next to him. "I'm goin' for Dude. You fellers hold 'em off 'til I get back."

Hack drew a long, black cigar from his shirt pocket. He rolled it around on his tongue, and then stuck it in his mouth. Digging a quirly from his vest, he thumb-struck the fire stick and, with cupped hands, lit the cigar. Hack held the match upside down out in front of him, letting the fire lick at his fingertips. The match burned upwards, engulfing his fingers in flame. Hack never looked at the match. The stick burned into black ash and fell to the floor.

"It looks like we got seven of you left," Hack said, blowing a great puff of smoke. "I recognize some of you. Y'all know you can't beat me on your best day, and I ain't near as good as the Kid. Plus we got one more gun on our side and he's a stone cold killer." Hack puffed again, blowing a huge cloud of smoke in the direction of the Quarry hired guns.

The Quarry bunch were not cowards by nature, but they were, in their own way, businessmen who were paid to use their guns. To most of them this did not look like a money-paying proposition. The tension was as thick as raw cane sorghum, and sweat poured off of the men like waterfalls. Somebody had to make a move.

"By the saints, that's enough." Stretch Cassidy stood at the bar, a little ways away from everyone so he could see the whole crowd. "I have gotten shot twice in these last few days and I killed a feller yesterday. I'm tired and sore and just about as mad as a man can get. I want all of you yahoos out of my saloon right now. You might think an old scattergun like this won't do much damage at this range, but this one is filled with double ought buckshot and it will take out some eyes, ears, and such. Plus, while you nitwits were jawin', I sent my bartender over to the doc's office to fetch my other shotgun. He's outside the door right now ready to come in blastin' if he even so much as hears a mouse sneeze."

The sight of two short barrels peeking through the swinging doors gave credence to what Stretch had just said.

"Bonner, you and yours back out of here now. Don't stop until you get across the street. When they're gone, then the rest of you can go."

Hack, the Kid, and Carlyle wasted no time in backing out of the saloon and hurrying across the street. The bartender gave the word and the Quarry gunmen backed out of the saloon in single file. When they were all gone, Max

O'Hara, the bartender, a man as Irish as the day is long, stepped inside and sauntered over to his boss.

"Well, there, Stretch, me lad, I reckon we showed those ruffians who can and who can't. Reminds me of the time I stared down those Indians back in '68."

"What does this have to do with an Indian fight?" said Stretch, leaning against the bar and gulping deep breaths.

"Well, me boy," said O'Hara, twisting the end of his thick red moustache. "On that day, I had no bullets in my gun, either."

Chapter 22

adger had been lounging in front of the hotel collecting his thoughts when he saw Max O'Hara sprint from the saloon into the doctor's office. He started toward the doc's, but had only taken a few steps when O'Hara burst back out of the office carrying Stretch's shotgun. Badger watched as the bartender ran up to the saloon doors and stopped.

Easing across the street, Badger worked his way close enough to the Golden Ace to hear what was going on inside. He was standing ready to join the ball when Stretch took control of the situation. When Hack and the other two advanced across the street, Badger trotted over to join them.

Jim approached Hack and Cormac. He gave the third man a cursory glance but did not recognize him. "Hack, what happened?"

Ott Carlyle's hand went to his front holster. It was empty. The side holster, likewise, held no pistol. His head jerked around searching for his six-guns. He found the weapons sticking in the Irish Kid's gun belt. He showed no expression as he looked at the Kid's smiling face, but his eyes glared out what was on his mind.

Cormac winked at him. "We almost got our bacon fried, Jimmy, boy, but thanks to your old friend here, we still got our scalps."

"My friend, Hack?" For the first time, Badger got a good look at the walking cadaver. "I don't believe I know this man, but I sure thank you, *amigo,* for helpin' my *compadres* out of a jam." Badger stuck his hand out to the man.

"Has it been so long that you don't remember me, Butler? I might have changed a little, but one thing hasn't changed at all." Carlyle turned to his side, showing Badger his lame arm.

Badger gaped at the man as realization struck him. "Ott Carlyle? You're Ott Carlyle? Good Lord, man! What happened to you?"

Carlyle's lips split into a mirthless grin. "I've been chasing you ever since I recovered from my gunshot wounds." He looked down at his lifeless arm.

"A man doesn't need a whole lot to survive on when he's got hate keeping him going. All I could think about for all these years was finding you and killing you on the spot."

Badger tensed up. "Why didn't you make your play when I walked up?"

"Because this grinning baboon here took my pistols."

Badger and Hack looked at the Irish Kid. Cormac rubbed the butt of Carlyle's guns and winked again.

The Quarry gunmen began to spill out of the Golden Ace. At the same time, Dude Miller showed up with Charlie Pratt in tow, as well as four more gunslicks. Miller went straight to the men in front of the saloon and began to palaver with them. After a few moments, he turned toward Badger and the others. Miller started across the street at a slow walk. The other twelve Quarry gunfighters spread out in a semi-circle around the Armstrong group. Charlie Pratt was not among them.

"Are you a man of your word, Ott?" asked Badger.

"Yeah, why?"

"If we give you your guns back, will you swear to not try and kill me until this brouhaha is over with?"

"Doesn't look like I have a choice," he said with a sour grimace. "I'll lay off of you until this thing is done, but if I live through it, all bets are off."

"Give him his guns, Cormac," Jim said as he started walking toward Dude Miller.

The Kid handed Ott Carlyle the pistols, barrels first. This time he didn't wink. Carlyle took the guns, spun the chambers to check for cartridges, and holstered the weapons. All three men spread out behind Badger and stood loose.

In the meantime, Charley Pratt had snuck around behind the saloon and entered the place through the back entryway. He sneaked through the storeroom until he reached the door leading into the bar. Edging the door open, he could see Stretch Cassidy and his bartender peering over the swinging doors, shotguns in hand. Charley crept up to within a few feet of the two men.

"Boys, drop them shotguns," said Charley, through clenched teeth. "And do it real easy-like. I'd plumb hate it if we lost both of our bartenders at the same time."

Charley sauntered up closer to the door so he could be heard outside. "Dude!" he yelled. "Everything is hunky-dory in the saloon. These boys are quiet as church mice." He laughed again, and prodded Stretch Cassidy on his injured shoulder with the barrel of his six-gun.

The saloon owner yelled and dropped to his knees.

Max O'Hara twisted around to face Charley and got a rap on his head for the effort. O'Hara staggered back against the wall, but he didn't go down.

"Be still and shut up," said Charley.

"Miller, this is between me and you," said Badger. "Let's leave everybody else out of it. We go head to head. One of us dies; the other rides out of Two Bucks City forever."

"What makes you think I will leave after I kill you, Butler?"

"My name ain't Butler, it's Bale Armstrong, Jr., and I'll take your word on leavin'."

"My word? Why, sure, I'll give you my word. And it don't make no difference who you are. I'm going to kill you, anyway." Dude raised his voice so all could hear him. "Quarry men, listen up, if this *hombre* kills me, you boys go on back in the saloon and have a drink in my honor. Mr. Quarry has about run his string out here in this country, anyway, and it's time you hardcases drifted."

"Watch yourselves, boys," Badger said to his men. "There ain't no honor on this street, today."

Mort Quarry had heard the commotion and stood just inside his office with the door cracked. He could hear everything that was being said. "How dare Dude say I'm through in Two Bucks City?" Quarry whispered to himself. "If the Armstrong brat doesn't kill him, I will, and then I will take direct charge of my men. This county will be mine, yet."

Badger Armstrong pursed his lips and breathed easy. He could feel the sun bearing down upon him and it felt good. He tasted the dust, blown up from a slight breeze. The particles mixed with the sweat pouring down his face, forming a salty gray paste at the corners of his mouth. *Salty*, thought Badger. He hoped he would still be alive to enjoy the simple pleasures of life when this was done.

'We ain't got all day, Miller, pull iron or leave town."

"Well, Armstrong, I been thinking about that." Dude Miller's eyes narrowed. "Maybe, we could talk this out. What do you think?" Miller blinked and grabbed for his pistol. He fired before he was ready; the bullet flew wide.

Badger's draw was smooth, and his aim was accurate. His six-gun barked twice, and two finger-sized holes materialized on Dude Miller's shirt. Before the blood could flow from the wounds, Miller was face down in the street.

When the gunshots went off, Charley Pratt jumped like he had been hit by one of the rounds. He took his eyes off of Max O'Hara for an instant to see who had been shot. The big bartender slammed his right fist square into Pratt's mouth; his front teeth shot out like bats leaving a cave.

The breeze had died, and the silence roared in Badger's ears. The count was still four guns to twelve, and none of the Quarry gunmen had shown any inclination to head inside the saloon. It was still bad odds for him and his bunch.

All at once a man came running down the street. It was Mort Quarry, and he was yelling to beat the band.

"Hold it right there!" Quarry hollered. "Don't let that murderer get away. Stop him!"

The Quarry gunslingers opened up and let their boss get through. He stopped in front of his men.

"We all saw what happened. The Armstrong boy shot and killed Dude Miller in cold blood. You'll hang for this, Armstrong. As the first citizen of Two Bucks City, I demand you hand your guns over to me. That goes for the rest of your gang, too. That man that's down, someone check on him. If he's alive, get his weapons too."

"Man down?" said Badger. He gave a quick look behind him to find the Irish Kid and Hack Bonner still standing. Ott Carlyle was not so lucky. He was on the street sitting with his back to a watering trough. Blood leaked from just below his breastbone. Odd wheezing sounds escaped from his open mouth. His quest for Jim Butler was done.

Badger turned back to face Mort Quarry and his men. "Quarry, you're finished in this county. I've sent for a Texas Ranger. He ought to be ridin' in here any day now. You have nothing left to fight for, Quarry. Your *segundo* is dead. Your cowhands have pulled up stakes, and what gunfighters you have left don't know whether to whittle or spit. Give it up, man."

Mort Quarry's right hand shot inside his coat, clutching for the .41 caliber pocket pistol concealed there. The deafening blast of two twelve gauge shot guns being fired simultaneously caused him to drop the revolver to the ground and duck for cover.

"That'll be enough of that," said Shank Halsey, cracking a long-barreled twelve gauge Colt shotgun. He popped the empty shell casings out and reloaded in one deft movement. Beside him, Rusty Puckett did the same.

Behind the two Double-A-Slash riders rode a half dozen more. What they may have lacked in skill, they more than compensated for with weaponry. Each man carried a shotgun or a rifle as well as a short gun.

Following close behind the riders was a wagon loaded down with Mexican farmers. Three people crowded the wagon seat. Maria held the reins, and Miguel sat opposite her. Between the two and holding on to them rode Bale Armstrong, Sr.

Maria guided the wagon close to Badger and halted the horses. The Mexican men jumped from the wagon and formed a cordon around it. Each man was armed with a pitchfork or an axe.

Bale Armstrong looked straight at Mort Quarry. His voice was weak, but loud enough to be heard. "Quarry, you took one of my sons away, but you brought one back to me, too." He glanced at Badger, then back at Quarry.

"You stole my cattle, you threatened my hands, and you insulted my companion, Maria. I should kill you, but the West is changing. The time of the gun is almost over. Men like you and me, we're history. I'll let the law take care of you." He paused, looking at Maria and the Mexican farmers surrounding the wagon. "No, we'll let the law take care of you. We'll hold you until the Rangers get here; then Two Bucks City will be done with you."

Mort Quarry turned in a circle, looking for someone to side with him. His gunmen were mounting their horses and riding away. The townspeople stood and watched, doing nothing. Each one turned their eyes away when Mort Quarry looked in their direction.

Quarry raised his hands and started walking toward Badger. "Son, you beat me," he said. "I give up. You're the better man, today. Let me shake the hand of my conqueror; it's the least you can do."

Badger glanced down at the offered hand. It was a mistake. He caught the blur in his peripheral vision and dived backwards. Quarry's roundhouse left hook caught the brim of Badger's hat and sent it flying.

Jumping back caused Badger to lose his footing. Quarry jumped on him like a crazed maniac, stomping and kicking at Badger's ribs. Badger rolled up in a ball trying to lessen the blows. One well-placed kick struck pay dirt, cracking a rib and causing Badger to yell out. The pain was agonizing, and Badger quit moving.

Confident he had the Armstrong boy down for the count, Mort Quarry raised his foot to crush Badger's temple. When he did, Badger sprang from his balled-up position, driving his head flush into Mort Quarry's groin. The huge man grunted and dropped to his knees.

Badger scrambled to his feet and, in spite of the pain, began to throw wicked left hooks and whistling right crosses to the body of the kneeling man. Quarry was beaten, but still Badger pounded him. He grabbed the bloody man by the throat and drew back his right hand to hit him one more time.

Melissa's face jumped into his mind, and he turned loose of Mort Quarry. The banker's unconscious body leaned to one side and toppled into the dirt.

Epilogue

Badger sat on the edge of the bed as Doc Withers wrapped his cracked ribs. Hack and the Irish Kid stood to the side.

"I ain't sayin' that *hombre* don't deserve killin'," said the Kid, "but your daddy was right. Let the law hang him."

Badger winced every time the doctor wrapped the bandage around the cracked part of his ribs. "My daddy," he said. "Who'd have thought it."

Mort Quarry was locked up in a small room in the saloon. Double-A-Slash hands were to guard the prisoner twenty-four hours a day until the Rangers came for him. Charley Pratt, minus his front teeth, was willing to tell everything he knew about his ex-boss if it would save him from the gallows. Bale, Sr., and Maria had gone back to the ranch to prepare a place for Badger.

Bale was still shaken by the return of his oldest son but, with Maria's persuasion, he was willing to give Badger a chance.

"Doc," said Badger. "What's gonna happen to Melissa?"

"Well, son," said the doctor, his face stretching into a grin. "Why don't you ask her."

Badger turned to see Melissa step in through the front door. He struggled off of the table and hobbled to her side. "Melissa, are you okay?"

She nodded her head and hugged Badger. "I'm hurting, but I will get over it. It's hard to believe what my father had become. I realize now that he wasn't the man I thought he was."

"I'm sorry," said Badger, not knowing what else to say.

"I have much to do to try and rectify what my father did. I have to start right away."

As Melissa moved to exit the office, she turned and looked at Badger. "I am going to need assistance in rebuilding my company's reputation. Will you consider helping me?"

Badger gave her his best possum grin. "Anything you need, Melissa, just call on me."

"Good," she said. "When your ribs heal, come see me. My ranch house is in dreadful condition and I am going to need a handyman to fix it up." She closed the door and was gone.

Badger turned and looked at the doctor and his friends. All three had blank looks on their faces. So did he.

-THE END-

LEE PIERCE is the author of *Bounty Hunter's Moon, The Treasure of Peta Nocona,* and *Rough Justice.* He was born and raised in north central Texas. He grew up with a deep appreciation of the land, and living on small farms and one-horse ranches as a youth taught him the value of hard work. After high school, Lee joined the U. S. Army and eventually graduated from The University of Texas at Arlington after attending part- and full-time for nine years on the G.I. Bill. He has written and performed songs and cowboy poetry for many years. Lee lives with his wife, Cathy, three cats, two dogs, and three horses in Dos Caballos, New Mexico.

WWW.LEEPIERCE.INFO

About
Barking Rain Press

Did you know that five media conglomerates publish eighty percent of the books in the United States? As the publishing industry continues to contract, opportunities for emerging and mid-career authors are drying up. Who will write the literature of the twenty-first century if just a handful of profit-focused corporations are left to decide who—and what—is worthy of publication?

Barking Rain Press is dedicated to the creation and promotion of thoughtful and imaginative contemporary literature, which we believe is essential to a vital and diverse culture. As a nonprofit organization, Barking Rain Press is an independent publisher that seeks to cultivate relationships with new and mid-career writers over time, to be thorough in the editorial process, and to make the publishing process an experience that will add to an author's development—and ultimately enhance our literary heritage.

In selecting new titles for publication, Barking Rain Press considers authors at all points in their careers. Our goal is to support the development of emerging and mid-career authors—not just single books—as we know from experience that a writer's audience is cultivated over the course of several books.

Support for these efforts comes primarily from the sale of our publications; we also hope to attract grant funding and private donations. Whether you are a reader or a writer, we invite you to take a stand for independent publishing and become more involved with Barking Rain Press. With your support, we can make sure that talented writers thrive, and that their books reach the hands of spirited, curious readers. Find out more at our website.

WWW.BARKINGRAINPRESS.ORG

Barking Rain Press

ALSO FROM BARKING RAIN PRESS

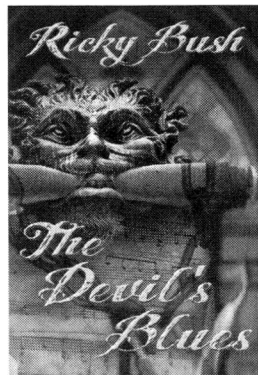

BOUNTY HUNTER'S MOON
LEE PIERCE

The Treasure of Peta Nocona
LEE PIERCE

WINNER TAKE none
Greg Comer

PADRE: THE NARROWING PATH
JENNIFER LEEPER

James M. Jackson
CABIN FEVER
A Seamus McCree Mystery

Ricky Bush
The Devil's Blues

VIEW OUR COMPLETE CATALOG ONLINE:

WWW.BARKINGRAINPRESS.ORG

79500675R00114

Made in the USA
Columbia, SC
03 November 2017